"DRAW!" RANCE SCREAMED

Joe Coffin turned away ever so slowly. By the time he heard the cocking of the revolver he was diving to his left. A bullet kicked up dust behind him as Coffin came up, the Peacemaker braced in both hands. He squeezed off a round and the bullet shattered Rance's gun arm.

The young man howled and fell. Grabbing his pistol with his left hand, Rance fired again but the shot was wide. Calmly, Coffin lifted the Colt and shot Rance in the leg, just below the knee.

Coffin shook his head in disgust, then bellowed, "If any of you people in this godforsaken town care for this stupid young buck, you best take his gun from him. I gave him two chances. I ain't fixin' to give him a third!"

**SADDLE UP FOR ADVENTURE
WITH G. CLIFTON WISLER'S
TEXAS BRAZOS!
A SAGA AS BIG AND BOLD AS TEXAS ITSELF,
FROM THE NUMBER-ONE PUBLISHER
OF WESTERN EXCITEMENT**

#1: TEXAS BRAZOS (1969, $3.95)

In the Spring of 1870, Charlie Justiss and his family follow their dreams into an untamed and glorious new land — battling the worst of man and nature to forge the raw beginnings of what is destined to become the largest cattle operation in West Texas.

#2: FORTUNE BEND (2069, $3.95)

The epic adventure continues! Progress comes to the raw West Texas outpost of Palo Pinto, threatening the Justiss family's blossoming cattle empire. But Charlie Justiss is willing to fight to the death to defend his dreams in the wide open terrain of America's frontier!

#3: PALO PINTO (2164, $3.95)

The small Texas town of Palo Pinto has grown by leaps and bounds since the Justiss family first settled there a decade earlier. For beautiful women like Emiline Justiss, the advent of civilization promises fancy new houses and proper courting. But for strong men like Bret Pruett, it means new laws to be upheld — with a shotgun if necessary!

#4: CADDO CREEK (2257, $3.95)

During the worst drought in memory, a bitter range war erupts between the farmers and cattlemen of Palo Pinto for the Brazos River's dwindling water supply. Peace must come again to the territory, or everything the settlers had fought and died for would be lost forever!

Available wherever paperbacks are sold, or order direct from the Publisher. Send cover price plus 50¢ per copy for mailing and handling to Zebra Books, Dept. 2605, 475 Park Avenue South, New York, N.Y. 10016. Residents of New York, New Jersey and Pennsylvania must include sales tax. DO NOT SEND CASH.

ARIZONA COFFIN
JOHN LEGG

ZEBRA BOOKS
KENSINGTON PUBLISHING CORP.

*For Eddie and Lynn Perkins
as thanks for your unwavering
and unassuming friendship;
with much love for you both*

ZEBRA BOOKS

are published by

Kensington Publishing Corp.
475 Park Avenue South
New York, NY 10016

Copyright © 1989 by John Patrick Legg

All rights reserved. No part of this book may be reproduced in any form or by any means without the prior written consent of the Publisher, excepting brief quotes used in reviews.

First printing: March, 1989

Printed in the United States of America

Chapter 1

Joe Coffin threw down his cards in disgust and finished off the remains of his mug of chock beer. Another lousy hand. Damn, if his luck didn't change, he thought, he'd about burst. Things had gone badly ever since he had gotten that telegram from his old friend U.S. Marshal Tom Pike in Prescott. It was just one thing after another.

He sighed and ordered another mug of chock. He grimaced as the tall, slick-looking man across from him raked in another pot. Coffin knew damn well the dark-eyed man dressed mostly in black was cheating, but he could not prove it at the moment. At this point, he wasn't sure he really wanted to anyway.

As Coffin reached for his fresh drink, the cards were being dealt again. Coffin's eyes bored into those of the tall man across the table. He sipped his chock and set the mug down carefully. As he waited for his cards, he began rubbing his stomach softly, a habitual—and to many, a misleading—gesture. But as he did, the hand wound ominously close to the butt of one of the .36-caliber Colts in the shoulder rig he had had made specially some years back. His index finger tapped the ivory handle twice, and then the hand resumed its circular motion.

All the while, he never took his dark, almost black, eyes off the stranger's. The tall, dark man nodded. It was perceptible only to Coffin. Coffin almost grinned. The man had gotten the message.

Three different men won the next three pots, but Joe Coffin

was not one of them. He drained the last of his chock. "That's it for me, boys," he said, standing. He picked up the short, flat-crowned hat from the table and slipped it on.

He noticed the tall stranger dressed mostly in black breathe a sigh of relief. Coffin turned and took one step before spinning back. "By the way, boys, I'd keep a close eye on that dude," he said pointing to the gambler.

The four men at the table looked up at him, questions in their eyes. "Why do you boys think he's won damn near every hand since we set down?"

They glanced from him to the gambler. One looked at Coffin and said, "You sure, mister?"

"Yep. Can't prove it, but I know it for a fact."

The gambler stared at him with flat, hate-filled eyes, glancing from the twin butts of the Colts in the shoulder rig down to the cross-draw holster with the huge .44-caliber Remington on the front of his left hip, and then to the .45-caliber Colt Peacemaker at Coffin's right hip.

Though Coffin was less than five and a half feet tall in the high-heeled boots he wore, the gambler knew better than to try throwing down on him.

"Hell, it ain't like that at all," the gambler stammered, looking from one poker player to the next. He softened his eyes, trying to look innocent. "I just been lucky, that's all."

He was still trying to talk his way out of it when Coffin turned and strode off. There was a slight smile on his lips. He might have lost most of the little money he had carried into this saloon in Adobe, New Mexico Territory, near the Arizona Territory line, but he had the satisfaction of knowing the gambler would also lose most of what he had. If he won more than a pot or two the rest of the night the others would string him up.

Coffin stepped out into the soft fall night. There was a chill in the air, up here in the high desert, but it was refreshing. He breathed in deeply, letting the cool, crisp air clear the heat, smoke, dust, and closeness of the saloon from his head. It would be winter before long, he knew.

Well, he thought, spirits recovering, it might've been a hell of a bad couple of weeks, but it was bound to get better. It had to—it sure couldn't get much worse. He thought back over the weeks, almost grinning.

He had received the wire from Marshal Tom Pike on a Tuesday, and set out within an hour. He had been hungover, his mouth foul and his stomach roiling. An hour out of town, he was bent over, still atop his horse, vomiting, realizing with sour sureness that he should never have left Denver.

He more or less made a camp and suffered there through the rest of the day. Sleep helped, and he felt a heap better when he awoke. Then he found out he had forgotten most of his food. Not wanting to face Ella, whom he had left standing high and dry to set out on this quest, he ate a bit of hardtack and jerky. But there was no coffee—not even stream water—to wash it down.

Finally on the trail again. He was grumpy, still tired and irritable.

The journey had gone downhill from there, what with two rainstorms that soaked him through; a sudden, early blizzard that trapped him without food for two days; a day's wait for a rain- and snow-swollen wash to recede enough to let him cross; the argument with the puma over a freshly killed deer carcass; the horse's thrown shoe; the struggle up and across Wolf Creek Pass; the wary, tension-filled journey across Navajo land . . .

"Hell," he muttered, drawing out his fixings and deftly rolling a cigarette. He fired it up and sucked the smoke deep into his lungs, enjoying the tobacco's harsh bite on his tongue.

Spurs clanking, he strode to his horse, which was tied to the hitching post nearby. "How ya doin', old boy," he said softly, scratching the broad forehead between the horse's doe-soft brown eyes. He took the reins and started leading the horse down the dark street.

"Where you goin' with my horse?" he heard somebody yell behind him. He ignored it.

Then it came again, with an added, "Hey, you. You there with that chestnut."

Coffin hesitated fractionally, then kept walking. They

couldn't mean him.

"You, goddamn it, you short little bastard. Where you goin' with my horse?"

He was sensitive about his height, though not overly so. Still, he knew now that whoever was talking was addressing him. "Damn," he muttered. Was this string of bad luck and hard times ever going to end? he wondered.

He turned slowly, eyes alert, horse's reins still in his left hand. He saw two men, both dirty, unshaven, and vicious-looking. Both wore two Colts at their hips.

One, slightly taller, older, and more sinister-looking than the other, said, "I ast you where you was goin' with my horse, mister."

Coffin stared at him. The man was just under six foot tall, Coffin guessed. He wore tan cord pants, patched at one knee, and a stained wool shirt under a plain tan vest. A dirty scarf was around his neck, and a battered, stained Stetson on his head.

"You ain't talkin' to me, are you?" Coffin asked, almost politely. But there was a coating of iron on the words.

"Who'n hell else would I be talkin' to?" the man said, pleased at his rapier wit.

"I got no idea who you're talkin' to," Coffin said. All the frustrations and anger of the past week were simmering just below the surface, ready to boil over.

"Watch him, Cort," the other man said, and Coffin took a moment to size him up: medium height, stocky, young, missing two front teeth, a week's worth of stubble coating his cheeks, chin, and upper lip. Levi's under batwing chaps; high-heeled, pointed-toe boots liberally covered with cow and horse manure; a hip-length duster, tan, open, showing a tobacco-stained flannel shirt.

"I'm talkin' to you, goddamn it," the first one said. "That's my horse, and I'd be obliged if you was to hand him over."

Coffin almost smiled. He had seen this before. A man would challenge someone, usually loudly, saying the man was going off with his horse. The other man, embarrassed, or maybe too drunk to know what was going on, might just hand over the animal without question. If the owner argued, the "horse thief" would just throw up his hands, saying he made a mistake—sorry, pard—and move on.

If it worked, it was an easy, and relatively safe way to steal horses. If it didn't, usually no harm was done. Occasionally, however, the thief would want to press it. Coffin hoped this wasn't to be one of those times, but he was beginning to suspect that it would be.

"You got it wrong, mister. This here's *my* horse." Coffin's voice was harsh, and he let it soften fractionally. "Maybe in the dusk here, you mistook it for yours."

"Goddamnit, I said that's my horse. Now give it over, boy." His eyes were darkly clouded, and Coffin noticed a nervous tic in the man's cheek.

"Go play your game somewhere else, mister," Coffin said harshly. "I ain't of a mood for such foolishment." He turned and started walking away, horse in tow, noticing that several people were standing on the wood sidewalks, or peering from lantern-lit windows.

"Hold it right there, goddamnit!" Cort roared.

"Shoot him, Cort," the other snarled.

"Shaddup, ya dumb bastard," Coffin heard Cort mumble.

Then Coffin heard a hammer being thumbed back. In a flash he had dropped the horse's reins and fell, rolling to his right. He heard Cort fire, and knew the bullet had gone right by where the center of his back would have been.

He spun and came to a stop, sitting in the street, a .36-caliber Colt in each hand. Cort fired again, just missing Coffin. Then the younger man tried, and fired wide.

Carefully Coffin fired once from each weapon. Cort and his companion snapped backward a step, as a slug tore into each of their chests. Both tried with little success to bring their own weapons back to bear.

Coffin stood, and moved closer. Then he fired once more from each pistol.

A bullet plowed into Cort's face, at the bridge of the nose, smashing him back a few more steps. He slumped down, sideways, and lay twitching, tangled in himself.

The second bullet ripped into the other man's throat, flopping his head to the side. He sank to his knees and then pitched forward and a little to the side, landing bent over like a bridge.

Someone hove into view, and Coffin cocked the pistol in his right hand, ready.

"Whoa, boy," the man said, holding out his hands. Then he tapped the badge on his chest. "Sheriff Tinker Grimes. Now set your pieces away."

Coffin looked around. Few of the faces surrounding him were hostile. Even Grimes didn't look all that angry, though the three deputies with him might be trouble if they put their minds to it.

Joe Coffin uncocked the one pistol and placed both back in their holsters. "It was self-defense, Sheriff," he said quietly.

"What happened?"

Coffin explained it quickly and briefly. When he was done, Grimes nodded. "Reckoned it was some such."

"Then I'm free to go?"

"Free to ride on out of town."

Coffin swiped a hand across his mouth and chin. "I was aimin' to get me a room for the night. I'll be ridin' out come mornin'. First thing."

"You'll be ridin' out now, mister."

Coffin's eyes hardened. "That ain't very friendly, Sheriff," he said, noticing the three shotgun-wielding deputies shift a little. "Seein's how I didn't do nothin' wrong."

Sheriff Grimes shrugged. "Didn't say ya did, boy. But you'll be ridin' out just the same."

"Mind tellin' me why? Seems like I done you and your town a service. And all I want's a bed for the night."

Grimes chewed his lip for a minute before saying, "Cort Stiles belongs to a gang. The gang don't get here often, but Cort's got kin over this way. That was his cousin, Arvis, with him."

"So?"

"Well, like I said, the gang don't get over this way much. I'd like to keep it that way. Word gets out you killed Cort, and then we let you stay in town, well, them sons a bitches he rides with just might come a callin'. That'd be a pity."

"Shit, Sheriff, I . . ."

The three deputies thumbed back the hammers of the

scatterguns they carried.

Coffin's eyes narrowed. The sheriff had given him a good reason for leaving, and he probably would have been persuaded to do so in a minute. But this rankled him. He bit back a retort. He had enough sense to know not to tangle with three scatterguns.

"That ain't necessary, Sheriff," he said finally, calmed.

"Didn't reckon so. But it pays to be cautious."

Coffin nodded, but stood. Time dragged on, and still the five men did not move. Finally a smile cracked Grimes's face. He waved his hand, and the three deputies carefully uncocked their shotguns.

Coffin nodded again, and turned. Scooping up the reins to his horse, he vaulted easily into the saddle. Since he was so short, and the horse rather large, it was an impressive move, and Coffin often used it to effect.

He touched the brim of his hat and rode off. A fine ending to a perfectly rotten couple of weeks, he thought ruefully.

Chapter 2

U.S. Marshal Tom Pike spit a stream of tobacco juice into the brass spittoon next to his desk. It landed with a dull clang. "Reno Holder and his boys got to be stopped," he snapped.

Joe Coffin gazed out past the lettering on the office window on the busy corner of Gurley and Cortez streets, catty-corner from the territorial Capitol building, in Prescott, Arizona Territory. It was a bustling town of more than two thousand residents.

It had taken Coffin a week after being tossed out of Adobe to reach Prescott. He had spent an uncomfortable night outside the town of Adobe in the chilly air. But he'd survived, and he thought maybe his luck might be improving.

The weather stayed fairly good considering it was about the beginning of October—only one shower, and several days later a frog-strangler of a rainstorm. He saw no one on the trails, unless he was nearing a town. Using his head, he would pull into a town—if he was lucky enough to come on one—get a room, have a meal, and maybe a woman, and then go back to his room. He wisely figured that the less time he was on the street or in a saloon, the less likely he was to get into trouble. The rest of the trip was made in peace.

"What've they done?" Coffin asked, turning back to face Pike.

"They started out rustlin', then moved on to holdups. Banks, stages, trains. Don't matter to them."

"Hell, Tom, you didn't bring me all the way out from Denver

just to catch some goddamn rustlers and train robbers."

Pike drummed his fingers on the desk. "No, no I didn't," he said finally. "But they've turned more vicious lately. Pure devils, they are. Started killin' too often, too easy. They gunned down two men while holdin' up the bank in Cottonwood. They killed another one three days later while holdin' up a stage over on Ash Creek."

"You send a posse after 'em?"

"The towns did. Both times. And the three times after that." He paused, anger rising. "Holder and his boys been pilin' up a hell of a record the last couple of months. Half a dozen sheriffs and deputies been killed in the last two months by Holder and his men. Finally I sent out my own posse—six deputies and a dozen or so men from Prescott here. Two deputies bought it, and two townsmen. So I sent out more men. Three more deputies was killed, and another townsman. I'm runnin' out of men, Joe."

Coffin nodded slowly. "How many of 'em are there?"

"Seven."

Coffin took the news in stride. "Where do I start lookin'?"

Pike waved his hand vaguely. "Mostly north and east of here."

Coffin shrugged. "How much you payin'?"

"Thousand dollars a head."

"Alive? Or dead?"

"Don't make me no nevermind."

"You got pictures on 'em?"

"Sure." They were right under his hands, and he held out the sheaf of Wanted posters.

Coffin took them and glanced hard at each, learning the faces. The men in the drawings were a jolly lot, Coffin thought as Pike quietly told Coffin about each man.

"Now, Pete St. Johns is a fat, drunken degenerate who likes killing close up, usually with a knife. Don't know how many he's killed, but it's a right tidy number.

"Bill Curly's a Navajo half-breed. Long ago in his young, hate-filled life he lost the traditional Navajo way of walking in harmony. He's a mean bastard, big Bill is.

"But Bill ain't nothin' when you start talkin' about Buck

13

Schiebel. This is one stone-cold son of a bitch. Man's got no emotions, far's anyone knows. And he's got a problem with the women, if ya know what I mean. Don't know any other way of bein' a man 'cept killin'.

"The next is—"

"Dead," Coffin interjected. "You owe me a thousand, Tom."

"What'n hell're you talkin' about?"

"I killed him week ago over in some place in New Mexico called Adobe. Bastard tried to steal my horse."

"You killed Cort Stiles and didn't know who he was?" Pike asked, somewhat amazed.

"Yep," Coffin grinned. "His cousin too."

"Which one?"

"Arvis."

Marshal Pike laughed, his heavy voice loud in the small room. "Well, I'll be damned." He chuckled. "And didn't know who it was."

"Nope." Coffin rubbed his stomach, the gesture familiar to old friend Tom Pike. "Sheriff there told me Stiles belonged to a gang. Threw me out of town so's the gang wouldn't think the town was bein' nice to me for killin' off such scum."

"Sounds reasonable to me," Pike said seriously. "Holder and his men got a heap of folks scared. Well," he added, after a slight pause, "I reckon you'll get your thousand for Stiles. But I'll have to call the sheriff over there. You know his name?"

Coffin told him, and Pike wrote it down with a thick pencil.

"What about the others?" Coffin asked.

"Well, let's see. Next is Ian O'Kelly. This red-faced Irish bastard got his start killin' in the slums of New York City. He continued it as a border raider for either side during the Civil War. After the war, he drifted west and hooked up with Holder.

"Will Greenaway's a product of Quantrill's raiders. He'll kill when pushed to it—he's usually a back-shooter, though, since he's got no balls to speak of. But his prime pleasure is rape. He can do things to a woman even the Comanches and Apaches ain't thought of.

"Then there's Holder. He's about forty and, some say, a handsome cuss. He's fond of the ladies, fancies himself a ladies' man, he does. Seems the ladies like him too. His father was a veteran of San Jacinto who went bad soon thereafter and was killed when Reno was a boy.

"Word has it that Holder killed his first man when he was fourteen. Gunned down a freed slave, but in Texas it meant little—still does, for that matter—and Holder was made into something of a hero. It did something to his head, and soon he took to killing just for sport.

"During the war he joined Quantrill's men. After that, he just kept up his lawless ways. The law finally got too hot for him in Texas and Indian Territory, so he drifted out this way. Much to my regret, and everyone else's that's come across him."

"Sound like a right fun bunch," Coffin said with distaste. He hesitated, then asked, "Why'd you bring *me* here for this?"

"Needed someone like you."

"Bullshit. There's men like me all over. You could've found some closer to home. You can't tell me there ain't enough hardcases in Arizona Territory to take down this bunch."

"Joe," the marshal said seriously, "I could find a hundred men willing to take on Holder and the others. Some of 'em might even get one or two of the gang. But I don't know any of them boys like I know you. I know what you can do." He grinned. "Besides, I need somebody Holder's men don't know."

Coffin stood, holding the papers in one hand, rubbing his midsection slowly with the other. All the while he stared at Marshal Tom Pike. The lawman smiled, knowing Coffin had made up his mind, but did not want to say anything just yet.

So Pike waited, watching Coffin's slowly circling hand. That action fooled a lot of people, lulling them with its innocence, and because it took Coffin's hand away from the .45-caliber Colt Peacemaker at his right hip.

The hand stopped. Coffin nodded once, and turned for the door.

"I got to deputize you, Joe," Pike said softly, stopping Coffin with his hand on the door handle.

"Then count me out, Tom."

"Can't. I need your help, Joe. But it's got to be done right."

"Bullshit." He stepped out the door.

Pike rose and walked to the window to watch his old friend—if anyone could be called Coffin's friend—walk down the street toward his horse.

Pike shook his head. People were amazingly stupid sometimes, he thought. They would watch Joe Coffin innocently rub his belly, and they would be calmed. They would look at his short stature, and somehow feel superior. A number of men had died because they refused to see that a man's height had little to do with his toughness or ability with a gun. Coffin was faster with a gun than anyone he knew, and he was the best shot Pike had ever seen.

Coffin was ambidextrous too, something that few people knew. By the time most people found out, it was too late, and the majority who learned did not live to pass on the knowledge.

In addition, Coffin was as strong as a bull and twice as tough. But too many men took his quiet demeanor, his small size, and his young, usually clean-shaven face as signs of weakness.

Pike turned away from the window as Coffin mounted the chestnut horse.

Coffin's face was grim, and his eyes constantly flicked back and forth, up and down, taking in everything around him, as he rode west down Gurley Street. He enjoyed the liveliness of the city, and the cool, pine-scented air. Maybe, he thought, he would move down here. It would be warmer than Denver, even in the winter.

He grinned a bit as he rode slowly past the intersection with Montezuma Street—Whiskey Row. He thought of stopping at one of the taverns and cutting the dust in his throat, but he pushed back the urge. There would be time enough for that later, he thought.

Two blocks farther on, he saw a general store named Goldwater's. Coffin tethered the chestnut and entered the dim interior, stepping to the side of the door inside, out of the glare, letting his eyes adjust for a moment before pushing into the wide, roomy store. Coffin strode purposefully through the store, the rowels of his use-dulled spurs clanking with a soft rhythm.

"Can I help you, mister?" a man asked. He was dressed in

dark wool pants and starchy white shirt, the sleeves of which were held at the biceps by black garters. He was of medium height and somewhere in middle age, hair thinning, but back still straight.

Coffin ordered all the supplies he thought he would need. "I'll be by to pick 'em up and pay for 'em soon's I'm set to leave. Tomorrow. The next day, maybe." He did not want to tell this shopkeeper that he had but a few dollars in his pocket, and that he was waiting to get the thousand dollars for killing Stiles before he left.

Finished, he asked where the livery stable was. Outside, he mounted the horse again. The sun had been brittle but bright when he had entered Goldwater's store, but clouds had moved in and now gave the day a dull gray tinge, and it had started snowing lightly.

"Damn," he growled to himself. "Just what I needed."

He rode to the livery stable, turning over his horse for caring. While there, he picked out a mule that he would use for packing his supplies.

Outside, on foot, he walked off toward Whiskey Row. Ducking into the first saloon he came to—the Nugget—he stomped to the bar. "Gimme a shot of whiskey," he said evenly. "And a beer to go with it."

"You sure he's old enough, Kal?" a man standing nearby said with a low chuckle.

"Might not be, by the looks of him," Kal, the bartender, said with a smirk.

Damn, why did it always come to this? Coffin thought in irritation. All he wanted was a little peace and quiet, a shot of rotgut and a mug of beer. *Damn.*

"Why'n't you run along, sonny," the man next to Coffin at the bar said. "Come back when you grow up some." The man was tall, perhaps forty years old, and looked both trail-hardened and trail-weary.

Coffin whirled and backhanded the man, who slumped against the bar, spilling his whiskey. Blood sprouted on his lip.

"Why you . . ." the man sputtered, pushing himself up. He took a step toward Coffin.

Joe took one quick step to the side and then kicked the man

sharply in the stomach. The bar patron doubled over, his breath gone in one quick explosion. His hat fell off at his feet.

With a sneer, Coffin grabbed the man's greasy hair in his left hand. He pulled the man's head up a little, so his pain-dulled eyes gazed up at Coffin's. "You have somethin' else you'd like to say, mister?" Coffin asked coolly.

The man shook his head, still unable to speak.

"Then *adios, muchacho*." Coffin snapped the man's head down and his own knee up at the same time. There was a resounding splat as the man's nose shattered in a burst of blood when the two connected. The man groaned once as Coffin let him fall to the floor.

Coffin turned toward the bar, eyes flickering across the mirror, making sure no one was going to make a play against him. Then he looked squarely at the bartender.

"Kal," he said slowly, distinctly, "if that hand of yours comes up with anything in it besides a bottle of whiskey or mug of beer, I'm gonna drill a hole right through the middle of your forehead."

Suddenly the .45-caliber Peacemaker was in his hand, the bore deadly still, aimed between Kal's eyes. The bartender sweated and moved his hand very, very slowly. The neck of a whiskey bottle appeared over the rim of the bar, and Kal gulped.

Coffin grinned. "You ain't as goddamned dumb as I thought you was, Kal." He slipped the pistol away. "Now, I'd sure appreciate that drink, if you can find it in your heart to provide it."

"Yes, sir." With a trembling hand, Kal splashed some whiskey in a glass. Then he hurried to draw a beer and bring it to Coffin.

Chapter 3

It was snowing lightly when Joe Coffin rode out of Prescott, pack mule in tow. And it was cold. Not frigid, but enough to sour his disposition. He hunkered down into his hip-length, wool-lined, canvas duster, thankful for the thick leather gloves he wore.

He headed east, and soon passed by Fort Whipple, under the watchful eyes of the cold, blue-jacketed soldiers. He tried hard to keep up his usual good humor, but it was becoming more and more difficult since it seemed that the bad luck was still dogging him.

He snorted in disgust, firing out two streams of smoky air. Hell, here he was feeling sorry for himself. And what for? He had his horse, his mule and plenty of supplies, a job to do, and still almost eight hundred dollars in his saddlebags. What more could a man ask for, except maybe a warm bed—preferably occupied by . . .

"Best get your mind off that, boy," he muttered to himself.

He'd had a good time, though, his last two nights there. It had taken Marshal Tom Pike a day to confirm that Cort Stiles had been gunned down in Adobe—and who had done the gunning down. Then it had taken the better part of another day trying to round up the cash.

Once Coffin had gotten his money, he'd paid for his supplies, and his mule. It had been far too late in the day to leave then, so he'd headed back down to Whiskey Row, with its wild, raucous saloons, and friendly, open women. First there had been Alma, and, a short time later, Ella, she of the soft chocolate-colored skin and round, soft . . .

"Damn," he snorted again, startling the horse a bit. He settled the animal and, with a mixture of anger at himself for being caught up in such thoughts and pleasure at their remembrance, he yanked off his gloves. He rolled a cigarette and fired it up, all the while scanning the bleak, gray horizon.

He skirted the southern rim of the Black Hills, so called—like their better-known counterparts far to the north—because the thick stands of pines made them look black from a distance. The snow, never very heavy, had sifted to a stop.

He heard the jangling, clanking, creaking approach of a stage, and he pulled off the narrow trail to allow it to pass. As it did, he could see the suspicious looks tossed at him by the burly, mustachioed man riding shotgun. He tipped his hat and grinned a bit.

The clouds began to break up late in the day, for which he was thankful, and long before darkness overcame him he pulled off the trail, deep into the ponderosa pines.

He unloaded the mule and unsaddled the horse. Hobbling both, he let them out to graze on the brown, stunted, sparse grass under the trees. He rigged up a lean-to from a piece of canvas stretched tight and tied to pine limbs under a tree. With a bed of pine needles, it would be comfortable enough. He tossed his bedroll into the lean-to and gathered firewood.

Though the clouds had splintered and fled off to the east, the wind kicked up and the temperature fell. Rubbing his hands to warm them under the gloves, he set out to find firewood. There was plenty, but he would need a lot to last out the night, since pine burned hot but fast.

After building a fire, he filled his small coffeepot from the spring nearby and set it on a flat rock in the fire. As he did, a jackrabbit burst from under a sage bush maybe twenty yards away. Coffin cleared leather fast with the Peacemaker, and neatly drilled the animal in the head, just under one giant ear. It was, he knew, a lucky shot, but he was proud of it nonetheless.

Quickly, he skinned and cleaned the carcass, tossing the bloody fur and entrails far away so he would not be bothered by the coyotes. Jamming a stick through the rabbit, he propped it up over the fire and tossed a handful of coffee beans into the pot.

Finally he sat back, across the fire from his lean-to, able to relax. From his saddlebags he pulled the Wanted posters on Reno Holder's gang, and looked them over, trying to memorize every feature of each man's face from the poorly drawn likenesses on the cheap paper.

Though he had had little trouble handling Cort Stiles, he was not lulled into thinking the rest of the gang would be easy to take down. While he was afraid of no man, he was cautious. It was why he was still alive when so many who had followed his profession were not.

It was dark, and an owl hooted off to Coffin's right. He smiled, comforted by the sound. He shoved the papers back into his saddlebags and poured himself some coffee. Slicing off a chunk of rabbit meat, he leaned back against his saddle and ate his simple meal.

Finished, he had another cup of coffee and rolled a cigarette. He pulled the coffeepot away from the fire. All it would need would be heating up in the morning. He tossed a rope over a small limb a good ways up in a tree and then attached the rest of the rabbit to it and hauled it up. He cleaned his Peacemaker and made sure it was reloaded, the hammer resting on the one empty chamber he always left in the cylinder.

Then he turned in, using his saddle for a pillow.

Passing through Smithville the next day, he stopped in the single small saloon. While sipping at his beer he overheard someone say that there had been trouble in the town of Piñon Springs.

"What kind of trouble?" he asked politely.

The old man, his mustache gray, his face a map of lines and creases, looked him over silently for a while, before saying, "Bank there was robbed."

"Know who did it?"

The old man searched Coffin's face. "Heard it was Reno Holder and his boys."

Coffin nodded, and drained his beer. "How do I get to this Piñon Springs?"

"Why do you want to know?" the old man asked, suspicious, a little frightened. A few other men began gathering around, their faces hard and unforgiving.

"Lookin' for them boys," Coffin said easily, though he had pushed off the bar and was standing alertly.

"Why?" The old man was very nervous now.

"I aim to kill 'em," Coffin said flatly.

"You a marshal or somethin'?"

Coffin shook his head.

"He's a bounty hunter, I bet ya," one of the others said softly.

"That true, mister?" the old man asked.

Coffin shrugged.

"Maybe you're really goin' to join them," the old man said, voice creaking with age and worry.

"I ain't," Coffin said with finality. When the others did not say anything for some time, Coffin said, "Even if I was, I'd probably remember that you folks helped me out. Might make Holder and his bastards leave this town alone."

The others relaxed a bit. Finally the old man said, "Ride east till you get to Fort Verde there on the Verde River. There's a road goes north toward Dry Beaver Canyon. Take that. It curls round to the east again at Black Butte. Just keep follerin' that road, you'll come to Piñon Springs soon enough."

"Thanks," Coffin said. He spun and moved out, spurs clanking.

The weather had improved some, with the coming of a late Indian summer, and the days were fairly warm, though the nights were chilly. Coffin did not delay, though he did not push the horse and mule either. Still, it took him six days before he rode into Piñon Springs.

He was just in time to see a funeral procession heading toward the small cemetery behind the church. The black, horse-drawn hearse led the slow, solemn march.

Despite the warmth of the day, Coffin slipped into his short duster and buttoned it halfway up. He wanted to hide the shoulder rig. If this funeral was somehow connected to the robbery by Holder's men, he thought it wise to not look too much like one of the desperadoes.

He stopped and tied the reins of the horse to a hitching post and stepped up next to the blacksmith, who stood watching the procession quietly.

"The mayor die?" Coffin asked, trying to sound friendly but not sarcastic.

The bulky, balding blacksmith looked him up and down, then growled, "No."

"Must've been somebody important."

"Just a man. A goddamn brave man."

"What'd he do?"

The blacksmith glared at him. "You're askin' a heap of questions, mister, about things that don't concern you."

"They might."

"They might what?"

"Concern me. I'm huntin' Reno Holder's gang. If this here's connected somehow, it'd help me out considerable to hear it. If it ain't, I'll keep my trap shut and talk to the sheriff later."

The blacksmith watched as the funeral march dwindled and disappeared around the side of the church. When the last of the procession was in the cemetery, Coffin, the blacksmith, and two men in front of the saloon across the street were the only ones left.

Finally the smithy said, "Maybe I ought not to say nothin' to you, mister, but if what you say is true . . ."

He paused, then said, "Holder and his goddamn gang of hardcases come through here a week or so ago. Robbed the bank and killed Seth Wilkes, the teller, in cold blood. Just gunned him down. Christ."

The blacksmith paused again, and in the silence, the two men could hear the preacher's deep intonations from over by the church, cut through with the sobs and wails of the widow and her children. A wind kicked up, cold and hollow.

"Anyway," the smithy went on, "Sheriff Patterson got up a posse soon's he could. Deputized a dozen men. They was on the gang's trail in less than an hour." He stopped to blow his nose on a giant red bandanna before going on. "Two days ago they come back with Hiram's body."

He waved one ham-sized hand—the one with the short, stubby, heavy hammer in it—in the direction of the graveside service that continued. "He was a good man, Hiram was. Never hurt no one. Didn't even carry a gun. He always done what he thought was right, though. Like this time . . ."

The blacksmith paused once again to blow his nose in the bandanna. His breathing was ragged as he tried to regain control of himself. When he did, he said, "Get them bastards, mister."

"I'll do what I can," Coffin said, uncomfortable under the pleading glare of the blacksmith, and the man's obvious emotion. "Where'd Hiram get killed . . ." He hesitated a heartbeat. "I mean, which way was the gang ridin' when . . ."

"Northeast. Gang ambushed the posse up 'round Chaves Pass."

Coffin nodded, and looked up at the sky. "You got a hotel or anything in town?"

"No, why?"

"It's kind of late in the day to be riding out. Thought I'd spend the night here, get me a good meal. Then I'd be fresh come mornin'."

"No hotel," the blacksmith said again. "But you can stay here"—he waved the hammer at the stable behind him—"if you're of a mind to. I got an empty stall. I'll fill it with fresh straw."

"It'll do. There someplace I can get some grub?"

"After the buryin's over, I'll talk to Miss Hallie. She's the best cook in town, and cooks for visitors, sometimes."

"I'd be obliged."

The blacksmith took the reins to Coffin's horse and mule and led them away. Coffin went to the saloon and had a beer before going back to the stable. The blacksmith had a stall cleaned out and filled with fresh straw. Coffin's saddle was on the side of the stall, hanging over the wood half-partition. The horse and mule were in separate stalls nearby, blissfully eating hay and oats.

The blacksmith came up and said, "I talked to Miss Hallie and she said she'd feed you whenever you're ready."

"Now's a good time as any."

The smithy led him to a small frame house at the other end of the small town. Miss Hallie Stickle was a horse-faced woman in her mid-thirties, with a shapeless block of a body, mousy brown hair with scattered wisps of gray, and long, work-split fingers.

But she was a damn good cook, and Coffin wolfed down large portions of charred beefsteak, potatoes, beans, and thick cornbread lathered in butter. He washed it down with several cups of coffee.

"That was real fine, ma'am," he said politely as he fired up a cigarette.

"Thank you," Miss Hallie said, trying to blush girlishly but failing miserably. "Where are you staying?"

"At the stable."

"You could stay here," Miss Hallie said with no embarrassment.

"I don't think that'd be right, ma'am," Coffin said, stumbling a little over the words. There was no way he would want to spend the night with this immense, slatternly woman, no matter how well she cooked. But he was not the kind to be mean either, and did not want to hurt her feelings.

"Like hell," Miss Hallie said flatly. She rolled a cigarette of her own, as deftly as Coffin had done it.

Coffin cast his mind around for words that would soothe her. They were not easy to find, but he did find some. "There's liable to be danger, Miss Hallie," he said softly. He tapped the shoulder rig and his two other pistols. "There might be folks in town don't cotton to a man such's me, especially after what's happened. It could be dangerous for you. . . ."

She knew he was lying, but it let them both save face. Her loins ached, though, for the feel of this hard, young man in her. There was no man in town who would have her anymore, and so she had to rely on strangers. But this was not to be one of those times for her, she realized with resignation.

"I'd appreciate bein' able to get breakfast here, though," Coffin said, trying to smile and almost succeeding.

She nodded curtly as she gathered up the dishes with more force than she had meant to display.

Chapter 4

As was customary, Joe Coffin was awake before dawn had fully broken. He felt well-rested, and thought maybe things might be getting a little better. He dressed and then swept out the stall that had served as his bedroom. Then he went to check over both the chestnut horse and the mule, making sure they had enough feed. While he was doing so, he heard the noise.

It wasn't the first time he had heard the sounds of a mob, and since the volume of noise was gradually growing louder, he figured it was heading in his direction.

Coffin went to the door and peered out. There were maybe thirty people—men, women, and even a few children—about halfway down the street heading toward the barn. He stepped back and stood very still, except to turn his head slowly, eyes and ears alert, surveying the room.

It was ominously quiet in the stable, with only the soft nickering and foot-shuffling of the several horses. The blacksmith who ran the place was not there. "Damnit," Coffin snapped, as he kicked the barn door shut and barred it.

He strapped on the shoulder rig, which he had left off while he was working. He checked each of his weapons, and began saddling his horse. Given a chance to make a break for it, he would, leaving behind his supplies, if necessary. He was not afraid of any of the people out there in the street. But he had seen mobs at work before, and they were unpredictable.

He had just finished tightening the cinch on his saddle when he heard, "You. In the stable. Toss out your guns and come on out with your hands up."

Coffin stepped close to the door, but at the side of it. "Go to hell," he yelled.

"Don't make it hard on yourself, boy. Just do like I say."

"Who're you?"

"Sheriff Turk Patterson. Now come on out."

"Why?"

"You're under arrest."

"What for?"

There was silence for a while. Coffin took the time to climb up into the loft, where he cracked open the hay-loading door there. He looked out. The sheriff was talking to the mob, trying to make himself heard over the clamor of voices.

Finally Patterson got most of the people calmed down some, and he turned and yelled at the stable door. "Look, mister. We lost two people here in the past week or so. We're thinkin' you might just be part of that gang."

"What'n hell makes you think that?" Coffin asked, startling them when his voice came from on high.

The people squinted up at him, the sheriff shading his eyes. "You been askin' an awful lot of questions about Reno Holder and his boys," Patterson spit out with a biting anger in his voice. "Maybe you got separated from them, and are lookin' for 'em."

"Could be," Coffin said more jovially than he felt. Damned if his luck wasn't still poor as the meat off an old bull. "But it ain't." There just had to be a way to change this string of mishaps, miscalculations, and other quirks that life had been saddling him with lately.

"Well, you throw out your guns and come on out peaceable. We'll let a judge decide all that."

Coffin laughed harshly, with little humor. "Horseshit. I come out there now, I'll be dead before I get across the street."

There was more arguing, while Coffin waited patiently, trying to ignore the grumbling in his stomach. He sure could use some food and, more importantly, some coffee.

Finally the sheriff turned back and looked up at him. "We'll burn you out, if we have to, mister," he shouted. "Now, you and I both know damned well that doin' so's gonna make a heap of folks unhappy, but . . ." He threw up his hands, and shrugged.

"None of this is necessary, Sheriff," Coffin called down. "You want to come in here and talk peaceable with me, I can explain it all and then you can check out my story."

"Well, I . . ."

"Go on, Sheriff," someone said. The crowd affirmed their support for such an idea.

"But, I . . ." Patterson said nervously.

Coffin sighed. It was never easy dealing with mob mentality. He took a deep breath and said, "I was hired by U.S. Marshal Tom Pike, over to Prescott, to run down Reno Holder and the bastards that ride with him. Why don't you send a wire to him, and check it out?"

Patterson looked uncertain. He had nothing to lose by doing so, but in the meantime, he'd still have a mob on his hand and a potential killer holed up in a barn.

The others were confused too, as it dawned on them that they might have an innocent man there, and with a simple way for them to find out. Of course, they couldn't let Coffin escape while they were waiting for the reply.

There was a gunshot. Coffin, who had presented small enough of a target at the upper door anyway, flatted down onto the loft floor. Then he heard, "Get outta my way, you damn fools."

He peered out and saw Hallie Stickle bulling her way through the crowd, scattering people. In one hand she held a Colt pistol, in the other a large picnic basket.

"Goddamnit, Miss Hallie," Patterson snapped, spinning in her direction, blocking her path. "What're you doin' here?"

"Bringin' food to that man in there, who's probably half-starved to death by now. Seems you ain't figurin' to let him out so's he can come on over to my place to eat. I aim to bring him his breakfast here."

"But, Miss Hallie—"

"Don't you but Miss Hallie me, Sheriff. You and these damn fools might be scared of him, but I ain't. He ain't here to harm none of us, and if any of you'd stop for a minute to think about that, you'd know it too. But if you can't see that, then go on and send your goddamn wire to Prescott. I'll set in there with him and keep him company while you do."

Upstairs, Coffin gulped at the thought.

Patterson said, "You'll probably let him go soon's I turn my back."

"Let the rest of these idiots stand here and watch. Just make sure you tell 'em that if they try comin' in there while you're gone, I'll shoot 'em, each and all. Now get your lazy ass outta my way."

The lumpy woman in a bright purple taffeta dress shoved past the sheriff, almost knocking him over. She got to the door and yelled: "Come'n open this goddamn door."

Coffin sat for a moment, letting his head—which did not want anything to do with this woman—argue with his stomach—which very much wanted some food—over whether he should let her in. Finally his stomach won. He slid down the ladder and, with a sinking feeling, he lifted up the bar and cracked the door open.

He stepped back, a pistol in each hand, as Hallie barged through the doorway. As soon as she was in, Coffin kicked the door shut again, and snapped, "Bar it."

"Put them guns away," Hallie said sharply, not in the least bit afraid of him.

"Just do it."

She shrugged and stuck her Colt into the partially opened bosom of her dress. Then she slid the bar into place. Turning, she said, "Well, where should we eat?"

He waved a gun toward the loft.

Hallie grinned lecherously and winked at him. Coffin gulped and began to sweat. Perhaps this had been a mistake, he thought. He could have made do with some jerky and hardtack from his stores. Even that unappetizing meal would be better than spending several hours with this lumpy, foul-smelling woman.

But Hallie was halfway up the ladder already, moving much more agilely than Coffin would have thought possible. With weak knees he followed her up, and took his former position near the door. He looked out and saw the sheriff just entering his small clapboard-fronted adobe office down the street.

With a practiced eye, Coffin looked over the crowd. Everyone was still there, he noticed, except for the sheriff. He turned back. Hallie had spread out a small tablecloth. From the huge picnic basket she pulled two covered skillets, a coffeepot with the snout plugged, two plates, and some cutlery.

Opening both skillets, she said, "Dig in."

One skillet contained eggs scrambled up with some kind of Spanish salsa mixed in; the other contained *chorizo* and some slices of ham. Coffin's stomach took the forefront, and he heaped up a plate with eggs, ham, and *chorizo* sausage. Leaning back against the door jamb, so that he was out of the way of those below but could still keep an eye on them, he started eating.

"Coffee?" Hallie asked, batting her lashes at him.

He nodded, mouth too full of food to speak. She poured him a cup and sat it next to him, brushing her hand against his Levi-clad leg as she did. Coffin almost choked on his eggs.

She sat back and filled a cup and a plate for herself. Coffin's eyes flicked back and forth, from the crowd outside to Stickle. The former began to dwindle as a few people wandered off; the latter ate more daintily than Coffin would have thought she could.

Coffin didn't really feel like it, but when he finished his plate full of food, he took what was left in the skillets. To be done probably would mean having to fend off this woman. So he ate more.

But there had to come a time when he had to finish, and he placed his plate back in the basket. Quickly he rolled a cigarette and lit it. Maybe, he thought, this would fend her off a while longer.

"Roll one for me?" she asked in a soft voice.

He looked at her, startled at the almost plaintive tone she had used. Deftly he did so, lit it, and then handed it to her.

"Thanks," she breathed. Her fingers brushed his as she took the cigarette and she almost winced, as if it was painful.

The two sat in silence, smoking. When they were finished, Coffin threw his out the door, smiling when two people had to scurry out of the way. Hallie carefully crushed hers out on the hay-covered wood floor of the loft.

Coffin pulled out his fixings hurriedly. "Want another?" he asked as he opened the pouch of tobacco.

"Sure," she sighed.

When he handed her the lit cigarette, she said in a voice barely above a whisper, "This ain't necessary, you know."

"What?"

"Lightin' one cigarette after another."

"I smoke a lot," he answered lamely.

"Bullshit. You just think I'll keep throwin' myself at you, and you want to avoid that."

"That's not true. I—"

"No need to lie about it." She smiled almost ruefully, and it softened her face a little. "I'm used to it. Even out here, where women are few and far apart, I can't get a man. Ain't no man in this town'll have me no more. Once in a while, if I push hard enough, I can talk some stranger into spendin' a little time with me." She drew in a ragged lungful of smoke.

"I'm sorry," Coffin said, sadly.

"Won't change your mind, though, will it?"

"No," he said quietly. "I know I owe you, though, for helpin' me out here and all, but . . ."

"But what?" she snapped, sarcastic, stamping out the cigarette with vicious stabs. "But I'm too big for you? But I'm too fat for you? I hear that a lot, ya know."

"But," he lied gently, "there's someone else. Back in Denver." Go easy, he told himself. Don't make it too big a lie.

Hallie's eyes widened, and her ruddy, fleshy face brightened. "Really?" she asked, almost excited. "I mean, you ain't got a ring or nothin'."

"Ain't married yet. Me'n Lisbeth'll be gittin' hitched soon's I finish this job."

Hallie's face showed hope. "I think you may be shovelin' a yard full of horseshit here, Joe, if that's really your name, but I don't care. Even if it's all a lie, at least you care enough to make up a good lie and try'n make me feel better. Ain't many men willin' to do that."

"My pleasure, ma'am," Coffin said, doffing his hat briefly. He glanced out the window. The crowd was still there. "Sheriff's back," he said over his shoulder as he continued to look out the door.

"Joe?" Stickle asked, pleading evident in her voice.

"Yeah?" he asked, snapping his head around at the tone of her.

"You said you owe me for helpin' you out." When he nodded, she said, "Well, there's somethin' I'd like ya to do for me."

"I can't, Hallie. I . . ."

"It ain't that." She paused, gulped, then plunged ahead, her eyes searching his with worried fervor. "But could we fake it?"

"What?" he exploded, stunned.

"Fake it. Put on a little sound show, like a mellerdrama, sort of." Her face had a new pinkish tinge now, but she went on. "Let them folks down there think we're . . . we're . . ."

"I know what you mean," he said with a slight cough. He sat silent for a few minutes, thinking. As he did, a grin began on his face, and grew and grew. Finally, he said, "Goddamn, yes. After the way they've treated both of us, I reckon we can gain you a little respect here with some playactin'."

Trying to fight down the giggles and laughter, they moaned and groaned and howled as if the throes of making wildly abandoned love. They capped it off when Hallie tossed one of her petticoats out the door.

The two, fighting back convulsions of laughter, peered over the rim to watch the garment waft down toward the shocked and revolted crowd. Coffin noticed there were no more children in the crowd, and only two women.

Coffin and Miss Hallie pulled back from the door and let their laughter out.

Chapter 5

"Joe Coffin. It's Sheriff Patterson."

Coffin poked his head out the door. He and Hallie Stickle had napped a while, after treating—if that's the word that could be used—the crowd below to two more sessions of their verbal lovemaking.

The crowd was gone now, Coffin saw. "What do you want, Sheriff?" he called down.

"Got an answer to my wire just a bit ago. Marshal Pike says you're tellin' the truth. You're free to go." He sounded like he wanted to be apologetic, but was afraid to be.

"Thanks a lot," Coffin called down sarcastically. He watched as Patterson drifted off, back down the dusty street toward his little cubicle of an office.

"Well," Hallie said to him as he turned back, "reckon you'll be leaving out right away, huh?" She looked terribly sad, lonely, and, yes, he thought, even small.

"Well," he said slowly, "I reckon it's a little late for me to be headin' on today." It was true, he told himself. After all, it had taken the sheriff more than eight hours to get an answer back from Prescott. "Besides, I'm hungry again." He smiled.

"Me, too." Hallie stood. "I am," she said with a poorly executed curtsy, "a respectable cook, sir. Would you care to join me at the supper table."

"Reckon I would." He had found that Hallie was nowhere near the horrible creature he had seen her as originally. No, she was witty, and full of bawdy humor. There was an underlying sadness that brought out sympathy too. She still did nothing for him sexually, but she was fine as a companion.

She smiled, and gathered up the few things she had brought that were still scattered around. When she finished, she said, "You can spend the night too, you know." She held up her hand to stop him before he could say anything. "I have an extra bed."

"All right," he said, not making light of her.

Downstairs, Coffin unsaddled the horse. When he unbarred the door, the blacksmith was waiting, looking rather sheepish. Coffin nodded, then said, "Make sure the chestnut and the mule are well taken care of."

He and Hallie stepped out into the warmth of the afternoon. She hooked her arm through his, first looking nervously at him to make sure it was all right. He nodded. So they sauntered down the street, the immense, shapeless, horse-faced woman clad in purple and the short, cocky, defiant man. They made quite a pair, but no one dared say anything.

After their dinner, Coffin walked to the small, shabby saloon. Standing at the plank bar, he drank two mugs of beer, smiling inwardly at the people. They were afraid of him. Anyone who had been hired by a U.S. marshal to run down a gang of murdering hardcases like Reno Holder's men—and do it alone—had to be one tough *hombre*. As did any man who would make love—three times in a single day—to Miss Hallie Stickle.

Coffin knew what they were thinking, and felt quite a bit of humor at it all. Especially the parts that the people were conjuring up.

The next morning, after another of Hallie's great meals, he rode out, sitting proudly atop the big chestnut horse. As he neared the edge of the very small town, he turned back and blew Miss Hallie a kiss with his hand. Then, with a roar of laughter, he galloped off, towing the stolid mule behind him.

He forded a stream, and soon after turned more eastward, skirting a rim of small mountains and buttes. It took several days, but he wound his way through Chaves Pass, learning nothing new at the small stage station there. Two days after that, he wound through Sunset Pass, between the two knobs of

Sunset Mountain.

Following the trail of the outlaws had not been hard, even though Coffin was not the best tracker around. Holder's men had made no effort to conceal their movements, plus there were numerous telltale signs, including the two bodies Coffin found and took the time to bury. He could not prove it, of course, but he figured the two men had been killed by Holder or his crew.

When he wandered into Red Cliffs, just past the Sunset Mountains near Clear Creek, it was late of an evening. Still, there was an awful lot of activity in the small, sandy town. He considered bypassing the place, since he did not want another reception like he had received at Piñon Springs. But he had to know if the Reno gang had passed by this way.

It was quite cold up this high at night, and so he was wearing his coat, covering up the twin .36-caliber Colts. He hoped it would help.

A tall, thin, though muscular man was just leaving the livery stable as Coffin rode up. "Can I still get my horse taken care of?" Coffin asked.

The man hesitated, then said, "Sure. Fourth stall on the left is open. Hay's at the far end. So's some oats. We can settle up come mornin'."

"Obliged." He touched the brim of his hat and walked the chestnut into the livery. When he had unloaded the mule, unsaddled the horse, rubbed both down, stowed away his supplies, and made sure the two animals had plenty of hay and oats, he left the livery. It was well into night, and Coffin was tired and hungry.

With saddlebags over one shoulder, and his Winchester in hand, he strode to the saloon. Like the one in Piñon Springs, it was small. A false wood front covered the adobe, which was unadorned inside for the most part. He walked to the bar—several planks resting on a half-dozen old kegs—and ordered a shot of red-eye and a mug of beer.

As he paid the bartender, Coffin asked, "There a place in town where I could get a bed?"

"End of the street, this side. Old man Tillman and his wife take in boarders. I reckon they got room."

"Obliged. How about food?"

The bartender looked him over. Coffin's dark eyes stared calmly back, but they were rimmed from tiredness. His face was stubbled and he was covered with dirt. "You look like you been on the trail a while, mister," the barkeep said noncommittally.

"Yep."

The bartender was used to quiet men, as he was used to loud men, and fighting men, and drunken men and . . . He had seen it all." We can rustle you up some grub here, if you ain't too particular."

"I ain't."

"Want it now?"

Coffin downed the shot and smacked his lips. "There any hurry?" he asked.

"Naw. My wife'll make you up somethin' when you're ready."

"Obliged." He polished off half the beer. "Reckon I'll see if I can get a room, then come on back."

"We'll be here."

Coffin drained the glass and left, walking up the dim street. The room he got from Old Man Tillman was about the size of a one-holer outhouse, but it had a bed, chamber pot, and water pitcher and basin. It also had a lock.

Joe set down his rifle and saddlebags. He took the money he still had in the bags and stuck it in a shirt pocket. The door might well have a lock, but that didn't mean he had to trust it—or the people who owned the place.

He went back to the saloon, which didn't even have a name, and went in. "Ready for your supper now?" the bartender asked.

"Yep. Reckon I'll take it at that table back in the corner yonder." He pointed.

The bartender nodded. "Something to drink?"

"Got any chock?"

"Nope." He looked around conspiratorially. "Hell, that Texas brew ain't worth feedin' to the hogs, you know what I mean."

Coffin grinned. "I'll have a beer."

"Coming right up."

Coffin took his seat. He had barely sat when the bartender brought him a foam-topped mug. Coffin nodded his thanks and took a deep sip. It was hot and close in the small bar, so he stood and shrugged off the short duster and hung it on the wobbly wood chair.

He was aware of the glances, surreptitiously pointed fingers, and whispers his action precipitated. He ignored it, staring fixedly ahead, sipping beer.

It was not long before a buxom, graying woman shuffled up and slapped down a tin plate overlapped by a charred beefsteak, a tin bowl piled with steaming, spicy beans, and another tin plate with a hunk of hot bread and a chunk of butter.

"Obliged, ma'am," Coffin said. He pulled off his hat and dropped it on the table. Picking up the cheap knife and fork, he cut into the steak. While he ate, he was aware that people were still talking about him, but he paid it no heed. Until one of the men edged closer to him. Most of the other dozen or so men in the place backed the man.

Coffin took one look at the man—an aging, gray-haired, reedy fellow with a pale complexion, stringy mustache, and too-big pants held up by a too-long belt. And a badge.

The old man cleared his throat, and asked in a shaky voice, "What's your business here, mister?"

"Supper." Coffin continued to eat, but as he reached his left hand for the bread, his right moved cautiously under the table and unhooked the safety strap of the big Colt's hammer. Just in case.

"That ain't what I mean."

"That's what you asked, Sheriff."

"Damnit, what're you doin' in this town?" the old man huffed.

"Eatin' my supper. Then gettin' what I hope'll be a good night's sleep over at Tillman's."

"You leavin' come mornin'?"

"Plan to. You got a problem with that?" His eyes bored into the sheriff's.

"Well . . . no . . ." the sheriff stammered, taken a little aback.

"Get out of the way, you old fool," a young, tough-looking

man said, pushing the sheriff out of the way. "You shouldn't've come back here, boy," he snarled at Coffin.

"Never been here before," Coffin said calmly, forking a piece of steak into his mouth.

"Like hell. You was with Reno Holder and them others that robbed the bank three days ago and killed my pa when we went chasin' after 'em."

"That's bullshit. Three days ago I was on the trail between here and Piñon Springs."

"Like hell!" the man screamed.

"Calm down, son," the sheriff said to him, but the man angrily shook him off.

"You say Holder robbed the bank here a few days ago?"

"As if you didn't know, goddamn it." He had not calmed any.

"Which way was they headin'?"

"See!" the man crowed. "See! I told you he was one of 'em. Look at him. All them guns and such. He got separated from them bastards and now he's lookin' for 'em again."

There was a growl of assent from the crowd.

"Is everybody in town as stupid as you?" Coffin asked, shoving another piece of meat into his mouth. He chewed slowly, eyes alert.

"Why . . . goddamn you . . ."

"You really think that if I was one of Holder's men I'd come moseyin' in here lookin' for him two days after he rode through and killed somebody? Don't you think I'd know where his hideout is? Or where they were gonna meet if they had split up?"

He spooned in some beans as the others thought that over, and the hard young man facing him sputtered, trying to come up with a retort. "I'm a bounty hunter, looking for them," Coffin said sharply.

"You'll get killed," someone said.

"The reward's big enough to risk my ass for. Now I'd be obliged if you all was to leave and let me finish my supper in peace."

The big young man thought to argue some more, but two other men hauled him away. The sheriff shuffled off last, after having searched Coffin's face for a while, looking for something. Coffin did not know if the old man had found what he was looking for.

The rest of Coffin's meal was eaten without interruption, and he sat back afterward with a cigarette and some beer. Before long, he drifted off toward his room in the boardinghouse, after finding out where he could have some breakfast in the morning.

As he made the short walk, he kept to the shadows, under the overhang of buildings wherever possible. It would not be impossible for him to think that the hotheaded young man in the saloon might be waiting in the dark for him.

But the walk was uneventful, and his night's sleep undisturbed—except for the one fearful dream in which he and Miss Hallie were married and . . .

He awoke in a rather foul mood. He had thought this task would be simple—by no means easy, but simple: Find Reno Holder, Pete St. Johns, Ian O'Kelly, Bill Curly, Buck Schiebel, and Will Greenaway, and either kill them or lasso them and bring them in to Marshal Tom Pike. But the six outlaws were proving difficult to find—though their trail had been easy to follow. And here he was being confronted in every town he entered. It did not make him feel comfortable.

It was with a sense of uneasiness that he left his room, with his saddlebags and rifle, in the morning. And he had a sense of urgency. He had to find these men soon. Real soon.

Heading for the livery stable, he heard the whistle of the train as it made its short stop in Red Cliffs. Inside the stable, he loaded his dwindling supplies on the mule, and saddled his horse. He would have breakfast, and then ride out.

He paid the liveryman and led his two animals out into the warming sunshine. Near the small restaurant, he tied the horse and mule and went in.

He was in a little better spirits when he came back out, until he heard, "You ain't goin' nowhere, mister."

Chapter 6

Joe Coffin took a deep breath and turned slowly. Sure enough, it was the young man who had confronted him in the saloon last night.

He seemed to be a little drunk. He shrugged off two friends about the same age, who tried to pull him away. Instead, he shouted, "Goddamn you, let's see how goddamn tough you are without all your friends behind ya."

"You're makin' a mistake here, boy," Coffin said coldly. He had no desire to kill this young man, but he would do so if someone did not grab the youth and haul him away. He looked around, hoping the sheriff or someone—anyone—else would take down this young man quietly.

But the only ones around were his two friends, one of whom grabbed the youth from behind, around the chest, and tried hauling him back. "Come on, Rance. Let's go on home. You'll only . . ."

Rance snapped his powerful arms outward, breaking his friend's hold. He spun and punched the youth, sending him sprawling. Then Rance turned back toward Coffin. "Well, bigshot, outlaw gunfighter. You gonna draw or are you afraid."

"You wanna live to be a man, you'd best turn you ass around and take it home, boy," Coffin hissed. Christ, he thought, that's all he needed now was to have to gun down some eighteen-year-old punk with a snootful of forty-rod. It might bring the whole town down on him.

"Shit. You're just chicken," Rance sneered.

The youth who had gotten knocked sprawling had finally picked himself up. "He's gonna kill ya, Rance, goddamnit. He's a killer."

"Run home, Tobe, if you're scared of seein' some bloodshed," Rance said over his shoulder.

Tobe backed away slowly, and then turned and ran. Coffin watched him with part of his vision. But most of him was still focused on Rance. However, he was aware of the few other people around him. No one would endanger him at the moment, but a number of people were peeking from behind curtains and such, watching.

The other youth stepped between Rance and Coffin, facing his friend. "Now, hold on, Rance," he said firmly. "This ain't doin' no one no good. It ain't gonna bring back your pa, and it sure as hell ain't gonna help you none to get killed. Let the law handle it."

"That old, useless fart," Rance snorted. "He couldn't catch a baby stealin' an apple if it happened right under his nose." Rance's eyes were bloodshot and wild. He wiped his hands on his pants legs. "Naw, I got to do this. Take care of it—"

"Don't do it, Rance. I ain't gonna let ya do it. You'll have to come through—"

Rance lashed out with a pistol and slammed it against his friend's cheek. The youth went down, not unconscious, but in pain, and bleeding. Rance slid the pistol back into the holster.

Coffin figured then that Rance was dead. There probably would be no stopping the bulky young man short of it. But Coffin figured he would give it one last try.

"Draw!" Rance screamed.

Coffin stood, arms hanging loose at his sides, not hovering too near either of his revolvers there. He was tense, but calm. He hoped Rance would not draw down on a man who was unwilling to draw. Coffin figured he could take the humiliation in this little town if it would spare this youth's life.

"Draw, I said! You puking yellow coward. Draw!"

Coffin remained standing stoically. The only signs that this young man was bothering him were a tightening of the jaws and a narrowing of the eyes.

Joe Coffin turned ever so slowly toward his animals. He took one step, when he heard a pistol being drawn. By the time Coffin heard the cocking of the revolver, he was diving off to his left, toward the center of the street.

A bullet kicked up dust a foot behind him, as Coffin came up on one knee, the Peacemaker braced in both hands.

Rance fired two more times, each time the bullet kicking up dust somewhere near Coffin. "Damn," Coffin muttered as he squeezed off a round. The bullet shattered Rance's gun arm between shoulder and elbow.

The young man howled and fell. He scrabbled up into a sitting position, and then awkwardly pushed himself up, grabbing the pistol with his left hand. Swearing at the pain that seared through him, Rance clumsily cocked the pistol with his left thumb and tried to draw a bead on his opponent.

Coffin had stood and brushed off his pants, but he still held the Colt in his hand, loosely. He watched in fascination as Rance took wavering aim at him. If only this youth had learned some self-control and patience, he would have made a good gunman. But he was too rash, and probably would not live to reach the age of majority.

"Don't do it, boy," Coffin said harshly.

"The hell with you." Rance fired, but the shot was wide by several yards. He thumbed back the hammer again.

Coffin pushed emotion out of his mind. Calmly he lifted the Colt and shot Rance in the leg, just below the knee. The young man screamed, buckling and falling.

Rance tried to get up again. All he could manage was a sit, but he had his old Remington pistol in hand. He was sweating hard as he worked to cock the pistol.

Coffin shook his head in disgust at what he was seeing. He pushed back his hat with the muzzle of the Colt, then bellowed, "If any of you people care for this goddamned stupid young buck, you best get down here and take his gun from him. I give him two chances. I ain't fixin' to give him a third."

Tobe ran out of a building, followed by the doddering Sheriff Parks. Tobe reached Rance just as the young man got the pistol cocked. "That's enough, Rance," Tobe said firmly, grabbing the pistol.

Rance tried to fight him off, but he had no strength left, and

Tobe easily pulled the gun away. Within moments a doctor was there, bending over Rance and muttering.

The sheriff stopped in front of Coffin, who calmly extracted the spent shells and replaced them.

"You are leavin', ain't you, mister?" the sheriff asked, fear clogging his voice.

"I had planned on it before Rance here went off half-cocked."

"You got to forgive him, mister. His pa was killed by the Holder gang when they rode through t'other day."

"I don't have to forgive nobody nothin'." Coffin was angry, and for the first time he let it show. "I come into town all peaceable, and all I get is some young punk with his balls in an uproar about somethin' I don't know nothin' about."

"I could run you into the calaboose." Sweat glinted above the sheriff's gray eyebrows.

Coffin laughed at the incongruity of the statement. The sheriff seethed. "Well," the lawman said stiffly, "we don't like strangers comin' in here and shootin' up our citizens."

"Then teach 'em to keep their guns in their holsters, and maybe they won't get shot," Coffin snapped. "Hell, if I wasn't such a nice fellow, that young pup over there'd be stiffenin' up in rigor mortis already."

The sheriff rubbed the back of his neck. Such doings were too much for a man his age. Twice in less than a week. He'd only taken the job because it was supposed to be easy. "Hell, I know," he finally sighed. "Rance's been lookin' for trouble since his pa got killed. It was only time before he threw down on somebody like you and paid the pound price for it. I reckon he was lucky it was you and not some of them others ya hear about."

Coffin was mollified, but only a little. "Which way was Holder headed when he rode out of here?" he asked.

"North, toward the Little Colorado."

"There anything up that way?"

"Not a hell of a lot. Train stops at the canyon—Canyon Diablo, a town up top of the canyon. Ain't been a town there for long—only since summer. Bad place, that 'un. Stage runs from there to Leroux Springs, west; and down to Prescott.

Thore's a little place called Aspen Wells off to the west a ways, Navajos farther north and the east. A few towns here and there. Lots of mountains, valleys, mesas. High desert."

"Don't sound promisin'."

"It ain't. Lot of nothin', least till you get over by the San Francisco Peaks. People've started ranching over that away. But except for a few small towns here and there, it's an empty place. There's no water in many places. Injins are still hostile, if they catch ya off to yourself. Ridges, switchbacks, gullies washes, drop-offs."

Coffin grunted and put the Colt away. He moved to his horse. Shoving a foot in the stirrup, he pulled himself on the animal. He glanced back at Rance, laying in a pool of his blood on the dusty, cold street, the doctor working over him. Coffin was not sure whether he wished the youth would live or die.

He rode slowly up the street, the feeling of gloom and uneasiness sitting hard on him once again. Maybe he should quit this job. It had brought nothing but misfortune. Maybe he should ride eastward, instead of north, back toward New Mexico Territory. Send a wire to Tom Pike from the first decent town he saw, telling Pike to find someone else for this. He still had more than seven hundred dollars in his saddle bags. That would keep him a while; longer if he could parlay it through gambling.

He almost chuckled at that. With the way his luck was running, his seven hundred-plus dollars would be zero-minus dollars in one sitting. But maybe, if he dropped this job, his luck would return. It was only since he had gotten the telegram from Pike that his luck had gone so completely sour. But if he didn't have this job anymore, perhaps, just perhaps, mind you . . .

A rider bolted past him, coming from the direction in which Coffin was headed. Joe stopped his horse and looked back. The rider raced to where the sheriff was standing a few feet from where the doctor worked on Rance. The rider came to a stop in a flurry of foam and dust.

Coffin twisted in the saddle to get a better look. The rider had stayed on his horse, and sat there talking and gesticulating wildly, pointing often in Coffin's direction, though Joe did not think the man was pointing at him.

"Well, damn," Coffin muttered, "I better see what this is all about."

He turned the horse and trotted back the way he had just come, stopping behind the horseman, just catching the man say, "two dead . . . another hurt real bad . . ." He choked to a halt, hoping to catch his breath.

"What happened?" Coffin asked.

"Train robbery," the rider gasped.

"Where?"

He pointed north. "Just before it gets to Canyon Diablo."

"There anything out there?" Coffin asked, since no one else seemed capable of it.

"Not a hell of a lot. Heap of rocky lava beds west beyond the canyon. And a big hole in the ground. Me and another fellow had our horses in a car. We heard the goings-on and saddled up. We opened up the door and jumped out, horses and all, first chance we got. He headed northwest toward Grand Falls and Black Falls. I headed this way, for here and, soon's I get through here, to Chaves Station."

He stumbled to a stop and gratefully accepted the bottle of whiskey someone thrust at him. He took a long swig.

Coffin took the time to look the man over carefully. He was of medium height, and slender, with the beginnings of a paunch. He wore a sensible Colt revolver, unadorned, riding high on his hip. He had on corduroy pants, and a plain brown wool shirt. A blue bandanna was around his neck. His clothes showed plenty of usage. An out-of-work cowboy, Coffin figured. Not one to be scared off too easily, but with enough sense to know you don't go up against a gang like Holder's without some edge.

"You folks got a wire here?" the rider finally asked. "I need to wire the federal marshal in Prescott."

Coffin almost smiled at that, but held himself in check.

"Yep," Sheriff Parks said. "Come with me."

"Just hold on a minute," Coffin said with steel in his voice. "You know who done it?"

"Hell yes. Reno Holder's gang. Who else'd pull somethin' like that?"

"You send anyone west to spread the alarm?"

"Naw. Wasn't but me and that other fella. Besides, them outlaws was headin' west, and there ain't nothing between where they did that robbery and Aspen Wells but the canyon and Apache Cave."

"Apache Cave?"

"Yep. South of the town of Canyon Diablo a couple of miles. Place got its name a couple of years ago when some Navajos chased a band of Apaches who'd been raidin' up in Navajo land into the cave. The Navajos blocked it off and set fires, burned all them Apaches to death. Ain't much to the cave, though, far's anybody knows.

"Canyon Diablo—the canyon is a hellish place. Steep walls, and only a few small trails leading down. Then there's the town. That's a hellacious place too. It—"

"I've heard," Coffin said roughly. "Anything south?"

"Nothing but the canyon itself. Good water and wood down at the bottom in some places, but most folks keep away from it."

"You sure it was Holder?"

"Yep. None of 'em wore masks. Never do, from what I hear tell. Ain't afraid of bein' seen. Hell, seems like they want to be seen. Makes people scared of 'em, I guess. Did me."

He poured another slug of red-eye down his throat, while Coffin thought. A cave, so close to the robbery, and right in the heart of where Holder's men had been performing their depredations. And just south of a town known as an outlaws' hangout. What a perfect place for men such as Holder's to hide. They could live in the cave, undetected, for months at a time.

"When did this happen?" Coffin asked urgently.

"Yesterday. Late. I rode all the night." He drained the bottle and tossed it down. "Now, Sheriff, where's that wire?"

Coffin yanked his horse around and kicked it into a run, the reluctant mule trudged behind, encouraged by the guide rope.

Chapter 7

Thunderheads were building far to the west as Joe Coffin trotted out of Red Cliffs. He felt a sense of urgency that he had never felt before. He didn't know why he felt it, only that he did, and that it drove him on.

He pushed on as hard as he could without wearing the animals down. It was dusty going in the sandy soil—until the boiling black clouds that clotted the sky unloaded their cargo.

Within minutes Coffin was drenched, the pounding water having seeped under his canvas duster, soaking through his shirt. A small pool puddled behind his buttocks on the saddle, seeping into his Levi's. The temperature plunged. Thunder boomed, and lightning crackled.

"Christ," he mumbled as he forced the horse along under the downpour. The animal accepted it, shaking its great-maned head frequently. But the mule brayed and balked, until it was being dragged along by the chestnut and the rope around the saddle horn.

"Goddamn it, mule," Coffin finally bellowed, angry. "I'd just as soon shoot your ass and have you for my supper as drag you along anymore. Now, come on, goddamnit, you cantankerous, mean-spirited, lazy-assed, no-good son of a bitch."

As was the way of mules, the animal paid the man no heed, and finally Coffin could not fight it any longer.

"All right, goddamnit, you win, mule," he growled as he pulled off into the sparse cover of some pines and a few mostly bare cottonwoods. He dismounted and tied the horse to a tree.

Then he set about unpacking the mule.

But the gray, short-tempered beast was not cooperative. "I've had about enough of you, mule," Coffin roared into the howling wind. Water ran off him as if he was standing under a waterfall, and he was in the poorest of humors.

He grabbed up a stout pine branch that was laying nearby. "You got but one more chance, mule," he snapped.

The animal brayed and kicked out with his feet. The supplies still on the animal's back went sailing, scattering about in the mud.

"Goddamn it!" He swatted the mule hard across the bony forehead. The beast squealed and brayed, almost falling to its knees. Coffin had no idea if his action would improve the mule's disposition any, but it made him feel a little better.

"Now," he said more softly, "you just calm down, and we'll get the rest of these supplies off you. Then you can roam a little."

Lightning splintered the somber sky, and thunder cracked, starting quietly, and then rolling across the land in a constant grumble. The mule bucked, snorted, and then raced off, canvas pack covering flapping wildly, supplies flying out every which way.

"Well, horseshit," Coffin snarled, anger and frustration fighting for prominence inside him.

Then he laughed. It was an uncontrollable urge that started down somewhere deep in his belly and just roared up like a steam engine gone wild. It charged up his throat and spilled out. It made no sense, but he could not help it. He whipped off his hat and let the rain splash over his head—which had been the only dry spot on him.

Then he whooped and danced, splashing around in the mud. The chestnut horse eyed him nervously. Coffin slipped and fell with a mighty splat on his backside in the mud. He sat laughing loudly.

Finally the laughter dribbled away, and Coffin sat for some moments in the slimy mud. Hell, he figured, he couldn't get any wetter or dirtier than he was.

He wondered about what had brought on such foolishment. He had not done such a thing since he was a boy. He stood, sloshing, and looked around, grinning. It was sure some mess, what with the mud and puddles and sopping pine needles and his meager supplies scattered to hell and gone.

He shrugged. Things had been so bad for so long that he must have needed the release. He did feel better, but if he didn't get dried off quickly, he'd probably catch his death of cold, he thought.

He gathered up the horse's reins and walked deeper into the copse, away from the creek, where the pines grew taller and thicker, and there were a few more cottonwoods, clinging to their last leaves.

He unsaddled the chestnut, hobbled it, and let it out to graze as best it could, while he went looking for firewood. He was lucky enough to find some dry, and soon had a fire going under a canopy of pine boughs. He rolled his blankets out near it, still under the low overhang of pine branches. He would be dry there.

Then he shucked off his guns and clothes. The pistols he kept close by his opened bedroll. His clothes he hung on scattered branches, as close to the fire as he safely could.

The clothing steamed as it began to dry. Coffin, naked and shivering with the chill, slid into his blankets and pulled them close around him.

It took some time, but eventually he stopped shaking, and was able to relax. Once he did, he fell asleep within minutes, his slumber unhampered by his empty belly.

But when he awoke, he was ravenous. It had stopped raining, but it had turned bitter cold, and the trees were coated with ice. His clothes were mostly dry, and so he dressed hurriedly, covering his goosebumpy flesh. As he pushed out from the cover of his impromptu lean-to, he saw the mule standing not far away, opened pack still tied to its back. It was munching pine bark and the sparse grass quietly, looking for all the world as if nothing had happened.

"Damn mule," Coffin muttered as he headed toward the animal. He finished unpacking what was left on the animal's back. Fortunately, his fry pan and coffeepot had gotten hung up in the rigging.

He searched around until he found a sack—mercifully still

mostly dry—of coffee and some hardtack, jerky, and bacon. He was all set. Rekindling the fire, he set breakfast to cooking while he went to see if he could gather up more of his supplies.

With the new day, the sense of urgency returned, and he ate hurriedly before packing up and heading out, riding hard through a biting wind. It was dark when he stopped and pitched camp in a grove of large, bare cottonwoods and stunted mesquite just off Clear Creek.

Earlier, he had taken the risk of being heard and shot two rabbits. He roasted one over the fire and hung the other high from a tree for his breakfast. When he was done, he moved away from the fire and into his lean-to. He did not want to be silhouetted against the fire if anyone was interested in his being there.

He had the other rabbit in the morning, washed down with hot, black coffee. The sense of urgency lingered as he packed his mule, but now it was tempered by caution. He was not sure, exactly, where the cave he was searching for was, but he figured it could not be much farther. If he had figured right, and the outlaws were holed up there, he would have to be even more watchful and alert than usual.

After saddling the chestnut, he left the two animals cropping the greening grass while he wandered around on foot, looking for sign. He saw none where he was, but that meant little. Finally he mounted up and moved out, more slowly than he had yesterday.

Within an hour he picked up some faint traces of the outlaws' tracks at an old campsite the outlaws had used. He checked around carefully, nodding as he picked out the individual hoofprints or footprints in the dust. The sign was at least a couple days old, and almost entirely obliterated by that other day's rainstorm, but it was there.

He climbed back on the chestnut and moved a little away from the covering of the trees which Holder's men had used for shelter. His eyes scanned the scrub-oak-, mesquite-, and paloverde-covered landscape. The day was chilly and the sun brittle bright, high overhead, making the land on the horizon shimmer.

Off in the distance, a bald eagle swooped and floated, wafting on the currents of cold air. Closer, a red-tailed hawk did the same. But there was no movement on the ground that he could see. No clouds of telltale dust; no smoke from a campfire.

Coffin finally cut the railroad tracks and followed them westward. By afternoon he had found where the robbery had taken place. With a grim smile, he started following the trail of the outlaws, moving slowly. The unrelenting, though not very warming, sun beat hard on his back, and his eyes, shaded by the wide brim of the flat-crowned hat, watered in the constant, unflagging brightness.

An hour later, he dipped below the lip of the canyon, following the narrow, rocky path downward along the yellowish-gray stone wall of the canyon. The trail was steep and treacherous, but he kept a firm grip on the chestnut, which moved confidently, if slowly.

As he rounded a sharp curve, he suddenly jerked the horse's reins, stopping short. Something—he did not really know what—had caught his attention. A fleeting movement, perhaps only the passing shadow of an eagle on the stone cliff.

He sat, waiting, watching, patient. But there was nothing but the unrelenting sunlight, and a few wispy strings of clouds above, streaming eastward.

He rubbed his belly, waiting, but still there was nothing. "Damn," he snorted. "Probably a deer or somethin'."

It was late in the afternoon, and he and his animals were tired. However, it would be a while yet before he made it to the bottom of the canyon. He hurried on a little, not wanting to be caught on this perilous trail in the dark.

But, still, he was uneasy. His well-trained senses usually were not fooled. And he was sure he had not seen an animal.

As dusk approached, he reached the canyon floor. A stream cut through it, and there was still grass. There were small pines, and a number of aspens and cottonwoods still clinging to a few leaves.

He saw a big cottonwood about half a mile ahead, and he moved toward it, eyes ever alert. There was grass by the massive tree.

He stripped the pack off the mule and the saddle off the chestnut, and staked both animals out. This was not a day to hobble them and let them wander. He rigged up his canvas lean-to, and sat to a cold meal of jerky and hardtack. There would be no fire tonight to give him away with its smoke or, later, light.

As the sky turned from azure to orangish-pink to purple, Coffin watched to the west, hoping to see movement, firelight, smoke, something that would indicate that the outlaws were up ahead somewhere.

But all he saw were the night birds coming out, and the last of the summer's buzzing insects. Three deer, looking furtive and skittish, as they always did, stopped at the side of the river, looking around before sinking their muzzles into the water to drink. Behind Coffin a coyote howled, and was answered by another some distance to his left. An owl hooted from up in the cottonwood.

The stars came out in profusion, looking close enough to touch, as the last of the light faded beyond the mountains. With a growl of discontent, Coffin turned in.

He awoke well before dawn began to glimmer over the high eastern rim of the canyon. He lay in his bedroll, staring up at the sky, head resting on his folded arms, listening to the sounds of the creatures of the night as they went about their business. It was a sound he liked, when he could allow himself the time to enjoy it. But the soft padding of a coyote, the quiet step of a deer, even the snuffling of a black bear not too far away were comforting to him.

It was too bad, he thought, that he had to do what he did for a living; how unfortunate it was that there were men like Reno Holder or Pete St. Johns or, especially, Bill Curly—someone who had been born in harmony and who had lost it. If only people could be good of heart. If only they could . . .

He pushed himself up as dawn tinged the sky with pale pink. People were not good of heart, he knew, which was why he did with his life what he did. He got no thrill from killing, but he enjoyed it, often, when he squashed a malignant human insect like Ian O'Kelly or Buck Schiebel. It was the way of life— men like Reno Holder preyed on others, and men like Joe Coffin hunted them down and exterminated them. It was a never-ending cycle, in which Coffin was a willing and active participant.

Gloom began to settle on him, and he angrily tried to shake the feeling off. He dunked his head in the stream, grateful for its cold bite. It cleared his senses, and boosted his spirits, though another cold meal of jerky and hardtack came perilously close to sinking them once more.

He loaded the mule, who seemed to have become more cooperative since Coffin had lodgepoled him with that log. Then he saddled the chestnut. As he fit the bit into the horse's mouth, he patted the animal affectionately, and said, "Well, boy, maybe today's the day we'll run them bastards down."

The horse nickered softly, and Coffin grinned. "Yep, we'll find 'em, all right," he said to the animal.

He heard a stagecoach rattle by up on the rim as he mounted and left. He moved slowly and cautiously, eyes flickering from track to rim to sky, seeing everything and evaluating it, filtering it through his knowledge and experience until it fit into its rightful place.

Just past noon, he entered a small side canyon. There were chunks of lava there, but mostly the rock was still the yellowish-gray of the canyon walls, running almost in stripes.

He worried a little about being heard, but there was little he could do about it. He had to press on. It was difficult following the tracks on the hard rock, but there was only one way for the outlaws to have gone. He entered a flat area, and found plenty of sign that the outlaws had been there, and recently too. Fresh horse droppings and freshly cropped grass told of it.

Several hours later, he heard something: a soft, mewling-type sound. He stopped fast, eyes searching frantically. He saw nothing and moved on, slowly. He heard the sound again, and then almost regularly.

Then he saw a crack in the rock, its mouth gaping black and ominously, under a massive stone bridge. He heard the noise again, and realized it was coming from the hole. He stopped and looped the rope from the pack mule around his saddle horn.

Coffin dismounted and groundstaked the chestnut. Drawing the .44-caliber Remington, he held it upward, ready, thumb on the hammer, and moved toward the foreboding opening.

Chapter 8

Flattened against the rocky wall, Joe Coffin edged into the dark, musty passageway. The mewling sound grew louder, and it was full of despair. It turned into desperate sobbing as he moved a little farther into the narrow rock channel.

He stopped and waited, but heard only the sobs, and a little soft rustling. There was only one person down the passage, of that he was sure now. Still, it paid to be cautious.

He moved on slowly, back scraping one dank rock wall. His eyes adjusted to the gloominess, and when he followed the wall as it curved around to the right, blocking the meager light that filtered in from outside, he thought he could see a dim glow a short way down the passage.

Now that he was around the curve, the breathless weeping was quite audible, and seemed to be growing stronger.

He licked his lips and wiped the sudden sprouting of sweat from his forehead. Then he shuffled forward.

There definitely was a pinkish-orange glow ahead, and as he moved silently up, it soon became evident to Coffin that it was coming from a flame. Mesquite wood, Coffin's mind checked off automatically, acknowledging the scent.

The passage narrowed more, and Coffin went through the slim opening. Beyond that, the cave widened as he neared the fire, and finally he came to a lip in the wall. He peered around it into a cavern, maybe thirty feet across.

Coffin noticed the woman first. It would have been hard not to. She cowered at the far side and was nearly naked. She was clad only in a battered pair of flat-heeled, black, high-topped shoes, and a shabby, shredded, pale brown dress that was bunched down around her smooth buttocks.

Under her mass of long, flaming-red hair, Coffin could see a rope knotted around her neck. It was attached to a ring imbedded in the cavern wall.

Coffin could see nothing of the woman's face. She was partially turned away from him, and her head hung down. Her bare, freckled, attractive shoulders shook as she cried. One leg was stretched out, uncovered, and it was filthy and scratched. Her other leg was curled up beneath her.

The woman was unaware of his presence, and he would have felt guilty under normal circumstances, staring at her like this. But these were not normal circumstances, and he felt he had to know everything about this place—including its occupants—before he could decide what to do.

Coffin broke off his gaze from the woman's back, and he took a look at the rest of the cave.

Around the curve of the cavern wall a little way was a body. That of another woman. She too was almost entirely unclothed. The bottom of her dark-green skirt was pushed up almost to her waist, exposing her legs all the way to mid-thigh. Her plain, white blouse was ripped open, baring her small, budding breasts.

She also had red hair, and was, Coffin guessed from his distance, about fifteen years old.

There were heaps of all kinds supplies scattered haphazardly about the cavern, and various kinds of booty from the gang's many robberies. Tack lay in jumbled piles, some half-covered with saddle blankets.

The rocky floor glimmered in the firelight under its covering of bottles and shards from broken ones. There also were some bones and shards of bones scattered around the floor—human ones—and Coffin guessed they were the remains of the Apaches who had died there. The walls were blackened with soot.

The place smelled foul. Coffin had thought Reno Holder, at least, if not the others, would have taken a stronger personal interest in cleanliness and hygiene. But either he did not, or he had been too preoccupied with the activities surrounding the two captives to have worried about it.

But worse, the place smelled of death too.

Coffin also was surprised to see that Holder had taken as his hideout a cavern with no rear exit. Coffin had not thought Holder would be one to do that. But, Coffin reckoned, perhaps they did not fear discovery.

Coffin shrugged. There was little use in dwelling on such thoughts. He had to get this woman out of there, and then hightail it to safety with her. The outlaws might be back at any time, and he would purely not like to be cornered there, facing six heartless killers.

The woman looked, even from where he stood, as if she was in a bad way, and he was not sure she would even make it. He shrugged again. There was only one way to find out.

He stepped into the open cavern. His boots crunched on broken glass, and his spurs jingled. The woman's head snapped up and her face spun to face this sound.

Her eyes were as big as dinner plates. Horror lurked in those gaping, brilliant blue eyes, just daring someone to come along and remove it.

She was attractive—no, beautiful—Coffin thought, though her face was screwed up from the fear and tears, and dirty. She was a little over twenty, he guessed. Her bare breasts were large, though not overly so, and pointy, capped by ruby tips, and they rode proudly above the slight swell of belly. They jiggled somewhat too, with the lingering sobs. Unconsciously she brushed back a wisp of cinnabar-colored hair from her forehead. She tried to say something, but no words came out.

Coffin gulped. He had been prepared for a lot of things, but a beautiful, naked, scarlet-haired woman was not one of them. He slid his pistol away and moved toward her.

She scuttled back like a crab, until her back came against the wall. The movements only accentuated her nudity, though the torn dress did slide down to cover a little more of her legs.

He moved closer, holding his hands out. "I ain't gonna hurt you, woman," he said softly.

She whimpered and tried to crawl into the rock wall.

"I ain't one of them others," he said still softly, though rage was bubbling just below the surface. How could anyone do . . . "I ain't one of them, I swear it. I'm after them bastards."

"No, no, no," the woman whispered, moaning. "Please no . . . no more . . . please . . . no more . . . I can't . . ." She broke into tears again, great wracking sobs that wrenched her shoulders and upper torso. There was nothing sensual in the swaying of her breasts this time, Coffin thought, angry at himself for having thought such a thing in the first place.

He stood, not sure what to do. Biting his lip to keep back the anger that threatened to burst out of his chest, he finally turned and looked to the body on the floor. The woman was dead, all right. Had been for at least several hours, probably longer. She was as beautiful as the other woman, though younger, and Coffin figured them to be sisters.

The younger woman had suffered greatly before she had died, and her face reflected it. There was no calmness and peace of eternity there—only horror, fear, and pain.

The outlaws had worked her over good, down to even carving their initials in the soft flesh of her belly and bosom. Her pale thighs were scratched and scraped by rock and dirty fingernails. There was a bullet hole, coated with coagulated blood, in the soft valley between her breasts.

He looked lower, and wished he hadn't. Pete St. Johns had been at work in the poor girl's nether regions with his knife. It was a sickening sight, even to the hardened Joe Coffin, who thought he had seen all the worst that men could do when he was only fifteen and fighting in the Civil War.

"Jesus goddamn Christ," he breathed, pushing himself up. Only animals would do such a thing, he thought. No, he added silently, no animal would do this. Only a monster. A sick, rabid ogre without a shred of humanity left inside.

Joe Coffin was not a cold-blooded killer. All of the men he had killed had been armed, and all had been trying—or would have tried, given half a chance—to kill him. But he swore then and there that he would kill every one of the men who rode with Reno Holder when he caught him—unarmed, willing to fight or not. That would be his gift—such as it was—to this unfortunate, unknown slip of a girl. He would kill those outlaws without feeling or compulsion; it was that simple.

He found a blanket and spread it gently over the dead young woman. He was shaking from grief, disgust, and rage as he turned back to the living victim. She was staring at him with those wide, blue eyes, as if taking stock of him again.

"I was after those bastards before," he said in a whisper. "But now I have a reason." He shook his head, trying to bring himself under control. It was not easy, but he managed it.

"I'm comin' over there now, woman, and cut you loose," he finally said in even tones. "I ain't gonna hurt you none. You got to believe that."

Apparently Coffin's earnestness—and the concern he had shown for the dead young woman—was reassuring, since she relaxed the tiniest bit.

"You'll be all right," he said softly as he knelt next to her. "I'm gonna get you out of here soon's I can, and get you back to a town somewhere. They'll take care of you."

He pulled out his dagger—a long, twin-bladed affair—and slit the rope a few feet from her neck. Then, with the utmost care, he sawed at the rope covering her neck. As he did, he could see the carotid artery throbbing. Her breathing was quick and shallow with fear.

Then he was through the rope, and he gently peeled it away from her. She smothered him in her arms, crying and screeching; her body trembled violently.

Coffin was taken aback, but he endured it stoically. After a while he began stroking her hair and holding her tight. His hand touched the bare flesh of her back, and it sent a ripple through him. He fought back the feeling.

"You'll be all right," he said over and over, not knowing what else to say. But his strong, gentle hands and his quiet voice soothed her.

The woman's sobbing dwindled and her shivering diminished until she was quiet and still in his arms. The only sounds he heard now were the woman's soft breathing, and a drip of water from somewhere in the cave. He worried that the outlaws might return at any time. Yet he could not bring himself to disturb the woman.

So still and quiet was she that Coffin thought she had fallen asleep. So he waited.

But she at last roused herself, wiping at the still-glistening eyes and her running nose. Her bright eyes were pools of liquid blue. They were beautiful, he thought, despite the red-laced white surrounding them.

"I'm sorry," she said, her voice stiff from phlegm and emotion. "I don't know what . . ." She trailed off.

"No need to say anything." He pulled a dirty bandanna from a hip pocket and handed it to her. "Sorry it ain't clean," Coffin said gruffly.

"It's just fine," she said, taking it and blowing vigorously several times. As she did, Coffin stood and rummaged around, until he found an almost-clean shirt and a canteen of water. He brought them back to the woman.

"Here," he said holding them out. "You can clean yourself up some."

She nodded and took the two items. She poured water onto the shirt and then scrubbed her face. She repeated the process several times.

"I'm Joe Coffin," he said quietly.

She looked up at him, trying to straighten her hair as she did. The action made her naked breasts sway, and suddenly Coffin's mouth was dry.

"I'm Kate McCoombs," she said, no hint of sauciness in her voice. She studiously avoided looking at the blanket-covered body close by. Instead, she busied herself with trying to fix her hair, and then scrub her face some more. She appeared to be totally unaware of her undraped condition, or the stimulating effect it was having on Coffin.

He waited a while, watching her, before realizing that she was still in shock, and was keeping herself busy so she did not have to think about what had happened to her. He kept patient, but finally he had to say, "We'd best get movin' soon, Miss McCoombs. I reckon those"—he hesitated—"bastards will be back sooner or later."

It was as if he had slapped her in the face. The color drained from her cheeks and lips and her breathing was rough. She started to topple, but Coffin leaped and caught her before her head hit the ground. In catching her, one of his hard, callused hands had landed cupping one of her breasts. He took a deep breath and moved his hand as rapidly as he could, but the tingling lasted in the limb for some time.

He pushed her into a sitting position, where she stayed, staring straight ahead. He left her that way and wandered around the room, looking for anything that might be usable—food or clothing, water, pots, whatever.

He built up the fire after breaking up an old crate for fuel. He was still worried that Holder's men would return at any time. Well, he finally shrugged, if they did, they did. He could not ride off and leave this woman to their tender mercies, nor could he ride off without burying the younger one.

He put some beans and water in a pot and set it over the fire. He found a skillet and set bacon to cooking. As it began to sizzle, he looked at the woman. She was in the same position. He shook his head, worried for her.

"I'll be back in a minute," he said to her, not knowing whether she even heard him. He went outside and got the horse and mule and brought them through the narrow entranceway and passage, and into the cave. He left them there and got feed bags. He dug into a sack of oats and filled each bag. He slid one over the horse's muzzle, and one over the mule's.

He turned the bacon over and stirred the beans. The woman roused herself slowly, looking at him as if she had just awakened from a long, deep sleep. She started to say something several times, but stopped each time. Suddenly she realized her nudity, and she tried to cover her bosom with her crossed arms.

Coffin got another blanket and brought it over to her. She was afraid to move her arms now, lest she bare herself again. So he carefully draped it across her shoulders. He turned back toward the fire. "Food's ready," he said. Figuring she had had enough time to cover herself, he turned.

He had been right. She hugged the blanket tightly to her.

"Hungry?" he asked, smiling a little for her benefit.

Kate McCoombs shook her head.

"You got to keep up your strength," he said sternly, though not harshly.

She shook her head again.

"There's much to be done here." He paused an instant.

"And elsewhere. You'll need energy for what's got to be done. Now come and eat."

She stood awkwardly and padded toward the fire. She sat across the flames from him, unsure of herself, of this man, of her situation. In fact, she was scared down to the soles of her feet. Past the initial shock now, she was beginning to feel again—and it hurt, badly. There were too many bad, frightful memories in this cave. Memories of . . .

She fought back the tears, and accepted the plate of bacon and beans that Coffin handed her. She nodded her thanks—barely. Huddled in her blanket, jumping at every sound, Kate McCoombs spooned down her meal.

From far, far off, they heard the sound of a train whistle, and Kate McCoombs shuddered. A look of pain drifted across her face and lingered.

Chapter 9

"We probably ought to be gettin' on the trail soon, Miss McCoombs," Coffin said after they had finished eating. "They could be back at any time."

He wasn't scared, but there was a tinge of worry in his voice. He would not like being trapped; had always been too cautious for that.

Kate McCoombs looked some better after having gotten some food in her. "They'll not be back for a while," she said, suppressing another shudder. "There any more of that food left?"

"Sure." He took her plate and spooned up more beans and the last of the bacon. Handing the tin plate to her, he asked, "How do you know they won't be back soon?"

"Heard them talkin'," she said. "After they . . . they . . ." Tears crept from her eyes and her breath caught in her throat. She gulped down several deep breaths to calm herself. Regaining some of her composure, she said, "One of 'em—the leader—said they were going to Aspen Wells to rob the bank."

Kate ate some beans, fighting desperately to keep from breaking down again.

Coffin nodded. He figured it was probably true, and if so, the outlaws would not be back for at least two days. "I know this ain't gonna be of any help to you after what you gone through," he said slowly, "but you're safe now here with me. I ain't gonna let no one hurt you no more. I'll get you to the nearest town—or to your home—soon's I can."

Life was returning to Kate's face, and it had a more determined cast to it.

"We'll stay the night here, if you think you can do that. . . ." Coffin looked at her questioningly.

She nodded tightly. Fear lurked behind the crystal-blue eyes, but she would not let it overwhelm her.

"First thing in the morning, I'll find a place to dig a grave for . . ." He was loathe to mention it.

Kate choked back a sob, then said in a firm voice, "Irene. She's my . . . was my sister." She faltered.

"You don't have to say no more." Coffin's voice was gentle, and his heart went out to this poor young woman.

"Yes, I do," she said obstinately. She set her unfinished plate of beans down. "I ain't lettin' you bury my sister out here in this godforsaken . . ." She paused for a breath, fighting for control. "Out here where she don't know nobody. I aim to see that she gets home, and is buried proper, with services and such."

"It ain't gonna be easy," Coffin started. But he ground to a halt when he saw the look on her face. "But we'll do it," he mumbled. "Where's home?"

"North of Leroux Springs."

"Where's that?"

"Northeast of the San Francisco Mountains."

He nodded. "We might have to see that Irene is laid to rest at a church somewhere before that," he said lamely.

"No." There was no tone in her voice, and Coffin knew better than to argue, at least for now.

Kate picked up the plate and began eating again. They sat in silence for a time, before Coffin finally stood and went to his animals. He unpacked the mule, and unsaddled the horse. Then he walked back out of the cave and stood looking around, watching for sign that anyone might be coming. There was none.

Dark was approaching in the cloudless sky. He gathered driftwood he found near some mesquite trees in the flat in front of the almost-hidden cave entrance. Arms full, he went back to the cavern.

Kate had finished eating, and had rinsed the plates off with water from the canteen. She had found Coffin's coffeepot and coffee, and had a pot brewing over the fire. Coffin was surprised. Kate seemed to be recovering far more quickly than he had expected. But perhaps it was still the shock of the events that was driving her, he thought.

He dumped the wood off to one side, and then, using his scuffed beaten boots, he kicked away some glass to clear places for them to sleep that night. He made sure, since he was under her watchful nervous glare, that he cleared spots well removed from each other, and well away from the blanket-covered body of Irene McCoombs.

"Coffee?" Kate asked, holding out his tin cup toward him.

"Thanks," he answered gratefully. He sat and sipped from the steaming cup, realizing that he was still tense. She sat too, with another mug.

"I'll take the spot over there," Coffin said, pointing toward the narrow entrance to the first cave.

She nodded, knowing that it would be safest for them both for him to do so. But there was still a lingering fear—fear that this man might turn out to be like the others, despite his mild ways and obvious concern for her welfare.

Coffin finished his coffee and set the mug down. Wandering around, he found another blanket and brought it to where Kate would sleep. He arranged his bedroll—and the saddle, which he would use as a pillow—in the cleared spot he had made. "Well, Miss McCoombs, I'm about ready to turn in."

She nodded. Coffin stripped off the shoulder rig, and then the waist gun belt. The former he hung on the saddle horn; the latter he laid next to the blankets. All four weapons would be within easy reach. He pulled off his shirt, baring his strong chest. He pulled off his boots and set them aside before crawling into the blankets. "Night," he murmured, but Kate did not answer.

Coffin was a light sleeper—had to be to survive—and he heard Kate moving around sometime in the night. It was dark in the cavern, the fire having burned down to faintly glowing embers. He reached for a pistol, but then realized she was probably just worried. He relaxed and sank back into sleep.

He awoke again when he smelled bacon and coffee cooking.

He sat up, rubbing his eyes. Kate was bent over the fire, which she had stoked expertly. She had a skillet of bacon cooking, with some corn cakes in another pan. The coffeepot full of Arbuckle's was bubbling away in the flames.

"Mornin'," she said, sounding at least alive if not cheery.

"Mornin'." He stood and pulled on his boots and shirt before hooking on his guns. He went outside to relieve himself, and to take a look around. Back inside, Kate had a plate set out for him, and she was eating.

"You seem a mite better," Coffin said tentatively as he sat and picked up the plate.

She nodded, mouth full of corn cake. After swallowing, she said, "I am. Thank you."

"I didn't do nothin'," he said.

"That's why," she mumbled, and Coffin looked embarrassed.

"It must've been bad, huh?" he questioned.

"Yep." She shuddered. But she was bound and determined now to not let it destroy her. She had hope in her heart again.

"Feel the need of talkin' about it?"

Kate shrugged. But she said, "We was on the train. We'd been over in Winslow, visitin' kin, Irene and me. We was on our way home, when . . . when . . ."

She paused, gathering her resources of strength and courage. Then she plunged on, the words boiling out at a furious clip. "We was on our way home, when those bastards held up the train. Just rode up to it when the train slowed as it got near Canyon Diablo." She shuddered. "A horrid place," she said, torn between fear and anger. "That's where the train stops, you know. Only recently made it that far too. Used to be you had to take the stage all the way. But last summer the train tracks made it to Canyon Diablo. Word has it that the railroad ain't got the money to go no farther."

She gulped a breath and plunged on. "We was ridin' along peaceful as can be, me with my knittin', Irene readin' her Good Book, when all of a sudden these men burst into the car, pointin' guns, yellin' and such.

"One passenger, a true gentleman by his looks and actions, tried to stop them, but they shot him down right off. Two of the outlaws went off to another car, but the others stayed in ours. They set about collectin' all the valuables they could find. Even"—she shook, despite the speed at which she was speaking—"cut off some old woman's finger to get her weddin' ring, which she couldn't pull off."

Kate stumbled to a halt, and drank some coffee, holding the tin cup with two trembling hands. Her nostrils were flared in fear and anger at the remembrance, but she would not stop in the telling of it.

"They took everythin' they could, and then they started manhandlin' Irene, pawin' at her and such, makin' fun of her 'cause she was readin' her Bible. I tried to stop them, but one of 'em—a big, hulkin', fat monster . . . the one who killed . . . later . . . he took his knife and . . ."

Coffin nodded. "I know what happened," he said gruffly, the picture of Irene's bloody crotch tearing at his mind.

She sucked in breath and raced on with her narrative. "Anyway, he cuffed me hard. Didn't knock me senseless, but took the starch out of me right fast." Anger and a loitering fear battled for supremacy within her. "God," she burst out, "I want to kill that son of a bitch. I want to take his knife and cut off . . ." She could not quite bring herself to say it, though the wanting of it was like a physical pain in her chest.

"They kept up sportin' with her, but not so bad for a while. Then the train stopped. Two of the outlaws grabbed me, and two others grabbed Irene and dragged us off the train. Irene might've spent a heap of time readin' the Good Book, but she was a feisty little one, she was." Kate almost grinned, but not quite. "She fought and kicked and swore. Lord, I never heard her use those words. Never had an inklin' she even knew them.

"When they dragged us off the train, the leader of those bastards shot the conductor, and then told the engineer to get going, and not to stop for nothin' till he was in Canyon Diablo.

"The outlaws had some horses up behind the rocks, and they dragged us up there. One of the men, an Injun-lookin' son of a bitch, threw me on a horse and climbed up behind me. The one with the knife—I think the others called him Pete . . ."

"Pete St. Johns," Coffin said, hate beginning to edge into his voice.

She hadn't seemed to have heard him as she pressed forward. "... did the same with Irene. Then we were off and ridin'. Before too long, we was here."

She stopped, tears pouring down her cheeks now, but they were tears of anger and hate, as well as those of fear and self-pity. Coffin began to think Kate might come out of this all right. She was getting a lot out of her system now, and if he could get her to her family—and if they supported her—she should do all right.

Kate finished off her coffee and placed the cup down. She pulled out Coffin's bandanna from under the blanket she was still using as a dress, and wiped at her face, and blew her nose.

"You don't have to say no more," Coffin said gently.

"I need to," she answered, surprising Coffin with the strength and fervor in her voice. "I got to get it out. I keep it locked inside me, I'll go plumb *loco*."

He nodded, letting her try to relax, gather her thoughts.

"They hooked me up to that . . . there . . ." She pointed, fear squirming around in her stomach like a snake, to the rope still hooked to the ring in the wall. "They kept Irene loose, to . . . to . . ."

She broke down then, sobbing and crying hysterically. Coffin sat uncomfortably, not knowing whether to go to her and try to comfort her or to sit back. He wanted to be able to help her, but perhaps the touch of a man—any man—would do more harm than good. So he sat, until she finally wept herself out.

"Each of 'em but one had his turn with her," Kate said suddenly, as if she had never stopped. "They done things that ain't possible for humans to do," she said through choking sobs, "all the time laughin' and hootin' and jeerin' and such. The worst was one the others called Will. He was . . . was . . . I don't know how long it went on, but it seemed to be hours, till finally that big, fat bastard . . . He couldn't . . . wasn't able to . . . So he took his knife and . . . and . . ."

Once more she broke down, glancing at the blanket-covered body of her sister. Coffin did not hesitate this time. He stood and circled the fire to get to her. Kneeling at her side, he gathered her into his strong arms and held her tight as her body shook with the pain that lanced deep into her. He did not talk, just held her in the warm, powerful envelope of his arms, trying, through osmosis, to draw the pain out of her and into him.

Finally she lifted her head. Her startling blue eyes once again showed whites laced heavily with red, and there were dark circles around the eyes. Her nose was red and puffy, and her lips, he saw, while normally full, were bloodless and chewed.

"Thank you," she whispered, peering deep into his dark, expressive eyes.

"You all right now?" he asked, realizing immediately how stupid that sounded.

But she nodded. He released her, and leaned back a little.

"Please hold me some more," she asked, eyes pleading. "I need someone to hold me."

"My pleasure, ma'am," he said without making fun of her. And he did as he was asked. She leaned her scarlet mane on his chest and rested, small tremors still shaking her periodically.

Then, into his chest, she said, "Then it was my turn. But they was some tired out, I guess, since they didn't pay me too much heed. Only the leader, and that Injun bastard, took me. They ate, then slept. After eatin' again in the mornin', they talked about robbin' the bank in Aspen Wells. The leader took . . . did . . . had his way with me again. Then they rode off."

"And left you."

"Yes," she whispered into his shirt. "I expect they were savin' me for later."

Coffin hugged her even more tightly.

Chapter 10

Joe Coffin tossed the remains of his coffee onto the fire, reassured by the expected hissing. "You able to ride, Miss McCoombs?" he asked.

"I expect so," Kate said. She still looked shaken, and her voice wavered.

He nodded and stood, walking toward his supplies. Kate began cleaning up the skillets. From his saddlebags, Coffin pulled his extra shirt and pair of Levi's. "Here," he said, handing them to McCoombs. "Why don't you try wearin' these, instead of that blanket? I reckon it'll be more comfortable for you."

She nodded her thanks, taking the clothes. She looked around, still scared, looking anxious.

"I'll turn away, Miss McCoombs," Coffin said softly. "I'll not look while you change."

Again she nodded silently, seemingly a little relieved. Coffin turned away, facing the opening leading to the cave mouth. With worried eyes on Coffin's back, Kate quickly slipped out of the blanket and tried to hurry getting on the shirt and pants. In her haste, her fingers were clumsy, making her job all the harder. But she finally managed to button up the shirt. It fit fairly well across the chest, but the sleeves were a little too long.

She tried to calm herself, never taking her eyes off Coffin's back, and rolled up the sleeves more slowly. She was still afraid that if he turned around he would see her. Teetering on legs still weak from her ordeal, Kate slipped on the pants. They were too long, and she rolled them up too, and the waist was too big. "All right," she said.

After he turned, Kate asked for his knife. With a question in his eyes, Coffin handed it to her. Kate turned and went to the wall where the rope that had held her prisoner lay. Steeling herself, she cut off a length. Handing Coffin back his knife, she took the rope and threaded it through the belt loops on the Levi's, and then pulled it up tight and tied it.

"There," she said. Being fully clothed again, rather than just wrapped in a blanket, seemed to have boosted her spirits considerably. And, though she still carefully avoided looking at the blanket-draped body of her sister, she began to think that she might weather this.

Kate went back to cleaning their breakfast mess, while Coffin wandered about the cavern, seeing if there was anything of use he wanted to take. There was little but two canteens of water, which he gathered up.

Kate was done with the cookware, so Coffin set to packing up the mule, taking only the necessities. He made sure he had the blanket Kate had used as a dress, and another blanket. The rest of his supplies, which by now were quite limited anyway, he stacked on the floor. Then he saddled the chestnut and hung the two extra canteens over the saddle horn.

Done, he said, "Maybe you ought to go on outside."

She stared at him, sparks of fear lighting up her sparkling blue eyes. "Why?" she asked, trying to keep the trembling out of her voice.

"Keep a lookout," he said blandly. "You see anybody—*anybody*—comin', you hurry back here and let me know. I'll be out, ready to leave in a few minutes."

Uncertain and afraid, she nodded and walked hesitatingly through the cave entrance. With each step, however, she got a trace bolder, as if her spirit was becoming free. There was nothing to hold her in that rock room, she realized. She was free! Free to leave, to go back to living. It was a heady feeling.

Coffin breathed a sigh of relief. He had not looked forward to having to tell Kate he wanted her outside so that he could load her sister's body on the mule without her standing there watching him. It would have been, he knew, much too traumatic for her at this point. He hoped that when he moved out of the cave, and the deed was done, that she would be more accepting of it.

He shrugged. It did not matter, he realized. It had to be done, whether Kate could handle it or not. Though he was short, Coffin had a big chest, and powerful arms. It was not hard for him to lift the slight, frail, blanket-shrouded body and toss it, none too gently, over the mule. He tied it down, making sure the unfortunate young girl was well-covered. With a last look around to make sure he had not forgotten anything, he took the mule's rope and the horse's reins and walked down the long tube of the cave toward the brightness of the cold day beyond.

Kate was sitting on a rock outcropping, scanning the canyon. She gave a little start of surprise when she saw the mule's burden. But she said nothing.

"Come on," Coffin said, standing next to the chestnut. "Climb on."

He boosted her up onto the horse and then climbed on behind her. She sat stiffly, hands white-knuckled where they grasped the pommel of the saddle.

"It'll be all right," Coffin said ineffectually into the tangled, dirty mass of flaming crimson hair. She had an earthy smell about her after all that she had been through, but her natural odor underlied it, and stimulated him. He shifted his buttocks uncomfortably on the saddle and took in one last great breath of her hair, before clucking the horse into motion. "Which way?" he asked.

Kate pointed southward. "There's an easy way out of the canyon there," she said. "It's the way the stages go."

They rode slowly, mule in tow. Coffin did not want to push the horse too hard, with its double burden. But he did not stop either, except twice when he shot rabbits that they would use for their supper, until it was almost dark.

Shortly after the sun had passed its zenith, they entered a weird land of chunked black lava. There was little grass on most of it, and few trees. Coffin worried some that the sound of the hooves of his horse and mules clacking on the hard, funny-looking rock might alert someone who was ahead—if there was anyone.

They stopped near a small spring, which had one small cottonwood growing on its bank, and two mesquite nearby. It was cool as the sun sank beyond the mountains to the west, and Coffin knew it would be cold that night. Coffin unloaded the supplies from the mule, but left the body on the animal. He hobbled the beast and turned it out to graze on the scant, short, brown grass and some sagebrush. He unsaddled the chestnut, rubbed him down with the few handfuls of browned cottonwood leaves he found, and then turned the horse out to feed too, after patting the animal. "You done good, old boy," he whispered.

As he turned back, he saw that Kate was wandering a little ways out of camp, gathering up what firewood she could find. He nodded, pleased to see her getting back into life. Then he set up the small canvas lean-to, attaching it to the small cottonwood.

By the time he finished, Kate was back with an armful of fuel. "Thanks," he said, trying to be cheerful.

She smiled wanly. "I'll get some more," she said, turning and walking away.

Coffin watched her for a few moments, before growling at himself in annoyance. There must be something wrong with him, he thought, to stand and stare at Kate, to be so stimulated by the sight and smell of her, after all she had been through. But still, he thought, glancing once more at her, his Levi's did look good stretched across her tight buttocks, and she certainly filled out his old flannel work shirt quite nicely.

"Jesus Christ," he muttered, gathering up some tinder. He snapped a match and fired up the tinder. When it caught, he added kindling, and then some larger branches. The fragrance of mesquite smoke wafted up into the growing darkness. It was a welcome smell, and the warmth was good too.

With the fire going, Coffin began skinning and gutting the rabbits. Kate returned with another armload of wood. She started to leave again, but Coffin said, "I reckon that'll be enough. Besides, it's gettin' dark."

She nodded, and absentmindedly shoved a lock of hair off her forehead with the meaty part of the palm of her hand. She took the coffee pot and filled it from the little spring. Filling it with some Arbuckle's coffee, she set it in the flames.

Coffin was done with the rabbits, and shoved a stick through each and propped them up over the fire. They began sizzling almost immediately, and Coffin almost grinned as he saw Kate watching the roasting meat with rapt attention.

The moon came up, and several coyotes howled off to the south. The two people sat in silence, listening to the night's concert of coyotes and owls. Several times Coffin thought he would say something, but each time, he decided against it.

Finally the meat was done, and they ate with enjoyment, though in silence. The coffee was hot, and good, though it would have been helped considerably, Coffin thought, with the addition of sugar. The last of his had run out some days ago.

After the meal, Coffin rolled a cigarette. "Want one?" he asked.

"No," she said, almost with horror. Good women did not do such things, and she wondered how he could have even asked her such a thing. Did he think she was . . . She sighed. Perhaps he did. After her kidnap and rape, what else could any normal man think?

He fired up the cigarette, watching the emotions flicker across her face. "I didn't mean to offend," he said quietly. "I ain't used to ladies." He sounded almost embarrassed. "Ladies don't usually have much truck with a man like me."

She looked at him, startled. "What do you mean by 'a man like me'?"

He smiled almost regretfully. "I'm a bounty hunter, ma'am." He doffed his hat in mock courtliness.

"What's wrong with that?" she asked, searching his face.

It was his turn to be startled. "Well," he stammered, "nothing, I reckon." He pulled in a mouthful of smoke, and let it drift out slowly. "But most decent folks don't take kindly to them. We get kind of looked down upon."

"But you do a necessary job."

"Well, yes, I suppose we do. Still most folks don't see it that way. All they see is a well-armed man who hunts down other well-armed men. Most folks don't see us as much different than the outlaws we're lookin' for."

"But you're more like lawmen than the outlaws. Aren't you?"

"I think so."

They were quiet for a little while. Coffin finished his cigarette and tossed the butt into the flames. He laid two more sticks on the fire and sat back, watching the flickering blaze, mind wrestling with the thoughts of this woman.

"Do you regret what you do?" Kate finally asked, breaking into his thoughts.

"No," he said. It was true. He had never thought about it much, but there was a thrill in what he did that he could get nowhere else. The thrill was in the chase, for him, not in the killing that so often followed, as it did for so many others in his profession.

"Are you good at it?"

He grinned. "One of the best, ma'am." He had a mocking tone, but he was proud of it, and she could see that plainly written in his face and eyes.

"Then you should not worry about what others think of your job," she said firmly. "It is a right and proper job."

"Thank you," he said sincerely.

"Are you really after the men who . . . ?" She could not finish the sentence.

"Yes."

"How? Why?"

"Seems they been havin' themselves a pretty good spree the last couple of months or so. Not only are they killin' people every time they pull a job, but they're killin' a deputy or two every time a posse sets out after them."

Kate sucked in her breath, but said nothing.

"That type of thing tends to raise the hackles of most marshals and such."

"I would think so," Kate said, outraged.

"The federal marshal down to Prescott is an old friend of mine. He lost several men to this bunch of shit-eat—oops, pardon me, ma'am, for such language."

"It's all right. Understandable, I'd say." She almost smiled, and it brightened her face.

"Anyway, he wired me and asked if I'd come lend a hand

runnin' these sons of bitches down. I'd been on their trail for a couple weeks or so when I found you...."

She shuddered, but fought back the fear. "I'm glad you did," she whispered.

His heart sang. But all he said was, "It's been a long day, Miss McCoombs. And tomorrow will be no better. You'd best turn in. I put blankets for you in the lean-to."

"But what about you?"

He stretched out his bedroll, and grinned. "I'm used to sleepin' in the open. I'll be fine."

"But it'll be cold," she protested mildly, looking up at the star-filled sky.

"I'll be all right here by the fire."

She nodded, accepting, and stood. "Well, then, Mr. Coffin, I'll say good night to you."

"Good night, Miss McCoombs." He unstrapped his guns and took off his shirt before laying down in his blankets. But it was some time before he fell asleep, what with all the thoughts of this striking, red-maned woman roaring around inside his skull.

Chapter 11

It was one hell of an angry town they entered when Joe Coffin and Kate McCoombs rode into Aspen Wells two and a half days after leaving the cave-scarred lava beds.

The town was on the edge of the weird formations left by the lava, as the land changed from rocky lava to high plains leading up to the snow-covered San Francisco Peaks. There were plenty of trees—mostly aspen, bare now, their branches clacking in the wind; and ponderosa pines; and cottonwoods near water. And there was much sage and other brush.

Reno Holder and his five evil compatriots had, indeed, paid their respects to the people of the small, windswept town. And three of the town's more illustrious citizens were dead as a result of that unfriendly call.

As Kate and Joe walked the chestnut slowly into town, they were watched by angry knots of snarling townspeople. Coffin could feel Kate stiffen with renewed fear and apprehension.

"Don't go frettin' over this," Coffin said.

"You've seen this before?" she asked over her shoulder, startled.

"More times than I care to remember. When you have a profession like mine, you get used to such things. People hate you because they fear you."

"But they're staring at me too."

"Yep. Most of 'em reckon you're probably some kind of scarlet woman who's runnin' 'round with a hardcase. Others probably think you're some kind of outlaw woman I'm bringin' in as a prisoner. And I reckon a few even think you been caught up somewhere by someone and most likely sorely abused. They'd be right on that one, of course."

She shuddered, but firmed her shoulders.

"Of course, when they find out that's really what happened, they'll pity you. But they'll hate you too. Not because they fear you, but because you've become a fallen woman, not fittin' for any decent man's home—or bed."

He was being harsh, but he felt he had to be. These people had no spark of friendliness in their eyes, and times would be hard here. He could handle that, he figured, since he had been forced to do so many times before. But this was all new for Kate McCoombs, and he had to try—and very quickly—to get her used to the treatment she would be given by many of these falsely pious folks.

"But I didn't . . ."

"Don't matter. See, it ain't so much what you done or didn't do. It's what they think happened, and what they think the others will think, and so they have to think it too. Most of 'em, if you got 'em off to themselves, would probably feel sorry for what you went through and really try to help. But if one thinks his neighbor thinks you should be treated like somethin' used and needin' to be thrown away, well, he'll think that too. 'Cause these people got to live with each other every day."

"But—"

"It ain't right," he said, cutting off her prostestations. "But it's the way it is. Neither you nor I can change it, so you got to adjust to it, and live your life as best you can."

He stopped in front of the sheriff's small adobe office. The sheriff stepped out, flanked by two shotgun-toting men, each of whom had a deputy's star on his chest. Coffin guessed they had been deputized only in the last day or so. Both were young, and seemed strong, though they probably had not seen much killing. Still, they would need to be treated carefully. You never knew when someone untrained would fly off and do something foolish.

The sheriff was tall and lanky, with a potbelly sprouting. Like the two deputies, he wore a holstered Colt; unlike them he did not carry a shotgun. He was tough and hard, with a battle-scarred face, and lines of determination around his eyes and mouth. This was one, Coffin thought, who had seen pain and death and killing before. He would not be put off by blood, if the need came to it.

"Sheriff," Coffin said, touching the front brim of his hat with two fingers.

"You got business here?" the sheriff asked. His voice was harsh and had a gargly sound to it, as if someone had tried to mash his voicebox, and partially succeeded.

"Some." Coffin did not care for the man's tone. "This woman"—he tapped Kate's shoulder—"and her sister was took by Reno Holder and his gang of bushwhackin' bastards when they held up the train a few days back over near Diablo Canyon."

He scratched his nose, gazing levelly at the sheriff, whose features had not softened any. "They were held in a cave in a side canyon off the main one a few miles south of the train depot. It appears the gang was using the cave as a hideout.

"Both was sorely abused by them sons a bitches. When I found 'em, the girl"—he jerked a thumb over his shoulder at the blanket-wrapped body draped over the mule—"was dead. Miss McCoombs here was in poor shape, but not overly much."

"That true, ma'am?" the sheriff asked, turning his harsh gray eyes on Kate.

Kate shuddered again, the fear beginning to coil in her belly once more. This man, she thought, was little better than Reno Holder, what with the small smirk at the thoughts of her being ravished by a group of other men. He had the look of a man who might join in such things, given half a chance.

"Yes," she said, choking back the gush of fear that lurched up her throat.

The sheriff returned his gaze to Coffin, who whispered to the woman, "Get down."

"What?" she asked, half turning.

"Get down." The voice was still not loud, but the urgency in it could not be mistaken.

Kate swung her right foot up over the pommel and the horse's neck. With both legs on the same side of the horse, she slid down until she was standing again. It was a strange feeling after all the riding. Her legs were a little weak, and she stumbled. She grabbed onto the hitching rail to keep herself upright.

People had begun to gather behind Coffin, and it made him uncomfortable, as did not having the protection of the woman in front of him. But at least now his hands and weapons were free. It would be folly to get involved in a gun battle now, he knew, but he would not be shot down without a fight, if that's what the sheriff was planning.

"Supposin' I don't believe a word of that crap?" the sheriff asked.

Coffin shrugged. He gently rubbed his stomach.

"Supposin' I was to figure you was one of them goddamned outlaw bastards, and you was comin' in here with that woman and a body just so's you could get a little reward money."

Coffin shrugged again. "Miss McCoombs will tell you I'm tellin' the truth," he said simply.

"She looks mighty scared to me," the sheriff said, eliciting a grumble of assent from the crowd bunched behind Coffin. "Might be that you got her so scared she'll agree to anything you say."

"Could be," Coffin said thoughtfully. "But it ain't."

"I still think you got the look of one of them outlaws, boy," the sheriff said. He had not changed his stance, nor had he moved the thumbs from where they were hooked in his belt. But his voice had taken on a harder tone.

"So do you, pard."

There was a collective gasp from behind Coffin, but he ignored it, instead keeping an intent watch on the sheriff and his two deputies.

The sheriff almost cracked a smile. "All right," he bellowed to the crowd, still not moving. "Y'all go on, get movin'. Go on back to your homes or your business. This ain't your affair here no more."

He waited patiently while the people broke into grumbling knots and drifted away. They were not appeased, but the sheriff did not really give a damn. Nor did Coffin.

When the people were gone, the sheriff said, "Lon, take the stiff down to Earl's." As one of the deputies stuck his scattergun just inside the door and headed for the mule, the sheriff said, "Earl's the undertaker." He paused, then he grinned. "Well, he ain't really an undertaker. But he's the closest thing we got."

As Coffin handed Lon the rope to the mule, he said, "You'll get the mule back to me in good shape, won't you, boy?" It was not really a question.

Lon nodded and walked off, leading the mule.

"What's your name, mister?" the sheriff asked.

"Joe Coffin. Yours?"

"Lyle Bordus." He waved his hand, and the other deputy disappeared inside the small office behind him. "Why don't you light and tie, Mr. Coffin. Step into my office and set a spell. We'll chat a bit over the bad things been occurring in these parts of late." Though it was couched in civil terms, there was no denying it was an order.

Coffin thought for a moment to refuse. To simply turn the horse and ride out of this festering little town. But nothing would be gained by that, he knew. And he might be able to pick up some information from Sheriff Bordus. "You got somewhere I can take my horse? He needs feed and water."

"Sure. Bart," he called. When the other deputy popped his head back out the door, he said, "take Mr. Coffin's horse down to the livery. Make sure he gets good care, hear?"

The deputy nodded and stepped out onto the dusty street—Aspen Wells was too small to have sidewalks.

Coffin climbed down from the chestnut. He pulled off the saddlebags and tossed them over his shoulder, then grabbed the Winchester from the scabbard. He nodded to Bart, who led the animal away.

Bordus turned and entered the office. Coffin nodded at Kate, who followed the sheriff. Coffin went in last, wary, despite the sheriff's seemingly newfound friendliness.

The inside of the office was adobe. At back were two cells side by side. Three feet in front of them was a barred barrier with a door. Against one wall, nailed high on the adobe, was the rifle case in which six Winchesters reposed. There was a small, wood desk, covered with papers, keys, pistols, a plate with a half-eaten steak, three tin coffee cups, and a horseshoe. There was a potbellied stove in the front corner farthest from the desk. And two dozen Wanted posters were tacked to the short side wall next to the kerosene lantern.

Bordus took the creaking swivel chair behind the desk and sat. Coffin pointed to a simple, straight-back chair in one corner, and Kate McCoombs sat down, looking rather relieved. Coffin sat in the remaining straight-back chair after dragging it to the front of the desk.

There was silence for a while, as they all took stock of each other, and listened to the sounds filtering in from outside—the clatter of a carriage, shouts, children playing, the far-off hammering of the blacksmith.

Finally Bordus said, "Now why don't you tell me what's really goin' on, Mister Coffin."

Coffin shoved his hat back, and said, "I told you outside."

"So," Bordus said, drawing out the word, "you're gonna stick with that story, eh?"

"It ain't a story," Coffin said coldly.

"That true, miss?" Bordus asked, swinging toward Kate.

"Yes, sir."

"You sure?" he questioned harshly. "If this man—or any other—is coercin' you in sayin' such things, you don't have to be afraid no more. I'm the law here, and I'll make sure you're protected from whatever riffraff comes along."

"What he said was true, Sheriff," Kate said carefully. She still did not trust this man.

"What was you doin' on that train?"

"Goin' home. Me'n my sister had been visitin' kin."

"Where's home?"

"Over near Leroux Springs."

"You old Lester McCoombs's daughter?" the sheriff asked, suddenly alert.

"Yes," Kate answered proudly.

Sheriff Bordus nodded. "Well, hell, that explains a lot. Lester was near frantic when that stage pulled in and you and your sister weren't on it. He's offered a reward for your return. Five hundred dollars."

She looked a little surprised. "Is there a telegraph office in town?"

81

"Yeah," Bordus grunted, almost with some humor, "but it ain't worked in six, seven months. Sorry." He didn't sound it. After a short spell of silence, he said, "What's your part in all this, Mr. Coffin?" His face was hard. "You don't look like no shinin' knight like you read about in those books."

"You read books?" Coffin asked sarcastically.

Bordus only grimaced.

"It ain't none of your business, really, Sheriff," Coffin said. "But there ain't no harm in tellin' it." He explained it all quickly and succinctly.

"So the big, bad bounty hunter was gonna bring these badasses to heel, eh?" Bordus laughed in a gravelly rumble that was not a pleasant sound to hear. "Well, maybe not so big."

Coffin's face was blank, but his eyes smoldered with anger. He took some moments before saying anything, lest he let his anger get the better of him. Finally, slowly, he said, "Well, Sheriff, seems all your kind can't do nothin' about Reno Holder and his band of hardcases except get your asses shot up everytime you cut their trail. So finally they had to get somebody could do the job."

He tried not to gloat as the rage colored Bordus's face, but it was difficult. "Besides, you ain't much of a sheriff, I reckon, if you let them bastards ride in here, shoot hell out of your town, kill several of your people, and let them ride on out."

Bordus went for his pistol, but Coffin was far faster, and suddenly the sheriff found himself staring at the muzzle of a Remington Frontier .44 less than half a foot from his nose.

Chapter 12

"Just ease your hand up, Sheriff," Coffin said calmly. When Bordus complied, Coffin moved the revolver back a little and said, "Now, I ain't here to call you out, Sheriff. I come this way 'cause I found this woman in a bad way and her sister dead. The sister needs a proper buryin' and Miss Kate needs some carin' after. I aim to ride out soon's possible on Holder's trail."

Coffin slid the pistol away and sat back in the chair. "There ain't no call for us to be fightin' over those badasses, Sheriff."

"I ain't ever gonna forget this, Coffin," Bordus said.

"Nobody has to know what went on in here but us. I ain't gonna say nothin', and I reckon Miss McCoombs ain't gonna either. So there ain't no harm."

Bordus relaxed a little. "You aim to bring them in alive?" he asked.

"I ain't plannin' on it."

Bordus thought for a while. He was not a stupid man. This cocky little bantam sitting across from him was right—no one had to know that he had been faced down by the man. And if this bounty hunter could bring Reno Holder to heel, well, maybe he could take some credit for it.

"How can I help you?" he asked finally.

"Mostly point me in the right direction. But if you know anywhere they might be holed up, I'd be obliged if you told me. I ain't all that familiar with this part of the country, and so wouldn't know where they could hide."

"The cave was a good place, I reckon," Bordus said. "Not

many folks go by that area. I'd say there's a good chance they'd go back there. Specially if they left this little filly"—he chucked a thumb in Kate's direction, though he did not look at her—"there for some sportin' later."

He did turn to Kate then, and said, "I'm sorry, ma'am, if I'm bein' rather crude in my talk, but such things has got to be said. If you'd rather, I can see if some of the other womenfolk in town will take you in for the time bein'?"

"No, Sheriff. I want to stay here and hear this. I grew up with five brothers, so I'm used to such speech."

"My talk might touch on things that you'd rather not hear. . . ." He left it hanging, the implication that they would have to discuss what had happened to her evident.

"I understand," she said on her third attempt. Her throat had suddenly become blocked and the room close. But she forced herself to go on. "I had a bad time of it, Sheriff. Worse than you—or any man—will ever know. But I ain't no delicate flower that needs to be coddled all the time. What you might be talkin' about was *done* to me. Do you understand that? *Can* you understand that? The talkin' about it might be unpleasant, but it sure as hell ain't nowhere near's bad as havin' it done to me."

Coffin was shocked—not that she would use such language or voice such things, but that she was so vehement. She had been quiet on their trek here. He knew that desire for revenge burned deep in her, but he also knew she was scared to her very core. Those men had already ravaged her. And they had done far worse things to her sister. If they were to catch her again—the thought was horrifying even to the well-blooded Joe Coffin. To Kate McCoombs, it must be stark, holy terror.

He admired her, though, standing up to Bordus like she had. It was not an easy thing.

"I'm sorry, ma'am," Bordus said, trying to be contrite. The wrecked larynx made it hard, though, since all his sounds came out like angry growls. "I just thought, you know, you bein' a woman and all . . . that you might want to . . . well, you know . . . be with other women who could . . ."

"I'll be fine, Sheriff. But I thank you for your concern. Now, please, you two get on with your business. Indeed, pretend I'm not even here."

Bordus cleared his throat, but it did not make the voice any more pleasant. "Well, Mr. Coffin, like I was sayin', the cave would be a real good hideout. And if I had somethin' like this tied up most likely, waitin', I'd sure as hell go back." His face flamed red, but he would not change his ways for any woman.

"Me too," Coffin murmured.

"One thing you got to understand, though," Bordus said, "is that this land hereabout for miles is cut through with canyons, gulches, washes, caves, mines, Injun ruins. To tell you the truth, Mr. Coffin, I'd not really know where to start, if I was lookin' for a hideout.

"Within a few days' ride of here, there's some Injun ruins and a heap of dry washes up to the north, where the Navajos still roam, though not like in the old days.

"Southwest is more mountains, and a bunch of canyons including Rattlesnake Canyon, Turkey Canyon, and one of the worst—Hell Canyon. The name of that one pretty well gives you an idea."

He stopped to roll a cigarette, and Coffin did the same. When the smokes were fired up, Bordus said, "To the south is mountainous country, thick with pines. Beyond that there's Dry Beaver Canyon, which ends down near Camp Verde. South of that is the desert."

Bordus paused, then asked, "How long you been chasin' them boys?"

"Several weeks. My first stop after hearin' something was Piñon Springs. They'd robbed a bank there. But those bastards are always one step ahead of me. By the time I got into Piñon Springs, they had already hit Red Cliffs. From there, the train, then here."

"Yep, they're a busy bunch." They all sat in silence for some time, smoking, thinking. Finally Bordus said, "If I was you— and don't get me wrong, I ain't tryin' to tell you what to do— but if I was you, I'd head on toward her folks' place."

He ignored Kate, who started at the idea. Coffin asked, "Why?"

"First off, you can get the reward for bringin' her back," he said bluntly. "Next off, they was headed in that general direction when they rode out of here."

McCoombs looked worried. "They were headed toward my folks' ranch?" she asked.

"Not to your ranch, miss. Just in that direction, sort of."

"We've got to go there, Joe," she said, surprising both herself and Coffin with the use of his first name.

"I ain't so sure, Miss Kate."

"We've got to. My folks might be in trouble."

"If Holder's men have ridden to your father's place," he said softly, "it'll be too late for us to do anything for them. Except maybe bury them."

Her face was pained, but she retained control of herself. "But I gotta know, Joe," she said plaintively.

Coffin looked at Bordus as if to say, thanks for getting me into this. Bordus looked back innocently.

A few moments later, the deputy named Lon came in. As he opened the door, the three people inside could hear angry noises from the street.

"What's goin' on out there, Lon?"

"Folks is mighty edgy, Sheriff. They don't like havin' either of these two"—he pointed at Coffin and Kate—"here. Not after what happened the other day."

Bordus looked disgusted. "Tell 'em I said to go on home. There's nothin' they can do here. There's nothin' they ought to be doin' here. These two strangers have been put upon by some of the baddest hardcases ever rode in this area. They don't need a town full of asses makin' their lives any more miserable."

"But, Sheriff, they ain't gonna listen to that—or me tellin' it to 'em."

"Bullshit. Just go on and do it. Tell 'em you'll arrest the first one of 'em who tries shovin' his weight around too much."

"Yes, sir." Lon left, looking decidedly unhappy. Coffin did not envy him his job.

"You ain't plannin' on stayin' around too long, are you, Mr. Coffin?" Bordus asked.

"Just till mornin'. I can use a good night's sleep and some hot grub. Been a while since I had decent of either."

"What about Miss McCoombs?"

Coffin shrugged. "I've done as well by her as I could,

Sheriff. I told her I'd bring her back to the first town we come by so she'd be safe. I done that."

Silence sat heavy on the three, until it was shattered by the babbling when the door opened again. The noise had grown worse. "They ain't listenin', Lyle," Lon said. "Bart's out there tryin' to talk to them now, but I don't expect he'll do any better at it than I did. Maybe you better go out and talk to them. They'll listen to you."

"Goddamn rabble," Bordus snapped. "What'n hell do they want anyway?"

"Him." Lon pointed to Coffin.

"Why?"

"Best I can figure from all the jabberin' that's goin' on, they're convinced he's one of the outlaws who rode through the other day. They want to string him up."

"Who's leadin' all this foolish shit?"

"Harmon Tuck, and his two boys."

"I should've known they'd havin' their stinkin' hands in the middle of this." He stood and put on his hat. "You two stay here," he growled. "Come on, Lon."

The two lawmen walked out. Coffin shifted his chair so he could keep an eye on the mob outside the window.

"What're you going to do, Mr. Coffin—Joe?" Kate asked.

He shrugged. "Wait to see what happens out there. It don't look good."

"I didn't mean that." She hesitated. "I mean about findin' the men who . . ."

"Ride on after them."

She swallowed hard. The idea had just hit her, and she was not sure she liked it. But still . . . "I want to come with you," she said, almost strangling on the words.

"No," he said flatly.

"But why?"

"I don't have to give you reasons why, Miss McCoombs. I said no, and that's all there is to it."

"Why, you son of a bitch," she exploded, shocking him.

"Now you just wait—"

"No, you wait. And listen." She stood and paced as she talked, as if that would help her think. "I want those bastards to pay for what they did to me and my sister. I want them to pay. To *pay!* You ain't after them for any reason other than the money. I got a reason—more than one reason—to hunt 'em down. But I can't do it myself. I need help. And right now, far's I can see, you're the only one who can give me that help."

"You'd only get in my way. You know what these men are. How they act. Ain't a one of 'em has an ounce of sympathy in him. Can you shoot? Can you fight, if pressed? Can you put out of your mind what they did to you and Irene when you come face to face with one of them?"

"You know well's I do I can't do those things. But there's one thing I got that you ain't got."

"What's that?"

"I . . ."

The door opened and Sheriff Bordus stomped back in. He grabbed up the two scatterguns that were resting against the wall right near the door. He handed one to Bart and one to Lon. The two deputies went back outside, and Bordus kicked the door shut.

"Goddamn fools, each and every one of 'em," he snapped.

"Bad?" Coffin asked.

"Yep. No use in denyin' it. I don't reckon they'll really pull anything, since most of 'em ain't got the guts to face down a couple scatterguns. But that damn Tuck and his boys are a thorn in my ass. He gets them people all worked up over somethin'. Then the three of 'em disappear just when the goin' gets rough."

"And what's all this mean?"

"It means I ain't gonna get no goddamn sleep tonight, is what." He tossed his hat on the desk and sat heavily. "Look, I hate to say this to you folks, but I reckon you both ought to spend the night here."

"In jail?" Kate asked incredulously.

"Safest place in town."

"Couldn't you protect us somewhere else?" she asked, growing fearful. It had never really occurred to her that the townspeople would want to harm them. That reality was like a dash of cold water on her face.

"Sure. But not as well as I can do it here. There's only one small window in the back, by the cells, and the two out here. The walls are adobe, even if the front is covered with wood. They'll not be able to get you in here. Between me, Lon, and Bart there'll always be at least two of us stationed outside all night. The third'll stay in here, probably gettin' some shut-eye, but still ready if we need him."

"I'll have a key?" Coffin asked.

Bordus nodded.

"Then I reckon you got yourself two houseguests for the night."

Bordus brought out a deck of cards from his desk drawer. "Do you play poker, Mr. Coffin?" he asked, shuffling the deck expertly.

Chapter 13

"The key?" Coffin asked as Sheriff Bordus led him and Kate McCoombs to the two small cells at the back of the sheriff's office.

Bordus grinned and handed him a key ring. "It's the largest one," he said.

Coffin nodded, picked out the key, and then, without showing any humor, tried it. It worked. He shrugged and tried it on the other door, just in case. It too worked with oiled smoothness.

"Satisfied?" Bordus asked.

"Yep." Coffin motioned Kate McCoombs into one cell, and he stepped into the other. Through the small window high up in the cell, he could see a star. It had turned dark several hours ago, while he and Bordus had played cards. Kate had napped a little and then wandered nervously around the room.

They had had a meal of chicken, gravy, biscuits, butter, milk, and coffee delivered by an elderly woman who looked like she wanted no part of all this but had been forced into it. They ate the food in silence. When they were done, Bordus went outside, scattergun in hand.

Lon had come in and eaten, and when he finished, it was Bart's turn. Finally, with both deputies fed and back on duty, Sheriff Bordus came back in. He and Coffin played more cards, chatting about nothing in particular, until Bordus said, "I reckon you two ought to be gettin' some shut-eye. There'll be two of us on guard outside all the time. We'll take turns comin' in and nappin' at the desk there."

Coffin nodded and stood, arching his back to stretch out the kinked muscles. He had won three dollars from the sheriff, and was feeling pretty good about it.

As he stepped into the cell, it was an eerie feeling. He had put many men behind bars, but never had he slept in a cell. He was not sure he liked it, but in he stepped anyway. He stretched out on his back on the creaky, iron cot. He pushed his hat down over his eyes.

"G'night," Bordus said after watching, possibly too intently, as Kate lay down and turned to face the wall.

"Night."

"Night."

Bordus turned down the two lamps in the office—one on the desk, one hanging on the wall—and went outside. A few minutes later Bart came in and sat in the sheriff's chair. Resting his shotgun against the juncture of the wall and the desk, he leaned back, pulled down his hat. Within minutes he was snoring softly.

Coffin relaxed. He was used to situations of danger, and so was able to put such things from his mind and take advantage of each opportunity to sleep. He let the comfort of sleep settle in over him, thinking briefly that all this had been much more trouble than it probably was worth. Never had such a string of bad luck dogged him. But there was peace in sleep, and he let it draw him in.

Kate's voice woke him. "You awake, Mr. Coffin?" She was talking softly, so as not to awake Bart.

"Yep," he grumbled. He was not happy with this.

"I was serious when I said I want to go with you, Mr. Coffin."

"I said no before and I meant it. I see no reason to change it now." He wished for sleep.

"I never did get a chance to finish before, when we were talkin'. I told you I had somethin' you didn't have."

"Yep. And what is that?"

"This."

He swung his legs off the cot so that he was facing her. Each cot was against the outside wall, so the entire length of both cells separated them, but that was not much. In the dull light he could see her standing, facing him. He was puzzled. "This what?" he asked, feeling stupid.

She waved her hands, palms upward, from neck to knees. "Huh?"

"You ain't really this dumb, are you?" she asked in exasperation. "Me! My body!"

Coffin thought he saw her pink up some in embarrassment. Then he snorted in a half laugh, half indication of disgust. "You think them boys are gonna come traipsin' after you just 'cause you're a woman? Hell, you've got nothin' they ain't seen—and abused—before. Unless you forgot," he added pointedly.

She sat, suppressing a shudder. "No, I ain't forgot. But not all of them had . . ."

"I know. But just 'cause they never finished what they started, don't mean they was plannin' to rush right back there and do so. If they were, they would've caught us still there."

"But—"

"Now, you listen to me, Miss McCoombs. Think back on what they done to you and your sister. Especially about what they done to Irene." Her face got pale in the glimmer of the low lanterns. "Now, do you really think they give a damn about you—or your beautiful body?" He paused a heartbeat and then went on. "Such things as they did to Irene ought to teach you that those bastards don't give a shit about you nor any other woman. You're nothin' but a body to 'em. You might have the most beautiful body this man's ever seen. But that don't make a rabbit's ass to them. You're just somethin' for them to use and then toss off, like an old bandanna or somethin'. They might take a beautiful woman given the choice, which is why they probably took you and Irene off that train and not somebody else.

"But without a choice they'll take an ugly woman, an old woman. Hell, they're the kind that'd most likely take girls ain't even close to bein' women yet. You ain't got nothin' any other woman ain't got, and that's all that matters to them sons a bitches."

He knew he was being much harsher on her than he should.

But she had to see what kind of men these really were. That they had no humanity in them; that she could not expect them to act like other men would act, even if it was with evil intent.

Besides, there was no way he could, in good conscience, take Kate McCoombs with him when he rode out of town on the trail of Reno Holder's gang of heartless outlaws.

Kate sat quietly, head hanging low in embarrassment and rage. All Coffin could see was the mass of dark hair. Then her head snapped up. "Those bastards!" she hissed, eliciting a murmuring and shifting from the sleeping deputy. "They were gonna leave me there in that cave, tied up like some goddamn old cow, to die! Weren't they?" She was breathing heavily, and her face was flushed with anger.

"Most likely. I expect they'd be headed back there in a few days. Might've even gone back already. If they'd have found you alive—or even newly dead, knowing those festerin' bastards, they would've been happy to have used you again.

"Course they might've brought some new captives with 'em. In that case, they could've used you and Irene as examples of what they was about to do to the new captives. It would, I expect," he added dryly, "keep any captive from 'causin' 'em any trouble.

"And," he threw in harshly, still trying to make sure she knew exactly what kind of beasts she was dealing with here, "it would serve to scare hell out of those captives. That's a big part of the way they operate—they thrive on other people's fears. Reckon it makes 'em feel like real men to have some woman scared so bad she'll likely piss her skirts every time one of 'em looks at her."

Coffin drew in a ragged breath. He had taken this job because it was a job and he had nothing better to do, because it paid well, and because an old friend had asked. He'd figured to do his business, collect his cash, and then ride on back to Denver.

It was rare that he got involved in the job on which he was working—beyond being his usual cautious self. But now, he was being sucked into caring. Each time he thought of any of Holder's men, the more he wanted to kill that man—and all his partners. It was unlike Coffin to be this way, but he couldn't seem to help it. If any men he had ever hunted needed killing—

and there had been some real bad hardcases—it was this bunch.

"What kind of monsters are they?" McCoombs asked, despair and wonder in her voice.

"The worst kind, ma'am. It's why I ain't aimin' to take you along with me when I go after them. Now go to sleep."

He started to lean back, but snapped up again when she said, "No. I ain't goin' to sleep. And I am goin' after them . . . them . . . whatever in hell they are."

She drew in a deep breath. "I'd rather go with you. But if I can't, then by God, I'll make it back to my father's ranch as soon as I can. Once there, I'll get me a horse and a gun—a couple of guns—and ride out after them."

"Alone?" Coffin did not laugh, but scorn was evident in his voice.

"Yes." There was no denying the determination in that single, simple word.

Damn, she just might do it too, he thought. "Chances of you findin' 'em aren't very good," Coffin said.

"I'll make it easy for them," Kate said, fighting down the coils of fear that sprang up in her stomach. She almost panicked, but she managed to keep it under control.

There was only one way she could do that, Coffin thought. And for the first time since he was fifteen and in the midst of a major battle in the Civil War, he felt fear. Not fear for himself like that other time, but fear for someone else. It was why he had never married and started a family. The fear of losing them somehow was the one fear he could never deal with. Now he found himself caring for this woman, admiring—while at the same time thinking how foolish she was being—her bravery. It annoyed him to no end to be having these feelings. *Damnit, why did I get involved with this mess?* he wondered. It had been nothing but trouble right from the start. At least *that* was something that had not changed.

"Even if you do find 'em," Coffin said—he almost shuddered, and was surprised at himself—"you'll only get yourself killed straight off."

Kate shrugged, caught between despair and determination. "You can stop that from happenin'," she said so quietly he almost missed it.

"Why should I?" he asked roughly.

"Because," Kate mumbled.

"Damnit," he snapped. He jerked up off the bed and started pacing. With sharp, tense movements, he rolled a cigarette and lit it. It would, he knew, be sheer lunacy to take her along. Suddenly he stopped, and faced her through the bars dividing the cells.

"You're set on goin'?" he asked sharply.

"Yes." There was a firmness to her jaw. "I owe it to Irene to try to find those bastards."

"There's no way I can talk you out of this foolishness? 'Cause that's what it is—foolishness. Pure and simple."

"I'm goin'."

His shoulders slumped. "All right," he said quietly. "You win. I can't have your blood on my conscience."

Kate looked happy and frightened at the same time. She had won! Or had she? Whatever, she had gotten what she wanted.

"Best get some shut-eye, Miss McCoombs," Coffin said. "If you intend to ride with me, we'll be settin' out early come the mornin'."

The initial flush of excitement wore off rather quickly, and Kate realized she was tired. She nodded. "Thank you," she said. She sat on the bed and then stretched out on her back.

Coffin grinned. It was so easy, he thought. He wished he had thought of it earlier. Doing so would have avoided all this arguing. Then again, thinking of it now meant he had had to argue, and it seemed more convincing after all that.

Yes, he would take her with him. As far as her father's ranch. He would leave her there, for if Lester McCoombs was any sort of father, there would be no way in heaven or on earth that the beautiful, red-haired Kate McCoombs would be going one step farther, no matter what she said.

Coffin sat on the bed and unhooked his spurs. He dropped them with a small clatter on the floor. He took off his hat and dropped it atop the spurs. But he would not take off any of his guns tonight.

He lay on his back, closing his eyes and shutting out the world.

Coffin wasn't quite sure what it was that woke him, but his eyes snapped open, and his hand snaked to one of the .36-caliber Colts in the shoulder holsters and rested there. He waited a moment until the pounding of his heart—initiated by the sudden awakening—slowed to normal.

He heard it again. Very, very carefully he lifted his head and looked around. There was no deputy sleeping in the chair. The lanterns were as dim as they had been. The room was mostly quiet. He looked toward his right, and saw a large figure leaning over Kate McCoombs.

Coffin's eyes widened as he watched Sheriff Bordus place a hard hand over Kate's mouth. She awoke with a start, but with Bordus's bulk partially atop her, she could not struggle much.

"Quiet!" Bordus hissed in a whisper, looking frantically over toward Coffin, who had his head back on the bed.

Coffin lay there for some seconds before rolling over a little toward the other cell. Cracking his eyes open, he saw Bordus unbuttoning Kate's shirt.

Shaking his head in annoyance, and wondering at the sheriff's stupidity, Coffin swung silently up out of the bed. In two strides he was out of the cell. In three more he was at the doorway to the other; and in two more was just behind Bordus.

He lifted out the Remington. It was heavier than the Colt, and probably less likely to be damaged. He whipped the gun out from the side, and the length of the seven-and-a-half-inch barrel smashed against Bordus's temple.

The sheriff groaned and fell atop Kate, who suddenly had trouble breathing.

Coffin grabbed the back of Bordus's shirt and jerked him off the woman. Her dark-tipped breasts were bare where her shirt gaped open, and Coffin went dry-mouthed at the sight. He dropped the sheriff to the floor, and with a boot rolled Bordus over. The sheriff was on the verge of unconsciousness—not out, but incapable of doing anything.

"What do we do?" Kate asked, eyes wide. She sat up, absent-mindedly buttoning her shirt.

"Wait till he wakes up."

"Then what?"

Chapter 14

Sheriff Bordus sat up, resting his back against the hard cot of the cell. His mouth was slack, and there was a line of coagulating blood stretching down from his right temple, across his cheek, and around his jaw. His head pounded, and his face was ashen.

Joe Coffin and Kate McCoombs stood, leaning against the bars next to the cell door, watching the sheriff. Coffin held the sheriff's Colt lightly in his right hand.

"What are we going to do with him, Mr. Coffin?" Kate asked, eyes wide with fear tinged with hate.

"What do you think we ought to do with him?"

The sheriff looked up at the woman with pain-shaded eyes.

"I don't know," she mumbled. She wanted to kill him for what he had tried to do to her, but when it came down to it, she was not that bloodthirsty.

"Well, Sheriff," Coffin said, "What do *you* think we should do with you?"

Bordus shrugged. With an effort, he pushed himself up until he was sitting on the cot.

"What'n hell ever possessed you to try to such foolishness?" Coffin asked, curious.

"Hell, I don't know," Bordus gargled in his gravelly voice. He looked up at Kate again. "I'm sorry, ma'am," he said, apparently in earnest. "I truly am." He shook his head ruefully, almost ignoring the pain. "I just kept thinkin' of her in here, asleep, and how good she looked, and all."

Kate tightened, then forced herself to relax some.

"Then I thought of how abused she had been by Reno Holder's men there. I figured you'd also took your share of her. . . ."

Coffin's eyes expanded in surprise, then narrowed in hate. He rubbed his stomach, fighting the urge to shoot Bordus down where he sat.

The sheriff looked up at the short, stock, powerful bounty hunter, and grinned a quick, rueful smile. "Reckon I was wrong on that too, huh?"

Coffin nodded tightly, still angry.

"Shit," Bordus muttered. "Guess I figured wrong all the way 'round." He looked sad. "I reckon this ain't gonna make the matter go away, ma'am," he added, glancing at Kate's pale, angry face, "but I'm sorry. I ain't never done nothin' like this before."

He was silent for a little while, before saying, "I know it ain't right, but I just couldn't keep from thinkin' of you and what pleasures you could give a man." He winced at the pain, fear, and disgust that flickered across Kate's face.

Bordus swallowed hard. "And I know this ain't no reason, but"—he paused, not wanting to say this—"most women don't want nothin' to do with an ugly old cuss like me." He brushed a hand down the long scar on his face. "Between this, and my voice, ain't a whole lot of women want to spend any time with me. Gets kind of lonely after a spell."

"That don't give you no right to take such liberties with any woman who comes along," Kate said roughly.

"I know." Bordus seemed truly pained, and Kate felt a tug at her heart. She wanted to forgive him.

She looked at Coffin, who was staring at her. As if he could read her mind, he shook his head. She nodded.

"That still doesn't answer the question of what'n hell we're gonna do with you, Sheriff," Coffin said.

"You could just shoot me down," Bordus growled. "It's no more'n I deserve, I reckon. Or," he added, with a tinge of hope in his voice, "you could let me go."

"I'm inclined toward shootin' you for now," Coffin said with no hint of forgiveness in his voice. "But I reckon that'd cause more troubles than it'd take care of. I might consider lettin' you go"—and Bordus's eyes brightened—"if you help us get the hell out of here."

"Us?"

"Yep. Miss McCoombs is goin' with me."

"I thought you were gonna leave her in town till we could get word to her father."

"Changed my mind." He glared at the sheriff, sure he had seen something he did not like in his eyes.

Bordus stared at Coffin for some seconds. Then he nodded. "Right. Reckon you ain't about to leave Miss Kate here in town long's I'm around." He rubbed his aching head. "Well, you wouldn't have to worry about that no more, I swear. But I don't expect y'all to believe that."

Coffin cocked his head in acknowledgment.

"How can I help you?"

"Get my horse up here, saddled. Have the mule packed with some supplies. And get us a horse for Miss McCoombs. One that's been gentled well. Saddled."

Bordus nodded and stood. "I'll be back quick's I can."

"Reckon not," Coffin said with iron in his voice. "Have one of your deputies do it."

"Don't trust me?" There was resignation on his face.

"Would you?"

"Nope."

The sheriff headed out of the cell, followed closely by Coffin and Kate. Bordus opened the office door. He went to take a step out, but Coffin said, "Tell him from here."

Lyle nodded. "How's things goin', Lon?" he asked.

"Poorly. Crowd's startin' to stir again, now that it's light."

"Damn. The Tucks back?"

"Yep."

"They the ones stirrin' things up again?"

"Yep."

"Be out in a minute to help," the sheriff said, closing the door. "Damn." He looked at Coffin. "I need my pistol back so I can go out there and help them boys settle these folks down." Before Coffin could say anything, Bordus held up his hand, and said, "I know you got no call to believe me, Mr. Coffin, but

99

I give you my word that I'll not do anything against you or Miss McCoombs."

Coffin looked skeptical, so the sheriff said, "Look, you and her ain't goin' anywhere with that mob out there like that. I ain't got but those two deputies, and I can't send one of 'em chasin' after your things and all while me and the other try'n calm things down."

"Think you can calm 'em down?"

"I don't know," Bordus said with a sigh. "There's a lot of angry folks out there. This ain't the first time Holder's been through here. And with some asses like the Tucks goadin' 'em on . . ."

"What's in it for the Tucks?"

"Reckon they're lookin' for revenge wherever they can find it. Last time Holder's gang rode through here, they killed one of Ole Man Tuck's lifelong friends, who had taken over the bank after Tuck's older brother, Henry, was killed the first time Holder ran through here. But him and his two sons ain't got the balls—oops, excuse me, Miss McCoombs."

She nodded her acceptance of the man's language.

"Anyway, they're big talkers but little doers. And since, somehow, everybody's come to believe you're one of Holder's gang, the Tucks figure to use that for their purposes. It'll make them feel better, I reckon, if they can get revenge on someone—even if they've picked the wrong man."

"You had somethin' to do with that wrong thinkin', Sheriff," Coffin said harshly, unforgiving. "When I rode into town, you mentioned that. A lot of folks was listenin'."

"Christ. I really made an ass of myself this time, didn't I."

It really didn't require an answer, so no one said anything. Bordus rubbed his head, which still hurt considerably. "Well," he finally said, "I really do need to go out there and see if I can calm things down. If I can get Tuck and his boys to go home, the others'll leave most likely."

"What're the chances?"

"What're the chances of gettin' the card you need drawin' for an inside straight?"

"That bad, huh?"

"Yep."

Coffin didn't have to think about it long. There was little choice. He twirled Bordus's pistol on his index finger. When it stopped, the revolver's butt was facing the sheriff.

Bordus took it, checked the cylinder, and then dropped it into the holster.

"I'll be watching you out the window," Coffin warned.

Bordus nodded. He turned and put his hand on the door latch, then stopped and turned back. "I've wronged both of you in many ways," he said stiffly. This was not easy for him to do. "And so I've got to do a heap of makin' up for my mistakes. I'll get you out of here safe, no matter what it takes." He went out the door.

Coffin moved toward one window, and flattened against the corner. It would keep him out of the line of fire—if it came to that—while still giving him a clear field of vision. He glanced at Kate and with a hand motioned her back against the wall. She obeyed without question.

Through the closed window, he could hear Bordus yelling at the crowd, trying to make himself heard over the yelling of the crowd. Finally the sheriff shook his head, angry. He grabbed out his Colt and fired two shots into the air.

The heavy boom of the weapon reverberated a little, and by the time the noise of the second shot had drifted into the early morning sky, the crowd was quiet.

"Now go on home," Bordus roared as loudly as he could with his ruined larynx. "Each and every one of you. You got no business here. All you're gonna do is cause trouble for yourselves."

"Bullshit!" someone yelled.

With all the people and his angle of vision, Coffin could not tell who it was. But the voice continued, "We want that outlaw son of a bitch you got in there."

"He ain't no outlaw."

"The hell he ain't," the same voice hollered. "If he ain't, then why do you have him locked up in there?"

"To keep him—and the woman—safe from idiots like you and them two fool sons of yours, Tuck."

There was a grumble from the crowd. "He's a bounty hunter on the trail of Holder's bunch. He ain't done nothin' wrong here. All he's done is to bring in the body of a girl that Holder's men raped and then butchered. And he brought in another girl who faced the same at the hands of those outlaws."

There was an angry murmur that spread through the crowd. They were worked up, Bordus could see, and not of a mind to listen to him. They had had too much time to listen to the vindictive talk tossed so easily about by Tuck and the two sons.

"That's shit," another voice said. "He's one of Holder's gang and you're protectin' him. Maybe you're even in cahoots with them. Seems they never harmed you or any of your deputies when they rode through here those two times."

Bordus's muttered "Damn!" was drowned out in the bellowing of the crowd. He waited, hoping the people in the crowd—people he knew for many years, people who looked to him to do his job, people who had elected him three times—would come to their senses. But it was looking less and less likely, with the three Tucks whipping everyone into a frenzy like they were.

He said something Coffin could not hear to the two deputies flanking him, and then came back into the office.

"This don't look good at all," Bordus said, rubbing his still-aching head.

"No, it don't. Leastways for us, Sheriff."

"It ain't so good for me neither, Mr. Coffin. Did you hear what they're sayin' about me out there now? They're sayin' I'm in cahoots with Holder and his bunch!"

"Are you?"

"Hell, no!" Bordus exploded. Still, Coffin did not fully believe him.

Bordus moved to the window. The crowd, egged on by Old Man Tuck, had edged a little closer to the office door. He turned to look at Coffin. "Seems they're gettin' worse out there."

"What do you aim to do, Sheriff?"

"I ain't cer—"

The loud explosion of a scattergun stopped him, and he whipped his head around to look out the window. The deputy Bart had fired off a warning shot. Both he and Lon faced the crowd, looking grim. Each had his shotgun down, cocked and ready.

"Shit," Bordus muttered. "This is bad. I better get back out there and see if I can do anything."

"I don't reckon you can. But if you're goin', you better take one of those scatterguns with you."

Bordus nodded. Quickly he opened the case holding the six Winchesters and one shotgun. There were two other spots for shotguns—the ones Bart and Lon were using. From his desk drawer, the sheriff pulled a box of shells. He cracked the weapon open and loaded the two chambers. It clicked together with a sharp snap. Then Bordus took a handful of shells and dumped them in a vest pocket.

He took a deep breath as he walked to the door. "Well, here I go," he said as he opened it.

Coffin slipped to his spot by the window again, and watched. There was no way, he saw, that Bordus would be able to control this crowd. "Get down behind the desk, Miss McCoombs," he said hastily, heading for the door.

"What're you going to do?"

"Never you mind. Just do what I say." As she ducked behind the desk, Coffin opened the door and stepped out.

Chapter 15

Joe Coffin stepped out into the dusty street, and bulled his way forward until he was standing next to Sheriff Lyle Bordus. "Quiet 'em down, Sheriff," he said.

Bordus cocked the shotgun and fired the contents of both barrels into the air. Silence dropped rapidly, as Bordus pulled the spent shells from his revolver, and then slid new ones home.

"All right," Coffin bellowed into the quiet, as almost three dozen angry faces glared at him. "Where's this fella named Tuck? I hear tell he's the fool started all this ruckus."

No one stepped forward, but many of the people started talking among themselves and looking backward. The mob began drifting a little to the sides, until there was a passageway between the two hordes of humans.

Standing at the back of the funnel of humanity was a stocky man of medium height and graying hair. He wore a black coat and black wool pants. There was a once-white shirt, now grayish, under the partially unbuttoned vest, with a gold watch fob stretched across the ample middle.

There was a younger man on each side of him. Each was a little taller than the father, and looked strong and lean. Each wore dark-blue Levi's pants, and flannel shirts, one red, the other green. And each had a Smith and Wesson revolver riding low on his left hip. Coffin decided the two young men probably did not know how to use those pistols very well, but they most likely would be ready to show off for the crowd. That made them dangerous. It did not worry Coffin, since now that he knew it, he was prepared.

"Well," Coffin said slowly, an edge of hardness in his voice, "so you're the famous Tuck family of Aspen Wells, eh? Can't say as I'm glad to make your acquaintance."

The three Tuck family members stood stock still, sweating a little under their Stetsons.

"Real friendly folk too, I see." Coffin drawled sarcastically. The crowd stared from Coffin to the elder Tuck and back. They were still hostile toward Coffin, but at least they were quiet and relatively calm.

"Sheriff Bordus here tells me you three boys don't cotton to my bein' in town. And that you three got some real damnfool reasons for that. That right?"

The father nodded, but barely.

"Now, I don't know where you boys got the notion that I belong to Reno Holder's gang. I'm tellin' you—all of you!—that it ain't so. You can believe that or not, as you're of a mind to. But let me tell you that the only connection I have to those thievin', murderin' sons a bitches is that I'm huntin' them down."

There was much mumbling from the crowd now, as they talked over this new information. Some stared at Coffin, as if trying to determine from his looks if he was telling the truth. Others looked at the three Tucks, seeking guidance.

The elder Tuck and his two sons stood as if frozen, half smiles plastered on their faces.

The jumbled noise of the mob died down slowly, and soon everyone was staring at Harmon Tuck. The dark-visaged man was terribly uncomfortable having been placed in the spotlight. But he managed to say, "Don't listen to him. He's one of those outlaws who killed my brother. I know that. I saw him."

"Me too," the two youths echoed.

The people swung back toward Coffin. This was not going to be easy, the bounty hunter thought. He was a stranger here, and the three men he faced were, if not townspeople, at least local ranchers with plenty of connections to the town. And Coffin had nothing he could use to convince them. But he had to try.

"He's a liar," Coffin said bluntly. "I never been in this part of the territory before, let alone in this town."

One of the younger Tucks took two steps forward before his father could say anything. "Who you callin' a liar, you bastard?" he demanded, unfastening the leather loop over the hammer of his Smith and Wesson pistol.

"All three of you," Coffin said bluntly, freeing up the hammer of his .45-caliber Peacemaker. He began rubbing his stomach slowly, methodically.

The young man started to say something, but his father grabbed his arm and pulled him back. "Them's strong words, mister," the father said. "Mighty strong."

"They're true, though."

The three talked among themselves, the one son obviously arguing to be allowed to kill this short, bold man.

But the father finally prevailed. The son stood back, anger distorting his otherwise handsome face. "What do you want here anyway, mister?"

"My name's Coffin. Joe Coffin. And I don't want anything here other than to be allowed to leave in peace."

"Why'd you come here?"

"I told that to you people yesterday. To bring in that dead girl for a proper buryin' and her sister to get some care. All I wanted after that was to get a decent meal and a good night's sleep before ridin' out. My sleep was disturbed, but I did have a good supper last night. Now all I want is to have some breakfast, pack up my mule, and ride the hell out of here."

"For what?" It was the other son. "To go to some other town and kill more honest folks?"

Coffin looked up at the tall sheriff, and raised an eyebrow in question. "That's Horace," Bordus said. "The older of the two. The other is Hector. The big man's name is Harmon."

"Best get that notion out of your head, boy," Coffin said harshly. "The only reason I'd look up Reno Holder or any of his men is to kill 'em."

"The hell you say. I saw you kill my uncle."

"So," Coffin said with raised eyebrows, "now I've gone from bein' a member of the gang to bein' the one who shot your uncle down. That it? And I suppose next you'll have me standin' there with a smokin' gun in my hand at every robbery and killin' in this whole damn territory for the last fifty years."

106

"Goddamn right," Horace snapped. There was a drop of spittle at the corner of his lips, and his eyes seemed crazed.

"They always act like this?" Coffin asked Bordus.

"Since Harmon's brother was killed, yep. They really believe you were with those outlaws that time. There's nothin' you can say or do to change their minds."

Coffin stared up at him for some seconds before saying slowly, "You said before you owed me somethin'." Bordus nodded and Coffin continued. "You also worried that I didn't trust you." Again a nod.

"Well, I'm gonna have to trust you now, Sheriff. I'm gonna have to trust you not only to back my play, but also not to have them two deputies behind you blow me in half with them scatterguns."

Without a moment's hesitation, Bordus craned his neck around and said, "Lon, Bart. You are to back this man up all the way. You follow his lead, no matter what play he makes."

The two hard-eyed, though nervous, young men nodded.

"It might not go easy on you, Sheriff. Slugs get flyin', some innocent people might get in the way."

Bordus shrugged. His face was hard again. "Deal me in."

Coffin nodded and turned back to face the crowd. Faces waited expectantly. Some were eager to see what would happen; some afraid. But all of them expected something to happen real soon. Only a few turned and walked away.

"Well," Coffin said flatly, "you're a bigger liar'n your idiot brother is."

Coffin was a man with almost limitless patience. It was one of the reasons he was so good at his chosen work. But his patience was at an end. The run of bad luck was still dogging his tracks, and this whole job was beginning to take on a nightmarish hue. There had been too many people making wild accusations against him lately; too many people pulling, or trying to pull, weapons on him. He had finally had enough. Maybe by making a stand here he would worsen matters, but maybe he could end this nonsense for a time.

Horace looked as if he was ready to burst open from the rage that boiled up within him. But his father's hand stayed him from making a play.

"Let him go, Harmon," Coffin goaded the father. "Go on, let

him come at me. Then you'll have a son to bury along with a brother. That might keep you busy enough so that you'll let innocent people live in peace."

"You rotten bastard!" Hector roared, stepping out from behind his father. He had his pistol half out.

"Stop!" Bordus roared, but the end of the word was clipped off by the loud bang of Hector Tuck's Smith and Wesson.

The slug thunked into one of the log support beams for the small overhang on the sheriff's office, several feet to Coffin's right.

"Don't try it again," Coffin snarled as the crowd fell on the ground. Several women screamed.

Hector thumbed back the hammer. Almost reluctantly, Coffin snatched out the Peacemaker. "Don't," he said once more. But Hector fired. The shot was far wide again, so convulsed with rage was the young man that he could not aim.

Without hesitation, Coffin squeezed off a shot. The bullet smashed into Hector's chest, slamming him back up against his father. The elder man staggered back a step, but managed to stay upright and catch his rapidly dying son.

There was a collective gasp from the crowd, and a few more screams. Horace Tuck yelled, "Goddamn you!" and grabbed for his pistol. Calmly, Coffin spun in his direction, Peacemaker up and at arm's length, pointing straight at the young man's heart.

But Horace did not stop. Coffin could have killed him easily, but he hesitated. He was angry, but he did not want a bloodbath. Hector fired twice in succession, but Coffin was moving. He dove to the side. He rolled, came up on a knee, and then surged to a stand, Colt revolver out.

There were two loud explosions. The first bullet from Coffin's Colt hit Horace in the upper stomach, doubling him over while at the same time punching him back a few steps. The second ripped into the young man's skull as he was bent over. The youth was dead before his twitching body hit the ground.

Coffin spun, gun pointing at Harmon Tuck. Harmon knelt, facing the sheriff's office, with Hector's head in his lap. Shock was written on his face, and his cheeks were covered with tears. Coffin eased the hammer of the Colt down, and then heard several shots, including the heavy thump of a scattergun.

There were screams and shouts, curses and crying, as Coffin dropped onto his stomach and searched around. Bart was wounded, his bicep bloody. But two citizens were also dead. Three more people in the mob had pistols out and were firing toward the sheriff and his two deputies. Coffin snapped up his pistol and fired off the two remaining rounds in his Colt. He smiled in satisfaction when one of the gunmen in the crowd went down, a bloody hole where the front of his face was a moment before.

"Get inside!" Sheriff Bordus yelled.

Coffin saw the door of the office open, and knew Kate McCoombs must have been watching and had opened it to help them all. Lon helped the wounded Bart in, as Coffin jammed his Colt in the holster and pulled the Remington. He fired off two shots, leaped up, and started backing toward the office door.

He and the sheriff reached the door at the same time. "Go on!" Bordus ordered.

"You first."

"It's my town. Go!"

Coffin snapped off a shot and another gun-wielding member of the mob went down, dead. Then he was inside. The sheriff stumbled in a step behind him. Together they slammed the door and shoved the desk over to barricade it.

Coffin looked out one of the shattered windows. Most of the mob had dispersed already. Only two men besides Harmon Tuck remained, and they knelt one on each side of Tuck, guns out.

"Miss McCoombs? Are you all right?" Coffin called out, not looking.

"Yes." She sounded scared, and he glanced her way. And smiled. She might have been scared, but she was not helpless.

Kate had Bart sitting on the floor near where the desk had been. She had torn off his shirt and ripped it up. From a canteen lying nearby, she poured water on a piece of the former shirt, and wiped at the blood on Bart's arm.

"It ain't bad," Coffin heard Kate say as he turned back to watch out the window. "The bullet went all the way through. You'll be all right in a couple days, I reckon."

"Yes, ma'am," Bart mumbled.

"Well, that didn't work as well as I had hoped," Coffin said slowly. "How about you, Sheriff? You got any ideas?"

"About what?"

"Gettin' outta here in one piece."

"Can't say as I do."

"It's gonna get mighty hungry here before long," Coffin said, keeping a close watch out the window. His stomach was rumbling.

"We'll get somethin' soon," Sheriff Bordus growled from his post at the other small window."

"How?"

"I'll go get us something."

"You get shot in the head or somethin'?"

"Nope."

"You're either braver or more *loco* than most folks I know."

"Ain't nothin' of either sort."

"Well, unless you forgot, there was a heap of folks out there slingin' lead at us a few minutes ago."

"Not a one of 'em townsfolk. They were all cowpokes workin' at the Tuck place. Harmon hired 'em all. Everytime he comes to town he brings a bunch of them with him. Usually they're like bodyguards for him. Figures he's a big-shot rancher, so he needs some protection." Bordus snorted in disgust. "But when somethin' like this happens, he spreads 'em around the crowd, agitatin'."

They watched as several cowboys drove a flatbed wagon up. They tossed the dead cowpunchers in with little ceremony. But they were gentle when they placed the bodies of Horace and Hector Tuck in the wagon.

They watched as the wagon, now loaded, was driven up the street by two cowboys, who flanked Harmon Tuck on the seat.

"Once Harmon rides out with that wagon, I'll be able to get out and get us some things. I'll have to watch my ass, but I can make it."

Before long they saw the wagon pull out, heading northeast out of town. A few moments later, the undertaker's surrey followed.

"Well," the sheriff said, straightening his hat. "Reckon it's time for me to go. Lon, help me move this damn desk."

When it was back in its accustomed place, Sheriff Bordus reached for the door latch.

"You have seen that son of a bitch with the rifle across the street, ain't you?" Coffin asked.

Bordus froze. He stepped back to the window and looked. "Where?"

"Three doors up to the right of the saloon. Middle window."

Bordus searched with his eyes. "I don't see nothin'," he said after a little.

"He's there, though. I caught just a glimpse of him."

Bordus looked unsure.

"I'll take him out from here, if you want," Coffin said. He and the sheriff stared at each other, ignoring the three others in the room.

The sheriff shook his head, still uncertain. "Maybe he ain't one of them," he said slowly.

"There's one way to find out." Coffin grinned a little.

Bordus nodded and reached for the door handle again. "I just hope the bastard can't shoot worth a damn," he muttered. "Well, here I go."

"Wait a minute, Lyle," Coffin said. He went back into the cell and returned with his Winchester. "He wants to take a shot at you, he'll have to show himself. If he does, he's a dead son of a bitch."

"You really like killin', don't you?" Bordus asked, mildly surprised.

"Nope. But I don't worry over it neither. If I liked it, though, I'd wind up bein' somebody like Reno Holder."

Bordus nodded as Coffin set himself at the window, rifle at his shoulder. "Go," the bounty holder said.

There was the crack of a rifle as the sheriff opened the door and stepped out. A bullet splintered the wood of the door a bare six inches from Bordus's head. The sheriff jumped back in the door, as Coffin fired. There was a distant scream, and then silence.

"Think you got him good?" Bordus asked nervously, slamming the door shut.

"Yep."

"You sure?"

"Yep."

"Absolutely sure?"

"One way to find out." Coffin smiled.

"How about you try it," Bordus said with a crooked grin. "You're a smaller target."

Coffin raised his eyebrows, and Lyle grinned. "I'll be back quick," Bordus said, stepping out the door, showing no fear.

There were no shots, and the sheriff hurried down the street. He was back in less than ten minutes.

"Somebody'll be bringing us breakfast real soon," he said as he entered the door. "And Doc Keever'll be here too. How you doin', Bart?" he asked, moving toward the deputy.

"I'll pull through. Hurts like all hellfire, though," he said through gritted teeth.

Bordus nodded and went back to his post by the window. "Seems quiet," Coffin said as he did.

"Yep." He leaned the scattergun against the wall.

Before long, a middle-aged woman—who once must have been attractive, Coffin thought, before time and working too hard had caught up with her—arrived with two baskets laden with food.

As she left, Coffin, Kate, Bordus, and the two deputies dug into the hot eggs, oven-warm biscuits over which they poured gravy, fatty bacon, slices of ham.

Coffin and Bordus ate standing up at the windows, keeping watch.

A few minutes later, the woman returned. In one hand she had a huge coffeepot, carried by the pail-like handle; in the other she carried half a dozen tin cups. Stiffly she carried them in, not wanting to be there. Other people would talk about her, she thought, and she would not be able to face anyone in town again.

"Thank you, Miz Stewart," Bordus said with a touch of sarcasm as he held the door for her to leave. She sniffed at him. "You can pick up this stuff when you bring our lunch later. If we're still here."

"Hmmmph," Mrs. Stewart grumbled as she swept out of the small office, her plain black dress swirling around her feet.

The bounty hunter had finished his breakfast, and was calmly smoking a cigarette, surveying the still-deserted street. He looked almost serene. He felt Bordus staring at him and he turned. "Why don't you get yourself some sleep, Lyle. I'll wake you soon's it seems somethin's about to commence."

The sheriff nodded tiredly and headed toward one of the cells. Bart was already using one cot, so Bordus took the other. Lon headed for the window that the sheriff had just abandoned. "You might's well get some shut-eye too, Lon," Coffin said.

He nodded gratefully. Neither he nor Bart were used to such things as had occurred in the past several days. The fear and the tension and, yes, even excitement, were wearing on him. He sank into the creaky sheriff's chair, propped his feet up on the desk, and soon was dozing.

It was eerily quiet. Coffin had seen only three people on the street since the gunfight, and the only sounds in the room were the snoring of the deputies. Even the dogs of the town seemed to have become quiet.

Joe checked his pocket watch when he saw Mrs. Stewart approaching. Quarter past noon.

"The doc ever show up?" Bordus asked as he walked into the room, yawning.

"Nope," Coffin said.

"Damn. Mrs. Stewart, I want you to go on over to Doc Keever's place. You tell him I said that if he ain't here within half an hour, I'm gonna come back over there, drag him here by the neck, and once he's done here I'm gonna shoot him."

"I'm no errand boy for the likes of you, Sheriff."

"You go and do it, woman," Bordus said with quiet menace to his voice, "or I'll drop by and shoot your old man too."

She was white with fear, but she nodded and left.

About midafternoon, he saw dust moving on the road that Harmon Tuck had taken out of town. It looked to be a number of horses. He followed it as it neared. Then there was a wagon with Tuck at the reins. Behind him, on horses, rode almost two dozen well-armed cowboys.

"Miss Kate," Coffin said urgently, waking her from her nap on one of the straight-back chairs, "fetch up the sheriff. Now!" As she moved, Coffin called, "Lon. Get your ass up, boy."

Bordus came into the room and growled, "What is it?"

"We got company."

Chapter 16

"Lyle Bordus!" Harmon Tuck roared. He was standing on the wagon with a phalanx of mounted, well-armed cowboys in front of him. "Send out that killer, Bordus. We've got no trouble with you. We just want that outlaw bastard who killed my sons in cold blood here on the streets of our fine town."

"Bullshit," Sheriff Bordus mumbled, watching out the window.

"Lyle, don't tell me you don't trust that upstandin' citizen of Aspen Wells," Joe Coffin commented in mock surprise and shock.

"Shit." It came out as two words.

"I hope you got plenty of cartridges, Lyle," Coffin said. "Looks like we could be here for a spell."

"Got more'n enough."

"Bordus! You got five minutes to send that bastard out here."

"Or what?" Bordus roared.

"Or we'll come in and get him."

Both Coffin and the sheriff snorted in derision. Coffin took a quick glance around the small office. Bart was still on the cot in one of the cells. He was awake and ready; Lon sat in the chair behind the desk, scattergun close to hand; and Kate McCoombs sat primly in one of the straight-back chairs.

"The window, Lyle," he said softly, not wanting to alarm the others.

The sheriff looked back, then nodded. He turned back to

watch the mob of cowboys sitting anxiously across the street. "There a few of them boys missin'?" he asked.

"Three. They slipped off around that building straight across from us."

The sheriff nodded. Over his shoulder, he called, "Bart, get up on that cot and keep an eye out that back window. Lon, break up one of the chairs or somethin' and board it up."

The two did as they were told.

"Miss Kate," Coffin said. "Can you load a Winchester?"

"Of course."

"Best load up all there is in the cabinet then, in case we need 'em."

Bordus turned and tossed a key to the woman. "Good idea, Joe," he said. "The shells are in boxes in the bottom drawer of the desk there, ma'am."

Kate opened the cabinet and took down a .44/40 Winchester lever action. Sitting at the desk, she pulled open a drawer and brought out several boxes of shells. Quickly, but without the fumbling brought on by unneeded haste, she began stuffing cartridges into the magazine.

There was some hammering as Lon wrecked a chair and then jammed pieces of the wood into the small window frame.

Coffin waited patiently, slowly rotating his hand on his stomach. Only once before that he could remember had he been in such a predicament. Well, he told himself firmly, he had gotten out of that one, he should be able to get out of this.

"One more minute, Bordus!" Tuck called.

"You ready for this, Lyle?" Coffin asked.

"Yep."

"You sure? After this, you ain't likely to be the most popular man in town."

"I get rid of that loudmouth, agitatin' son of a bitch, things'll be just fine."

Coffin grunted. It was Bordus's problem. "How do you think they'll do this?" he asked.

"Ain't but one way they can—straight on. There's no other doors, and only that one other small window in back. That's boarded up, so I expect they'll just come chargin' at us."

"That's what I'd have thought too. But there's somethin'

115

about all this I don't like."

"Scared?"

"Course. But it ain't that. I can't see what's going on over by his wagon. There seems to be a few of those boys doin' somethin' there, but I can't see what it is 'cause all the others are in the way."

"Any guesses?"

"Shit. No need for guesses now."

The milling knot of mounted cowboys had parted, and several of the men had pushed an old, small, flatbed wagon out, the stub of its snapped-off tongue pointing straight at the sheriff's office door. In the back were several kegs of gunpowder. The men ran behind it, pushing, and at a shouted signal, they all shoved as hard as they could. The wagon rolled rapidly toward the door. And there was nothing to stop it.

Coffin and Bordus snapped their rifles up and, as one, fired off several rounds each. Neither knew for certain whose shot it was that set off the gunpowder, and it didn't matter.

The kegs went up with an ear-busting boom. The power of it blew the wagon into splinters, and knocked out what glass was left in the sheriff's office windows. It knocked both Coffin and Bordus back and down. Kate screamed and ducked behind the desk. Lon, still up on the cot working at the window, fell off the cot, swearing when he landed.

Coffin scrambled up, grabbed his Winchester, and leaped to the window. He saw three cowboys with a log in hand, almost at the door. The others were running toward the office. "Lyle, the door! Shoot through the door."

He lifted his Winchester as he spoke and started firing at the running cowboys. He heard Bordus's Winchester blasting, and from the corner of his eye caught holes being bred in the wooden door. Then he heard, "Move, Sheriff."

He glanced over to see Lon step up with his scattergun as the first blow of the log shook the door. Lon fired both barrels. There were several screams from outside, and the battering on the door stopped.

Coffin continued firing until his rifle was empty. "Miss Kate?" he called, as he set his Winchester down.

"Ready," she said, already standing next to him with

another loaded Winchester. There was fear in her voice, but she would not let it subdue her.

"Thanks," he said, snapping up the rifle. Kate reached for his and hurried back to the desk.

Bordus was back at his post by the window, and he and Coffin were firing rapidly, steadily—and with deadly accuracy. The street out front of the sheriff's office was already littered with bodies.

"Hold up, Sheriff," Coffin yelled.

Everyone stopped firing and the silence that descended was broken only by the moaning of some of the wounded out in the street. The cowboys who were unhit were behind two overturned wagons across the street.

"Everybody all right?" Bordus asked.

There was a chorus of yeses.

"Christ, I ain't seen nothin' like that since I was with Picket at Chickamauga."

"Rebel?" Coffin asked, surprised, though he supposed he shouldn't have been.

"Yep. And you're a Yankee. That a problem for you?"

"Nope. You?"

"No, sir. War's been over a long time. And right now we are ass deep in trouble."

"Wish everybody saw things so clear."

"Hmmmph. What do you expect 'em to try now?"

"Hell if I know."

So they waited some more. The afternoon clicked slowly by, and Coffin began to worry that perhaps old Harmon Tuck was planning to wait until dark before making another concerted charge.

Then he heard a soft scraping sound, from over on Bordus's side. "Lyle, the window!"

But it was too late. A flannel-clad arm appeared. The hand at the end of it flicked and then was gone. But a sizzling stick of dynamite lay sputtering on the floor behind Bordus.

Coffin started to go for it, but Kate McCoombs was faster. "Move!" she screamed as she leaped at the dynamite, scooped it up, and took the two steps to Coffin's window. Coffin flattened against the side wall as she came by and tossed the dynamite out the window. The two of them ducked, and three seconds later the dynamite went off.

Without thinking, Coffin grabbed Kate and held her. After the reverberations wore off, he realized he was holding her tightly. He looked embarrassed as he let her go. "Sorry," he mumbled.

"No need to be," Kate said as she stood. She was flustered, and she was not sure whether it was the close call with the dynamite, or the close call with the muscular Joe Coffin.

As Coffin went back to the window, thoughts of the woman's taut, full body clouded his thinking. He shook his head. Damn, he told himself angrily, this is not the time for such thoughts. He breathed deeply a few times, feeling another jolt of adrenaline kick in.

"Lyle, I figure they're gonna try that again and again . . . if we let 'em."

"My thoughts too. But what the hell can we do about it?"

"I reckon they'll have somebody come from each side this time, figuring we'll only be watching one way."

"And?"

"And we're gonna put a stop to this foolishment. I ain't fixin' to spend the rest of the afternoon dodging sticks of dynamite."

"And how do you plan on doin' that?"

"You'll see. Your Winchester full?"

"Yep."

"Lon, come on over here and take my place at the window. Make sure your rifle's full too."

When the deputy was standing next to him, Coffin said, "When I say it's time, I want you to commence firin' at those bastards across the street. And don't let up for nothin'. Have an extra rifle full and ready."

"What're you gonna be doin'?" Bordus asked, thinking he might know.

"I'm goin' out there and take care of any idiot with dynamite. So I'm countin' on you boys to keep those others pinned down so I don't get my ass shot off."

"I knew all Yankees was crazy," Bordus said.

"It's why we won the war," Coffin said with a loose grin.

"Shit," Bordus snorted.

"Miss Kate, you get the door for me. Stand here." He positioned her so that she could grip the door handle but was not in the line of fire. "Now, when I tell you, you yank that door open fast, and stay behind that wall there. I'll shut it when I get back in."

She nodded, but her face was pale with fright. If anything should happen to Joe Coffin, why she'd just . . . What in hell was she thinking? her mind yelled at her. This man was a bounty hunter. He had saved her, but that was all there was to it. She could not be thinking she was in love with him. Could she? No, her mind told her firmly. Such a thing was out of the question.

Coffin went back to the window. "Now be quiet, all of you," he said. He stood, alert, listening intently. He smiled grimly when he heard a sound. It was from his side this time—the sound of shirt material scraping on adobe.

He stepped back to the desk. Then he nodded at Kate. "Now!" he said.

As the woman yanked open the door, Sheriff Bordus and Deputy Lon began firing. Coffin ran. Just after passing the door, he dove, stretched full out, hands extended. He landed on his hands and did a perfect somersault, coming to a stop on his feet facing across the street.

Coffin spun, drew his Colt, and knelt in one fluid movement, turning toward the side he had been posted on. There was a man with a stick of dynamite in his hand. He was just setting a match to the fuse when two .45-caliber bullets ripped into his lungs.

Joe Coffin whipped around the other way and nailed the other man, who had lit the fuse of a stick of dynamite and was inching toward the window. One slug caught him just under the cheekbone; the other severed the spine at the base of the neck.

Coffin legged it into the office, skidding to a stop. Behind him, Kate slammed the door shut. There were two explosions, one after another, that shook the building. Kate staggered and fell from the blast, but Coffin caught her.

Both were breathing heavily, as he stood her up straight.

"You all right?" he asked, worry creasing his brow.

"Yes," she breathed.

The whole episode, from opening of door to Coffin's retaking his spot by the window, had taken perhaps half a minute.

Sheriff Bordus gave out with a Rebel yell, and said, with a whoop, "Whoo-ee, boy, you sure are something. Goddamnedest Yankee I ever saw."

Coffin grinned. "Did give them bastards something to think about, didn't I?"

"Yep. Look at 'em."

While the cowboys and Harmon Tuck were still hiding behind the wagons, two hired men were riding out of town fast. The others were arguing with Tuck.

"Can I see, Mr. Coffin?" Kate asked.

"Sure. And call me Joe."

"All right, Joe. If you call me Kate." She moved up to the window, standing nearer to him than was really necessary. He breathed in the perfume of her hair and skin as she leaned just enough to touch him.

Chapter 17

Joe Coffin and Sheriff Lyle Bordus got only a brief glimpse of Harmon Tuck as he climbed up on the wagon, behind a wall of cowpunchers. But they could hear him just fine when he bellowed, "You've had your chances, Bordus. But since I'm a forgivin' man, I'll give you one more."

The people inside the sheriff's office said nothing.

"You come on out with that outlaw bastard, and everything'll be square between us."

"He's desperate," Coffin said.

"Yep," Bordus answered.

"Means he could try somethin' even more foolish than he's already done."

"Could."

"You gettin' tired of bein' cooped up in here, Lyle?"

"Yep."

"Then let's say we end this crap here and now."

"I'm in. How?"

"What'll happen if we kill Tuck?"

"I'd lay several months' wages that them cowpunchers would turn tail and run. Wouldn't be worth it to them to stick around."

"That's what I reckoned."

"How we going to kill him?"

"See that cowboy with the green shirt and the gray hat?"

"Yep."

"You take him out. He goes down, Tuck'll be wide open. I'll

drop him and this'll be all over with."

"I don't cotton to killin' a man in cold blood like that," the sheriff said.

Coffin gave him a disgusted stare, and Bordus said, "Then again, him and his *compañeros* been tryin' to kill us all afternoon. Reckon it wouldn't be cold-blooded killin', would it?"

"Nope." Coffin turned to Kate McCoombs, who still stood close to him, unwilling to leave. "Best stand back, Miss Kate."

"Just Kate. Please?"

"Yes, ma'am. Now go on back behind the desk," he said gruffly.

"You set, Joe?" Bordus asked when Kate had cleared out of the way.

"Yep."

Bordus sighted down the Winchester, as Harmon Tuck continued to harangue them. He squeezed off a shot, and the targeted cowboy spun and fell off the far side of the wagon.

There were perhaps two seconds before the men on the wagon could react. In that small span of time, Joe Coffin carefully sighted and then placed a .44/40 Winchester bullet dead center in Tuck's chest.

Coffin snapped the lever down and then back up and got off another shot before Tuck fell completely. That slug skimmed off the top of the rancher's head.

Tuck flew off the back of the wagon like a stringless marionette. Still the men had not had time to react.

"Nice shot, Joe," Bordus said.

The cowboys finally reacted. All of them jumped off behind the wagons, and they could be heard arguing. After some minutes, one of them stepped tentatively from behind the wagons. He held a Winchester up. Its lever was open, and there was a piece of white cloth flying from the muzzle end. He started walking across the street.

"That's far enough," the sheriff yelled when the man was about halfway. "What do you want?"

"We quit, Sheriff. We've had enough. We'd just like to gather up our dead and ride on out."

"Can't let you do that," Bordus said, and Coffin looked at

him sharply. The sheriff was smiling wolfishly. Coffin also grinned.

"You boys are guilty of all sorts of wrongdoin' here. Attempted murder, shootin' off guns in the city limits, creatin' a public nuisance, annoyin' hell out of the sheriff. There's more, but you catch the drift."

"You'll have a hell of a time gettin' us all to come in there."

"Might be. But I could shoot you dead right now. That'd go a long way toward convincin' them others. Now throw down your weapons, all of you, and come on out where we can see you."

"Ah, come on, Sheriff." The cowpoke was sweating hard. He swallowed. "You know this weren't our doin'. It was Old Man Tuck. We was just doin' what he was payin' us for."

"I thought he was payin' you for punchin' cows, not murderin' lawmen and other citizens."

The cowboy spit and wiped the sweat off his brow with a large red bandanna. Things was supposed to be easy. They were supposed to come in here, shoot up the place a little, scare hell out of the sheriff and his two deputies. Then they'd drag that outlaw killer out and string him up. It was the way of things out here. Everybody knew that. The man had killed Tuck's two sons, it was that simple. He deserved to be strung up.

But nothing had turned out the way it was supposed to. Old Man Tuck was dead. Half the cowpunchers he had signed on were laying dead here in the street. This wasn't their fight anymore. But he would be damned if he'd turn the living half of his men over to the law to be hanged. If he could just keep the sheriff talking a while, he could start edging back toward the wagons. Once there, he and the others could scatter, heading for the buildings across the street. From there they could get out into the alley, steal horses if they had to, and ride like hell.

"Come on, Sheriff," he said, trying to force a soothing note into his nervous voice. "You know how hard jobs are to come by 'round these parts nowadays. It ain't easy for us boys to come on a good job." He shrugged, trying to seem nonchalant, though his mouth was dry. "We didn't want no part of this. But Tuck was payin' us and—"

"Let me think about it." Bordus pulled his rifle in from the window. He kept a watch out.

The cowboy started moving backward toward the wagons, very, very slowly.

"He thinks you ain't payin' attention, Lyle," Coffin said.

"I know. It's what I want him to think."

"You lettin' them go?" He was only a little incredulous since he understood.

"I ain't fixin' to lock all them boys up in here. Too much trouble. No judge or jury'd find 'em guilty anyway, 'less you or I could link one of 'em direct to the attack here."

The cowboy was three-quarters of the way across the street. "If I let them think they ran out on me, they'll be more likely to keep their distance from here," Bordus added.

"I could lay a shot down next to him," Coffin said with a mischievous grin. "That'll get 'em to thinkin' too."

A grin grew on Bordus's face. "That might be good," he said, the grin wide now.

Coffin stuck his rifle out the window and fired. The bullet kicked up dirt barely two fingers' width from the cowboy's left boot. The man froze.

"Goin' somewhere, pard?" the sheriff called out. "Just 'cause I'm thinkin' on things don't mean I ain't watchin' over you."

The cowboy said nothing.

"How long you gonna let him wait?" Coffin asked.

Bordus shrugged. "Let's see what happens."

After perhaps five minutes, they could hear one of the cowboy's friends from behind the wagon: "We'll lay down a cover, Earl. When we do, you haul your ass for this wagon."

Coffin and Bordus laughed, and ducked. There came a rain of bullets, hitting into the walls of the adobe office. Then there was silence. The two stood and carefully looked out the windows. A few of the more than a dozen cowboys were on horses and slapping the animals hard, riding hellbent for parts unknown. The others were trying to jump on their mounts and follow.

"Should we give 'em a send-off, Joe?" Sheriff Bordus said, chuckling.

"Yep."

They fired rapidly in the direction of the scattering cowboys, taking care not to hit anyone. And when the last of the cowpunchers had fled in a flurry of dust, Bordus and Coffin slid down the walls, laughing hard.

Kate McCoombs looked at them in some amazement, before she too joined in the laughter, her high, tinkly voice complementing Coffin's clear, deep tones and the gravelly growl from Sheriff Bordus. Lon and Bart chuckled, relieved that it was all over.

Bordus finally stood. "Well," he said, "let's go see what the town thinks of all this excitement." He opened the door and stepped out, followed by Coffin, Kate, Lon, and the wounded Bart.

"Well, well, well," Bordus said sarcastically, "look at this."

Quite a few of the townspeople, including women and children, were drifting around, stopping to look at the bodies scattered around the street.

"Good work, Sheriff," someone called out.

Others shouted agreement, and the mayor, a tall, bald, patrician-looking man dressed in dark check suit, vest, and pale blue shirt, strode over, hand extended. "Well done, Sheriff Bordus," he said jovially in his deep voice. "Well done."

He ignored the mayor's hand. "Bullshit," he snapped, eyes flashing. Coffin tried not to grin, as Bordus said, "You fractious son of a bitch. How dare you come over here all smiles and sweet when just last night me and my two deputies had to stay up the night to keep this goddamn horde of bloodthirsty bastards at bay. All of you are alike!" he roared. "Near everyone of you gutless sons a bitches were in the mob last night, achin' for a chance to string an innocent man up."

He was angry now, and it showed on his scarred face and in his scarred voice. "Ain't a one of you people come to help us. Hell, Stewart, I had to threaten you to bring us some food so we didn't starve to death. And you, Doc Keever, you stupid ass, I had to threaten you too."

Coffin watched the sheriff carefully. He knew Bordus was angry but he felt there was more behind this than he was letting on.

125

"Well, I've had it with all of you, goddamnit. Find someone else for this goddamn thankless job." He yanked the badge off, ripping his shirt in the bargain. He threw it on the ground at the mayor's feet.

Behind him, Kate gasped, and the people of the town stood in stunned amazement. Bordus spun on his boot heel and stomped back into the office. Coffin, Kate, and the two deputies followed, the latter looking worried. Hell, if Bordus really did quit, they might get stuck with his job, and after the past week there was no way either one of them wanted that.

As they filed into the room, Bordus burst out laughing.

"What're you laughin' at?" Lon asked, worried. He was young, and while he had drawn blood in battle, he was still new enough to such things that it bothered him.

"It's his way of gainin' back respect," Coffin said, starting to chuckle. "Them people was all against him last night. Today they wanted him to take care of the problems they helped create. All they do is want from him. Never want to give."

He glanced over at Bordus, who was nodding, though he was still laughing, the sound strange coming from that throat.

"Anyway, I reckon he's got no intention of quittin' as sheriff. Right?" Bordus nodded again, wiping the tears of laughter from his eyes, as Coffin continued. "So he put on a show for them. Hell of a performance it was too, Lyle. Better'n any I ever saw in the opry houses in Denver."

Kate began to giggle, and Bart was starting to stifle some chuckles.

"I reckon that the mayor, and anybody else who counts in this town, is gonna be in here any minute now beggin' Lyle to take his star back."

Bordus finally stopped laughing, and breathed deep to get himself back to normal.

"You are gonna take it back, ain't ya, Sheriff?" Lon asked, still nervous and worried.

"I reckon. But we'll see." He chuckled again.

"Well," Coffin said, "I thank you for your hospitality, Lyle, but I reckon me'n Miss Kate here ought to be movin' on."

Bordus grew serious instantly. "It's late in the day. Why don't you both stay the night here in town. Things'll be all right." He moved off the corner of the desk and stepped to directly in front of Kate. "You'll have nothin' to fear from *anybody* in this town, Miss McCoombs. I swear it." He looked terribly earnest.

Both Bart and Lon looked at him strangely. Coffin stood back, watching, waiting. It was up to Kate McCoombs now. The woman stared at the tall, scarred, glum-faced sheriff for some seconds. "Why, I think it would be nice to stay the night here, Sheriff Bordus," she said regally. She turned to Coffin. "What about you, Mr. Coffin? Do you think another night here would be all right?"

"Reckon so," Coffin said, rubbing his stomach. "Long's I ain't got to stay in that cell again." He grinned.

Bordus looked mightily relieved. "We'll find you some better accommodations. Bart, who don't you go on home, rest up, Lon, please go on down and see if Miz Bohrer will be able to put up Mr. Coffin and Miss McCoombs for the night."

Just after the two deputies left, there was a knock at the door.

Chapter 18

Though the outlaws' trail was rather old, it was simple enough to follow. The carnage the six men had left in their wake made it so. But it was not an easy thing for Joe Coffin and Kate McCoombs. Especially for Kate, who was not used to such things.

On their second day out, Kate also began to grow more and more worried. They had found three farms and ranches that had been attacked. At each, several people had been killed. And the trail they were following appeared to be leading straight toward Lone Pines, the ranch owned by Lester McCoombs.

Kate feared for her family, and she rode the petite bay mare in increasing agitation.

Coffin wondered why Holder's men were raiding farms and ranches, since there was little profit in it. And he worried that perhaps the killing was becoming a sport to them.

The going was slow too, since Coffin had to spend hours digging graves and burying the victims of the Holder gang's murderous spree. It was an unpleasant enough task, but the time it took angered Coffin. The longer it took him to find Reno Holder and his gang, the more bloodshed there would be.

For the first time in his life, he felt almost helpless, with frustration churning inside him. And at the center of it all was Kate McCoombs.

There was something about the headstrong, flame-maned young woman that had him caught up. It was more than her physical attraction and her beauty, though there certainly were those things to be sure. But there was something more, something deeper. She had an inner strength, resilience, and courage that made her that much more beautiful to him.

He growled at himself for having such mawkish thoughts. And he slapped down the rest of the dirt over the last of the graves at the third ravished homestead they had found.

Coffin wiped his face off with a hand, and then with his shirt. As he pulled the cloth away from his face, Kate was standing there, bucket full of water from the well in hand. He nodded gratefully and pulled out the tin dipper. He drank deeply of the cold water.

Though it was almost November now, it was still warm under the brilliant sun. All the exercise of the past several hours had left him bathed in sweat. When he finished his drink, Kate said, "Bend over."

He looked at her in surprise, until she hoisted the bucket a little, indicating she wanted to dump it on him. He nodded and bent at the waist. Kate poured the water over Coffin's head and back. He whooped a bit when the coolness of it first hit his skin.

He snapped back up, shaking his head at the same time. "Damn, that felt good," he said with a sigh. Some of the gloom lifted from him, and more cheerily he said, "Thanks."

She nodded, but said nothing. Her mouth was dry and her palms quite damp.

"Better get my clean shirt, though," he said, looking ruefully at the filthy rag in his hands. He turned toward the horses.

"Wait," Kate croaked, her throat arid. She licked her lips. She was more scared now than she had been since Reno Holder and his men had taken her. But it was a completely different kind of fright.

"What?" he asked, spinning around.

"Wait," she said, a little more firmly.

He felt utterly stupid, and he didn't know why. "What?" he mumbled again. "What's wrong?"

"Nothing's *wrong*." She set down the bucket and took the three steps separating them. Her heart raced and pounded, thudding loudly in her ears, and she was afraid she might faint. She could not believe she was doing this, not after . . .

Kate reached him. Looking up into his charcoal eyes, she rested her small, soft hands on his broad, muscular chest. He smelled of sweat and woodsmoke, horses and leather, work and maleness. It was wonderful to her.

But still she was unsure of herself. She rubbed small circles on his chest. Coffin sucked in his breath at her gentle touch, and he could feel himself reacting.

Kate tilted her head back. Her lips were slightly parted, and her eyes slitted, waiting.

Now it was his turn to be tentative. He knew full well what she was doing, but he could not believe she was doing it. He wanted her; God, how he wanted her. But he was not sure she knew what she was doing.

"Don't make me beg, damnit," Kate whispered, perilously close to tears.

"But I . . ."

"If you don't want me, just say so," she mumbled, dropping her head so she was staring at the ground. "I'll understand." She started to turn, the tears hot on her cheeks.

He grabbed her—a little too roughly, he thought—and that sent a stab of pain through him. But she yielded, willing, spinning into the warm cocoon of his arms. Her head went back once more, and her mouth parted, willing, wanting.

All Coffin's fears fled, and he smothered her mouth with his own, tongue searching out for hers.

Kate groaned around their locked lips, and felt dizzy in his strong, certain embrace. Her knees wobbled a little, and she was sure she would have fallen flat over if he was not holding her.

Coffin finally broke off the kiss, breathless. He stared at her, his face a mask of lust and concern, desire and worry. "You really want to do this?" he asked hoarsely, his throat thick with longing.

"Yes," she whispered, resting her cheek on his chest.

Her breath was hot on his skin. "You sure?" he asked, his voice strangled.

She pushed gently away from him. With quivering hands, she began to undo the buttons of his shirt, which she had been wearing since he had found her. She had a chance to replace it with something more feminine before they left Aspen Wells, but she had refused to do that. It was better for the trail, she had told Coffin and Sheriff Bordus. In reality, she just plain liked wearing Coffin's shirt—and pants. Within moments it was opened and she had shrugged it off, dropping it.

Her breasts rode high and proud, tipped with a red far darker than that of her hair. Splashed across the billowy white tops was a light dusting of freckles.

Coffin licked his lips, and drew in a few ragged breaths. How much better, he thought, to see her this way, when she wanted it this way, when she chose to bare herself before him, than when he had first seen her, at least as nude, but with rejection, despair, and pain weighing on her.

With firm steps, she strode to the horse and grabbed Coffin's blanket roll. She returned to where she had been and spread the blankets out. With every movement, she made her unfettered breasts sway enticingly.

Kate sat on the blankets and unlaced her boots and tossed them aside. With a saucy grin, she unhooked the pants and, without getting up, skinned her way out of them.

"Jesus," Coffin breathed as Kate stretched out. He followed—no, devoured—her with his eyes, from her scarlet tresses, across her freckle-specked, beautiful face, across her inviting perfectly shaped breasts, across the gentle small swell of her belly with its deep-set navel, across the vermilion pubic thatch, and down the length of her exquisite legs right to her tiny, well-formed toes.

He unstrapped his gun belt with the two heavy pistols, and laid it right next to the bedroll, where it would be easily accessible.

"Hurry," she whispered, afraid that she might change her mind.

He needed no more urging. With haste, he kicked off his boots and stripped off his socks and Levi's. With desire burning deep in his dark eyes, he stretched out alongside her, his mouth immediately searching out hers.

She gave of herself fully, with abandon and without a trace of guilt or regret. Only once, as he prepared to cover her, did she panic for a moment, her mind flashing back not so long ago to a dank, candle- and lantern-lit cavern and six slavering . . .

Kate pushed that thought away as a wave of pleasure shook her, and she moaned. Her desire built to a fever pitch, until she was screaming in fits of ecstasy, hardly noticing Coffin's groaning explosion.

He fell atop her, and then rolled onto his back, pulling Kate with him, unwilling to let her go. Her deep, startling blue eyes sparkled like never before. She tried sitting up on him for a while, but it had left her too weak, so she slumped down onto him, her breasts pillowing on his hard chest.

He stroked her hair, trying to catch up his own breathing.

"Is it always like that?" she asked after a while. She lifted her head and rested her chin on her fists on his chest just below his throat.

He twirled a thick strand of her hair in one hand, and folded the other under his head as a rest. "I wish I could say yes," he said, meaning it. "But it's not."

"Most times?" She looked only a little disappointed.

"Yep." He grinned.

"Should be all the time."

"Yep."

"They say practicin' makes you perfect sometimes."

"Who says that?"

"My mama, for one."

"Your mama never said no such thing about this!" he responded, laughing, making her bounce a little.

She giggled. "I do believe you're right, sir." She stared at him, her eyes beginning to smoke with renewed desire. "But it might be true." She smiled impishly. "And if it is, maybe we ought to get to practicin'."

"Well . . ." he said slowly, drawing the word out.

"Don't you 'well' me, boy," she said, eyes snapping with lust. She bit him on the lip, but not hard.

He growled playfully and clamped his arms around her. He rolled, until he was mostly atop her. "So you want practice, eh?" he said in mock fierceness. "Well, goddamnit, you'll get practice." He smashed his lips down onto hers.

She eventually got the upper hand again, as they rolled, and she was swept up in the passions as she rode him, screeching as little explosions of dynamite went off inside her body, culminating in a giant explosion, after which she sank onto him, exhausted.

After a long time, she rose up and smiled at him. He was half-asleep. She stood and got the cigarette fixings from his saddlebags and brought them to him. He grinned, waking. He sat up and rolled a cigarette, as she sat down opposite him. Their knees touched. She was some sight, he thought, sitting there naked and cross-legged.

"I thought you said it wasn't always like that," Kate said with a smug smile.

"It ain't," he answered, puffing out a small cloud of smoke. "But we've been practicin'."

"It outta be real good," she said, bursting into laughter, "after we practice a *few* times."

He laughed too, and thought how lucky he was.

But eventually they would have to re-enter the real world. He did not want to stay here, with the burned out building and the freshly covered-over graves. He crushed out his cigarette in the grass, making sure it was out. A cold wind had sprung up, and he realized again how late in the year it was.

"It's time we was goin'," he said softly.

She nodded. Kate did not want to leave there; she wanted to stay, naked and with him, forever and ever. But she knew it could not be so. She leaned over and kissed him hard, broke off, and then just barely brushed her full lips over his. "We *will* practice more," she whispered, her voice dripping with desire and promise.

He dressed slowly, also reluctant to leave, but knowing it must be done. As they mounted their horses and rode off again, he started to worry. He had done it now, he thought—fallen in love. Now there was just not only him to take care of, there also was the red-haired, desirable Miss Kate McCoombs. It was a good feeling and a bad feeling at the same time. Being in love with her was good, he knew, but having to worry about her was not.

Nor was worrying about what to do with her once they reached her father's place. He could not leave her there now;

not when his heart would be with her no matter where he went. But he could not take her with him either, for she might get killed that way.

It was the dilemma he had always been afraid of, and so had avoided. But there was nothing Joe Coffin could do about it now. His heart was made up; his mind would have to follow.

Clouds blew in from the west, dimming what had been a staggeringly bright sun, and the wind kicked up, pushing a small cloud of dust ahead of it. Ghost riders raced across the sky, and suddenly they could hear thunder booming off the massive mountain peaks to the west.

Just as they began making camp in a small copse of ponderosa and piñon pines, the skies opened up. They hastily finished their work, and ate a quick meal of venison from a deer Coffin had shot that afternoon.

"Time for more practice," Kate said with a lusty smile.

Coffin grinned. They stripped down and crawled under the small canvas lean-to and into the warm inviting blankets, as thunder shook the trees and lightning put on a show for them.

Chapter 19

"Why, Miss Kate?" Joe Coffin asked as they lay in the blankets, listening to the drum of the rain on the little lean-to.

"Don't you think you ought to just call me Kate now?" she countered, stroking his cheek. He had not bothered shaving in several days, and it was fuzzy under her finger.

"Reckon so." He grinned. "But you didn't answer the question."

"Well, I reckon I love you."

"I figured that, Kate. But why, after all you've . . ."

She stopped him by moving the finger around from his cheek to rest against his lips. She crawled up on him some and replaced her finger with soft, full lips. "Hush," she murmured, and snuggled up tight against him.

There was silence—except for the hiss and drill of the rain. They were well protected under the canvas covering and the low-hanging boughs of the fragrant pines. Those trees had also left a carpet of needles that provided a soft mattress.

Suddenly Kate began to speak. "It's different with you, you know, Joe."

"I hope so," he said with an ease he did not really feel, trying to keep his tone light.

She nipped his shoulder, but she shuddered at the same time, as the feelings flooded over her—love for him, disgust and fear over what had been done to her. "I wasn't . . ." she started, stopped, and then started again. "I wasn't pure when those men . . ."

Kate choked back tears. "There'd only been one before. We was supposed to be married. He went off a couple years ago, headin' for Denver and the gold fields there." She was crying now, unchecked.

Coffin lay silent, holding her, as she went on. "He never came back. We heard all sorts of stories—that he was killed by Utes or Apaches or Navajos on the way. That he made a strike in the mountains and was killed by claim-jumpers. That he was killed in a fight in a saloon. That he ran off with a woman he met in Denver. That he was still up there by himself, lookin' for gold.

"I never knew what to believe of all the stories. But as time went by, he became less and less important to me. I'd hardly thought of him in almost a year until those men grabbed me off that train and started taking me...."

She cried quietly, her slim shoulders shaking. Coffin let her be; kept his silence.

Finally the sobbing ebbed, and she lay breathing raggedly. For a while he thought she had fallen asleep. Then she suddenly started up again, "When those men"—she choked back the bile that rushed up her throat at the thought of what Reno Holder's men had done to her and Irene—"did what . . . they . . . did, I . . . thought I'd die from shame. I thought somehow it was my fault that they did it, that they killed Irene. That somehow I could have stopped them; that I must have enticed them somehow, led them on."

"You couldn't have—" Coffin started, defending her against her own demons.

"Shush. Now let me tell it my own way. I got to."

"Yes, ma'am," he said humbly.

"When you first came into that cave, I was afraid you was another of those men. Then I didn't care if you was. When you didn't do nothing at first, I figured you weren't one of 'em, and then I hoped you'd kill me. I figured if you was a good man, you'd do that—put me out of my shame and misery.

"Instead, damn you, you started takin' care of me, tryin' to help me. I thought I'd die for sure then of the shame. All kinds of things was in my mind—that you were gonna take me off somewhere and keep me in another cave or somethin' like those others, or that you were gonna take me into some town where they'd all cluck their tongues and pity me." She shuddered. "I couldn't stand that."

"Didn't have much of an opinion of me, did you?" Coffin asked, not sure whether to chuckle or be offended.

"Well, what'd you expect?" Kate snapped, regretting it instantly. She rubbed his cheek again. "Sorry."

"It's all right." He released her and sat up. She looked worried, until she saw he was just reaching for his cigarette fixings. He calmly rolled a cigarette and lit it.

Kate rested up on one elbow, looking at him, the covers pulled up almost to her neck. "By mornin', I was thinkin' I might be in love with you. At the same time, I thought what a silly idea." She saw the shocked, almost pained look that flicked on his face. "Not because you aren't lovable," she added hastily, worried that she had lost him. "But because of all I'd just been through. How could I love *any* man with that. Especially one that knew what had happened to me."

She sucked in a breath and bit her lip. "But more importantly, I wondered how any man could love me after all that, see?" Her eyes implored him to understand.

Coffin nodded, serene once again. "I was," Kate went on, sobs and tears beginning again, *"used."* She made the word sound infinitely filthy.

"You don't have to go on with this, Kate," he said softly.

"Yes I do," she sobbed. It took a while before she was calm enough to continue . "So I kept my feelin's to myself. But after a while back there in Aspen Wells, especially when I thought we were gonna die, I began to realize that you had some feelin's for me too. I knew you didn't just pity me, or see me as some kind of degraded, used . . . whore." She bit off the last word.

"I made up my mind then and there . . . I think"—and she even managed a grin—"that the exact time was when you came flyin' back in that door after takin' care of the two men with the dynamite . . . that I was gonna offer myself to you first chance I got."

Kate sighed. "I got several chances along the trail after we pulled out,. but I always lost my courage at the last minute. Until . . ." She reached for his bandanna and wiped her nose.

137

"I'm mightly glad too," he said hoarsely, tossing the cigarette out into the rain, where it hissed and sputtered. Coffin noticed some snowflakes mixed in with the heavy rain. He reached for her.

She melted into his arms, her love for him becoming a palpable thing.

It had stopped raining by morning, but it was a cold, gray day. Fog swirled around trees and rocks, and there was a thin blanket of snow on everything. When she awoke, Kate felt good; better than she had in a long time. The world and its dangers and fears, shrouded by the mist, seemed a faraway place.

But as Coffin and Kate rode along that day and the next—which dawned clear and chilly—they did so with increasing trepidation.

Midway through that second day, they found another ravaged farm, and after burying the five dead they found there, they moved faster, fear growing.

Coffin had never known a fear like this, and it both angered and frustrated him. It was not a fear of battle or blood or death. It was a fear rooted in his love for Kate McCoombs. He realized now that he had fallen in love with Kate almost from the very beginning. But because of her suffering he had suppressed it. But now that she had declared her love for him so openly—had bared her soul to him—there was no denying his own feelings any longer.

However, that made their lives all the more difficult. Though she tried to keep on a good face, he could see that she was nearly sick with worry the nearer they got to her father's ranch. There was little doubt anymore as to what they would find when they got there. The signs were too plain. But still, both kept up hope as best they could, always thinking that perhaps Holder and his men had veered off somewhere before they reached the McCoombs's ranch.

Kate was torn by her recently declared love for Coffin, and the growing fear of reaching her home. She had been through too much in the past several weeks to be able to handle what she was sure she would find when she and Coffin reached Lone Pines.

She rode almost numbly, oblivious to her surroundings,

including the majestic cones of the San Francisco Peaks.

"You never told me how you were able to be with me after what had happened to you, Kate," Coffin asked, trying to keep her mind off what was to come. He thought that perhaps it was not wise to remind her of her recent past, and what had happened, but he figured it had to be better than her speculating on the future.

"I don't know," she hazarded. It had, obviously, been on her mind all the while she was scheming to make love to him. Indeed, it was what had kept her from making herself available to him for so long. After the degradation and abuse she had suffered, she was both repulsed by the thought of another man taking her and intrigued by it happening—if done with love.

But she had also worried deeply if another man would even want her.

"Why would any man *not* want you?" Coffin asked, surprised at her fears.

"After what I . . ." she started. Then she saw the look on his face, and she smiled. He really didn't care that she had been abused, her body violated. She had not asked for it; therefore it was not a problem.

And she could see in his face too that he could not understand how other men would place such value on a situation not of her own making.

It was another reason why she loved him. He was fierce and proud and strong, and cared not one whit what other men thought of him. Once he made up his mind, there was no turning him back.

"Well, anyway," she said, smiling, "I knew I could do only two things. Crawl into a shell and live like an old maid in misery all my life. Or put what had happened behind me and live my life as normally as I could. I figured"—and she suddenly got shy—"that if you loved me, none of the rest would matter."

"I do," he said without hesitation.

"Then it's all right." She smiled again. "And besides, no one else has to know what happened to me. A few folks back in Aspen Wells might know, and I might get around to tellin' my family. . . ."

She froze, face white. She gulped and blinked back some

tears. "Well, I figured that since we're in love, you'd be takin' me back to Denver with you soon's our business is over. Up there, nobody but us will ever know."

There was no question that Coffin would be able to do the job for which he had been hired, and that there would be no one from the outlaw gang to ever spread the word.

"That's true," he said hastily, trying to get her thoughts off her family again. "You'll like it in Denver. It's high up, prairie, like here in some ways. The mountains all rise up west of the town maybe twenty miles or so. It's real pretty. Real . . ."

But she was not listening anymore.

They made camp in a small clearing in a forest of lodgepole and ponderosa pines that night. As they made camp, Kate looked around, seeing the San Francisco Peaks as if for the first time.

"We'll be there tomorrow," she said fearfully.

It was an uncomfortable night, with Kate worrying about her family, and Coffin worrying about Kate. Coffin thought about riding straight west in the morning, until he found another town. He could leave Kate there and ride on to her family's ranch by himself, see what was there before going back to get her. . . .

But, no, she would never allow that, he told himself. Kate McCoombs was a strong woman. She had handled herself well, for the most part, throughout her ordeal. Whatever the fates would throw at her now, she would be able to handle.

However, in the morning, he dawdled, delaying their departure. He was reluctant to be on the way, wanting to save her pain and the grief he was sure was just over the horizon.

"We can't put it off forever," she said after cleaning up their breakfast mess. It was as if she was reading his mind.

Coffin thought of joking with her, but he saw her tight, pinched face, devoid of color, and he knew he could not. He simply nodded and sped his preparations.

Within an hour, she was in a funk, her mind preoccupied with horrid scenes of death and destruction, her eyes unseeing. She simply followed along behind him, blue eyes dim and unfocused.

Coffin was the first to see the signs—a low-hanging gray

cloud of smoke around which swirled a flock of buzzards and vultures. He turned back to look at Kate, but she paid him no mind. Coffin said nothing about what he had seen; only kept riding toward the inevitable.

Two hours later, he heard a choking sob and a low moan behind him. He swung in the saddle, alarm written across his face. "Damn," he muttered when he saw her.

Tears were running freely down Kate's cheeks, and her face was a horrid mask of pain and despair.

"Damn," he mumbled, not knowing what to do. All this was new to him. He could stand up to an angry mob; throw down against a merciless killer; face a war party of hostile Indians. But this one small, frail woman was more than he could deal with. There was an aching in his chest that he had never experienced before, and he realized that it was the pain of loving someone and being totally incapable of helping her when she most needed it.

He turned back as they edged into a clearing, planted mostly with corn. Far off he could see the smoldering ruins of several buildings. The field was trampled some, and a cow, a large brass bell around its neck, wandered through the clearing, cropping at the plants.

Kate screamed, "No!" and raced her horse past him, leaving the mule behind.

Coffin kicked his horse, intending to speed after her and catch her. But he stopped himself. It would do no good to catch her now.

Reluctantly, wearily, he gathered up the rope on the mule and rode slowly after the woman he loved.

Chapter 20

"Joe!" Kate screamed.

Coffin dropped the rope leading the mule and jabbed his heels into the chestnut's side. The horse leaped forward. Good God, Coffin thought, how could I have been so stupid in letting her go ahead on her own?

He could not see her, and fear gripped his heart, swirling in his belly, thinking that Holder's gang was still there and had recaptured Kate.

He finally spotted her, down amongst the last of the corn stalks, kneeling. He yanked at the reins and was off the horse before the animal had fully stopped.

Kate was kneeling next to a man. He was a little younger than Kate, with the same flame-red hair. His face, contorted with pain, was coated with freckles.

"My brother Sean. He's hurt bad," Kate said, pain and fear coloring her beautiful face.

Coffin knelt and looked the young man over. He had been shot several times, and beaten some. "What happened?" Coffin asked as he sliced open Sean's shirt and looked over the wounds.

"Gang of outlaws," Sean gasped. "Came ridin' through."

"Who?"

"Don't know." His breathing was labored, and Coffin was stunned that the youth still lived, since he had taken at least two bullets in the chest, another in his right arm, and one in the left leg. He had lost a considerable amount of blood.

142

"Get the Wanted posters from my saddlebags, Kate," Coffin said. "You just take it easy, Sean. You'll be all right. We'll get you fixed up."

The youth nodded, and Coffin felt a pang of guilt. There was no way the youth would recover. Maybe if they had gotten him when it had first happened. But not now. He had lost too much blood, and was hovering on the edge of shock because of it. But Coffin could not bring himself to say that either to Sean or his sister.

Kate came back with the Wanted posters and gave them to Coffin. He showed them to the youth. "This the men?" he asked, certain he knew the answer already.

"Yes."

"Thought so." Coffin stuffed the papers in his shirt. "When was they here?"

"Ain't sure. I passed out for a while. Yesterday, maybe? Afternoon."

Coffin nodded, thinking. They really should bury the other bodies—if there were any, and he was sure there were. Sean would not last much longer, but Coffin could think of no easy way to explain that to Kate. He could think of no way to tell Kate that it would be useless to try to get Sean to the nearest town, wherever it was.

Besides, Holder and his men might still be fairly close if they had been here just yesterday. Which meant he could finally catch up to them—and quickly—if only . . .

"All right," he said, standing. "Kate, you stay here. I'll see if I can find a horse. We'll need one to get Sean for some help."

"Can't you do anything?" Kate asked, concern marring her features.

"Not here." He walked off, toward where the barn had been. It would, he thought, give him time to think of something else. It would also let him find any bodies before Kate did. He might also be able to pick up the trail of the outlaws. And by walking instead of riding his horse he would present a smaller target should the outlaws still be lurking about.

He found another young man, who must be another brother. Then an older man, whose graying hair could not hide the fact that he was the father of this red-haired brood. Off to one side of the ranch, where a log corral had been knocked down, he found another red-haired man, a little older than the first two. Coffin figured him for the oldest son of the family. He had been shot in the legs first, and was propped against a fence pole for the corral.

Coffin spit, for the bile left a bitter taste in his mouth. Holder's bunch must've had themselves a fine old time, Coffin thought, rage coursing through him. They had taken the time to ravish a pretty, dark-skinned young woman—Coffin took her to be the oldest son's wife—while they had made her husband watch. The young woman's body was in no better shape than Irene's had been when he found it.

"Shit," Coffin muttered. Not through all the horrors of the Civil War had he seen anything like this. Only a few times had he seen anything similar—when an Indian war party had ridden through an isolated farm or ranch like this one; or when an Army patrol had ridden through an Indian village. It disgusted him.

Coffin wandered back toward where the house had stood, and found Kate's mother nearby. And he found out where Kate had gotten her looks. The mother had been shot through the head, but at least she had not been defiled.

He saw a horse, and walked that way, talking softly, trying not to scare the skittish animal. But the horse was having nothing to do with him. Coffin went back, pained by the imploring look seeking help in Kate's eyes. "I found a horse," he said, his voice cracking. "But he's scared. I'll need to rope him."

Kate nodded dumbly, as she cradled her brother's head in her lap and stroked his face and hair. The youth looked almost dead already.

Coffin mounted the chestnut and rode out. The McCoombs's horse watched with wide, nervous eyes, and then took off. But the chestnut was faster, and accustomed to having Coffin on his back and anticipating his rider's needs. The chestnut kept the other horse just ahead. Coffin unrolled his rope and shook out the loop as he raced along.

"Come on, boy," he clucked. The chestnut needed no more words. He charged ahead, bringing his rider up along the other horse. Coffin tossed the loop the few feet separating him from the other horse, and it settled over the horse's neck.

It was but a few more moments before he had slowed the horse and was leading it back toward Kate and Sean. He knew before he reached them that the young man had died. He could tell it in Kate's hunched shoulders, and the way they shook. He knew she was crying, though she made no sound.

Coffin stopped his horse, and looping the rope from the McCoombs's horse around his pommel, he stepped down. His heart was heavy, and his movements slow. It made his insides roll with frustration to see Kate this way and not be able to do much about it.

He came up behind her and grasped her at the top of each arm, at the shoulders. He tugged a little. "Come on, Kate," he said softly. "You got to let him go."

She shrugged her shoulders, trying to get away from his hands. "No," she snapped, her voice muffled by phlegm.

"It's time you left him in peace, woman," Coffin said, still gently but more firmly. "It's best. Now come on."

Kate resisted some more, until finally Coffin pulled her up with sheer strength. She screamed and tried to keep a hold of her brother's head. But up she came under the powerful tugging.

Then she was standing, tears flowing unchecked, unheeded down her face, knowing she could not resist any more. Coffin tugged her around to face him. "Here," he said, handing her a bandanna from his pocket. "Blow your nose and wipe your face."

Her pain ate at him as he watched her. She tried to give him his bandanna back, but he said, "You keep it. You'll most likely be needin' it again." He tried to smile at her, but failed.

She moaned, and it tore at him. He could not even begin to fathom the loss she must be feeling, and that made him all the worse, for now he had guilt atop the other emotions. He felt tears welling in his own eyes.

"Damn," he growled. He grabbed her roughly and pulled her toward him. She did not resist, but instead took comfort in his strong arms, warm chest, and loving embrace.

Coffin was glad he held her close—this way she could not see

145

his tears.

But finally he pushed her away. He blinked several times to clear his eyes. Then, in a firm voice, he said, "Take the horses and the mule and set up a camp over there." He pointed back the way they had come—far away from the ranch and its grisly adornments. "You stay there till I come back for you."

"No," Kate said, stamping her foot. "No. I've got to see my ... Sean ..."

"You do like I say," he ordered.

"But if they're ... they're ..." Kate began crying again.

He nodded, and she stood weeping. When the tears slowed, she said, "I've got to take care of them ... see to them ..."

"I'll do it, Kate. I'll take good care of them."

"But I've got to say goodbye ... say a few prayers ... or somethin'. I just can't let them ... go ... without ... I've got to ... say ..."

"There'll be time for sayin' your goodbyes later, after I've ..." Joe said softly, unable to finish.

"But ..."

"Just hush yourself now and go do as I say. There's much for me to do first." He stalked over to the mule and pulled out the small shovel he had. He wished he had a larger one—it would make the job so much easier. But he had seen none lying around the ranch, and he figured any that the McCoombs family had had were in the smoldering rubble of the barn. This was all he had, and it would have to suffice.

Kate reluctantly turned and grabbed the reins of the horses, and the mule's rope. She led all four animals away, her back stiff, as if daring herself not to turn around again.

Coffin watched her until she was in the cover of the trees before he turned and took a deep breath, trying to prepare himself for the gruesome job he faced.

He walked toward where the house had been, looking around its outer fringes for a soft spot. In the back, he spotted a lonely grave. He nodded. It would be best for them all to be together. He jammed the shovel into the dirt near the grave so that it stuck. He peeled off his .36-caliber Colts and set them carefully down. He stripped off his shirt, shivering in the cold. Reluctantly, since this was an onerous task, he stretched and rolled his muscles, loosening them.

Coffin could not stall forever, and he knew it. With a deep breath, he grabbed the shovel and stabbed it into the earth. He pulled it up with the blade filled with dirt. Over and over he did it, the dirt piling up in a musty pyramid. Coffin liked the feel of the muscles working in his back and shoulders. And he enjoyed the sweat that soon began running down his back.

After a time, though, it began to wear on him. He did not make the graves very deep, but with six of them to dig, it was hard, grueling work. But soon he had them all dug. Wiping his face off, he went to retrieve bodies.

He would grab one, carry it to the makeshift cemetery, place it gently in the hole, and then go fetch another one. The oldest son's wife was the hardest for him. She had been young, and quite attractive, and he pitied her as he carried her naked, ravished corpse to the graveyard. He tried to cover her as best he could with the remnants of her dress, but there was little left of it.

Finally he filled in the graves as quickly and as dispassionately as he could manage. Maybe, he thought bitterly, he could get a job as a grave-digger soon, and quit hunting men for the money. He was getting quite good at the former these days, he thought angrily, and doing rather poorly at the latter.

The sun was almost gone by the time he smacked the last of the dirt hard on the final grave. He grabbed up his Colts and shirt and carried them and the shovel back to their camp.

Kate was pale, but composed. Probably numb from all that had happened lately, Coffin thought. He went to the creek nearby and washed himself off in the cold water. When he came back to the camp, he said softly, "You can say your goodbyes now, if you want."

She nodded and started off. In two strides he caught up to her. "This ain't your affair," she said, almost angry at him.

"Yes it is," he said simply.

She stopped and stared at him for a while. Then she shrugged and walked off again, Coffin matching her steps. When they reached the cemetery, Coffin pointed to each grave and gave a name or description. With each, Kate nodded.

Coffin stayed well back as Kate went to each grave in turn

and stood whispering. Coffin did not know if she was just saying goodbye, or if she was playing too. He decided it didn't matter. So he stood and waited, uncomfortable.

Kate stayed the longest time at her mother's grave. But then she was ready to go back.

"I'll put markers on 'em tomorrow," Coffin said sadly.

Kate only nodded and turned back toward the camp. Coffin was worried about her. She had not cried at any of the graves, and she was so solemn and serious that he was afraid she would snap.

It was a tough night for both of them, but they made do. After eating in the morning, Coffin hastily made some markers of wood, with the names written on them in charcoal. It was cold, and Kate, who had only a light coat, shivered. Snow fell lightly.

"What are you gonna do with me?" Kate asked suddenly.

Coffin could not tell whether she was worried or just curious.

"Take you with me. There's nothing else I can do."

"Disappointed?"

"Nope."

"Even though you didn't get your money?"

"I wasn't lookin' for the money. I might've been at first, but I've come to love you, Kate McCoombs. I'd take you with me now, even if we had some other place for you to stay."

Her smile was a pale imitation of what was normal, but it was a decided improvement on the gloomy looks she was wearing almost constantly now.

They saddled their horses. Riding to the cemetery, they stopped and planted the pine-stick crosses. Then Coffin led them across what had been the yard, moving to where he had picked up the trail yesterday.

"Wait," Kate said.

He turned and looked at her, worried.

"My brother and his wife had a place over there," she pointed southwest. "Less than a mile. Maybe the outlaws left it alone. If they did, we can get some supplies there."

He was worried about the tight rein she seemed to be keeping on herself, but he nodded and moved the horse in that direction.

The house was still standing, untouched. They let the two cows and the four horses loose, keeping the one he had roped yesterday as a spare. Then they raided the house for supplies—food, ammunition, some extra blankets since winter was upon them, and some clothes for Kate.

Kate took a few mementos, and her brother's .38-caliber Colt pistol and the old Winchester rifle.

"Ready?" Coffin asked after the mule was loaded.

Kate nodded tightly. Her shock and loss were gone, replaced by a rage that burned deeply and relentlessly.

Coffin almost nodded, seeing the look in his woman's eyes. She would be all right. He mounted up, thoughts of devastated farms, raped women, and slaughtered settlers searing into his brain. He should have put a stop to this long ago, he thought, and the frustration at not having been able to do so enraged him further.

"Let's ride," he growled, kicking his horse into a run, heading for the bloody trail Reno Holder's men had left in their ghastly wake.

Chapter 21

"You knew, didn't you?" Kate asked that night after she and Joe Coffin had made their camp.

"Knew what?"

"That Sean was gonna die soon."

"Yes." It was said quietly.

"That why you took so long to do everything? So we wouldn't have to take him anywhere?"

"Yes."

She was close to tears again, and she sniffed them back. "How did you know?"

"I've seen lots of men die, Kate." He looked away, up at the cold light of the stars. It was into November, and this high up, it was winter already, and most always cold. "He just had that look about him."

"We could've tried to get him somewhere," she said, her voice a mixture of anger and sorrow. "Leroux Springs wasn't but a couple miles off. Sometimes there's a doctor there. Maybe he was there and could've . . . could've . . ." She broke into weeping.

"He would've died before we got him half a mile, Kate," Coffin said, almost pleading with her to believe him. "And in a hell of a lot more pain. This way he passed on with you watchin' over him, comfortin' him. Hell, I would've done something for him, if I thought I could have."

She cried a while, and then the tears subsided, and she became perfectly calm. It was almost eerie. With red-speckled

150

eyes Kate stared at her man, and said with barely controlled rage, "We are gonna kill them, ain't we? All of 'em?"

"No."

Kate blinked dumbly and then stared at him with unseeing eyes. "Huh?" was all she could manage to say.

"*I'm* gonna kill 'em," Coffin said grimly.

"But I . . ."

"But you what? You want to kill them?" When she nodded he said, "That's plumb foolish."

She tried to object, but he cut her off. "Damn it, Kate, you know what these bastards are. They ain't some damnfool farm boys feelin' their oats and got carried away. These are men who make killin' a sport. They do it so well because they get so much pleasure out of it. These men truly enjoy killin'. Makes 'em feel like big men."

"You don't like it, and you're good at it."

He shrugged. "That's true. It ain't necessary to like killin' to be good at it. But most men who take as much pleasure in it as these men do get good at it."

She sat silent, gazing up at the stars. "You're all I got now, Joe, you know," she said at last. Her voice was sad, but there was no despair in it.

"I know," he said softly.

"You can't leave me, you know." There was no pleading.

"I got no desire to leave you."

"I need you, Joe. Now."

He rolled over to her and took her in his arms, a little unsure of himself. It was a feeling that was becoming more frequent for him—especially around Miss Kate McCoombs—and it was odd, since it was not like him to be that way. It annoyed him.

"It's all right, Joe," she murmured into the angle where his neck and shoulder joined. She pressed her lips lightly against the throbbing artery of his neck.

"You sure?"

"Um hum."

He felt the uncertainty slipping away, until only a nagging remnant of it remained. Even that disappeared by the time they were done and lying against each other, their breathing heavy. They snuggled close as the chill of the afternoon turned into the coldness of the autumn night.

When they rode out the next morning, it was still cold, and there was an inch of snow on the ground. Both were thankful for their heavy coats, as well as warm clothes. Kate had had the opportunity to take some of her sister-in-law's dresses from her brother's home, but she had not done so, partly because she was slightly taller and fuller of figure than her sister-in-law, but also because she had become comfortable with the fact that she liked wearing a man's—especially her man's—pants and shirts. But the ones she had been wearing were becoming rather threadbare, and so she had taken one of her brother's shirts, a pair of Sean's boots she had found at the older brother's house, and two pairs of her older brother's pants. They were much too large, but she would make do with them. And the coat.

They shivered in the biting wind as they rode, and Coffin thought that perhaps the trail they were following mostly south toward Oak Creek would lead them to warmer climes.

"Damn," Coffin suddenly muttered, pulling up his chestnut horse.

"What's wrong?" Kate asked, alarmed.

"Nothin', really," he said, climbing down off his horse to stare intently at the snow-covered ground, and the nearby bushes and trees. He moved around a little, always studying the ground and lower bushes with his eyes. "They split up," Coffin said. He pointed down the creek, through the falling snowflakes. "Three of 'em went that way. You know what's down there?"

"Nothin' much, till you come to Dry Beaver Canyon some miles away."

He nodded. "The other three went this way." He pointed almost due south. "What's there?"

"Oak Creek Canyon."

"Sheriff Bordus never mentioned that."

"No. Southwest there's other canyons that he did mention —Hell Canyon and Rattlesnake Canyon are the two biggest."

"I think we'll keep on south."

"Why?"

Coffin shrugged. "Just a hunch, I guess. I'm hopin' Holder

will be lookin' for someplace warm to hole up for the winter."

"It's as good a way as the other."

They rode a little faster and harder, a cold wind pushing them as they headed into the rocky, high-walled canyon.

They made a camp in a stand of tall, sturdy pines and bare cottonwoods and aspens on a small flat. The night turned rigid. The cold bit at their fingers and noses as they worked around camp, but their blankets and a good fire of pine kept them warm while they slept.

In the morning everything was blanketed with snow, which was more than half a foot deep. And it was still snowing, though not nearly as hard. Before noon, they worked their way farther into Oak Creek Canyon and onto a large flat covered heavily with large pines. The steep, rocky east side of the canyon dropped off sharply nearby.

Coffin stopped his horse, and Kate rode up alongside him. "See anything?" she asked.

"Yep." He pointed. About a mile away on the west side of the trail down into the canyon was a wisp of smoke.

"Think it's them?"

"Hell if I know, Kate," he said sharply, regretting it immediately. More calmly he said, "Could be them. It could just as soon be a couple prospectors. Or a couple Apaches."

She tried to ignore the stab of fear that lanced into her stomach and chest. She was not entirely successful at it.

Coffin sat surveying the land, looking for the best way to go about his business. "We'll leave the horses over by those trees"—he chucked his chin toward a thick stand of white-capped ponderosa pines not far from the cliff falling off and down to the canyon floor—"and then I can work my way along the rim there, behind the brush and trees and such, till I'm opposite them. I'll figure out what to do then."

"What about me?" Kate asked stiffly, her fear swamped by annoyance.

"You'll stay with the horses," Coffin said bluntly. He wanted no argument.

"But—"

"We went through this before, Kate," he said softly, but sternly. "These men are killers, pure and simple. They have no sympathy and no compassion. I ain't takin' a chance on you either gettin' killed or gettin' caught again. You stay here. I can move better on my own anyway."

She nodded, not happy. But he didn't care. His mind was already trying to set himself for what lay ahead. They moved slowly into the trees. Coffin loosened the saddles but did not remove them. "Leave the mule packed," he ordered.

He held her for a moment. Releasing her, he realized he had nothing more to say. He turned and walked off, following the ragged line of the top of the canyon wall, moving around evergreen trees, brush, and rocks, feet sloughing through the snow. Wind whistled across the flat and he was glad for the protection of the pines and his wool-lined duster.

He reached a spot opposite where he had seen the smoke and he peered out from behind a large ponderosa pine. Across a meadow, bunched up against a thick stand of pines, there were three men sitting around a small fire. Two tents were set up behind them, both snapping in the wind. The three men were talking and laughing rudely.

From where he was, Coffin could not tell who they were, but he was fairly certain they were among the men he was looking for. He stood for a while, trying to formulate a plan, until he realized there was but one choice.

He headed back the way he had come until he was out of sight of the men, then he crossed the meadow through the sparse trees. Carefully he worked his way back. Within minutes he could hear their voices, and he proceeded more cautiously, glad that the wind and the lightly falling snow masked the sounds of his approach.

Coffin heard something off to his left, and he froze, thinking that perhaps one of the men at the fire had gotten up and was walking around. But he only heard it the once, so he moved on, snaking from tree trunk to tree trunk.

He stopped behind another tree, and surveyed the little camp. Three of them. They were still there, passing a bottle of whiskey among them.

Since he had long ago memorized their features from the poor drawings on the wanted posters, he recognized all three immediately: Bill Curly, the murderous Navajo half-breed, had his back to Coffin; Reno Holder himself sat facing the tents, sideways to Coffin; and Ian O'Kelly, partially blocked by Curly's body, faced him across the fragrant fire.

Damn, Coffin thought with a touch of joy, *my luck must be changing. Reno Holder is the first one I come across.* Take him down, and the rest would be little more than simple murderers—dangerous, but without direction.

He pulled off the leather gloves, stuffed them in a pocket, and slid out the big .44 Remington Frontier. Then things became a blur.

"Hold it right there, damn you all," he heard as he was taking aim at Holder's head.

He almost cracked his neck whipping his own head around. Kate McCoombs stood about ten feet to his left, her eyes blazing red, her scarlet hair a tumbled mass around her head. She had her legs slightly spread, and was holding her brother's old pistol uncomfortably in both hands.

Out of the corner of his eyes, he saw the three men at the fire freeze momentarily.

Then Curly said with a sneer, "Hell, it's only a woman," and all three men moved.

"Shit, goddamnit, son of a bitch," Coffin said. He fired off a quick round, which winged Curly in the arm. The half-breed howled but did not slow as he headed for the cover of the trees that curled in a small half-moon around the camp—and the horses tied there.

Holder and O'Kelly had each leaped up and then half-dove, half-jumped in opposite directions. Kate stood, swinging her pistol back and forth, trying vainly, almost desperately, to draw a bead on one of the three. She fired twice wildly, hitting nothing. Curly was gone now, and Holder and O'Kelly were behind trees, taking aim at Kate.

Coffin burst out from his cover and ran, flat out, spurs clanking. His gloves fell out of his pocket, but he did not know it. He slid a couple of times in the snow but kept moving. He was almost to Kate when he heard two pistols roar. He gasped as fire burst into searing flames in his chest and then a leg, knocking him sideways.

He managed to keep to his feet until he slammed into Kate,

155

knocking her down. He fell heavily in a heap atop her. Kate screamed. Coffin heard more shots being fired, the sound a blurred roar. Half-covering his woman with his own bleeding body, he snapped the Remington up and fired off two rounds at Holder. But the outlaw leader was well hidden behind the tree, and the bullets thunked harmlessly into the trunk.

O'Kelly leaped out, two pistols blazing, from behind his tree and headed for the horses tied nearby. Over his own pounding heart, and the roar of the guns, Coffin could hear Bill Curly racing away down the canyon.

A red gauze seemed to be covering Coffin's eyes, making it hard for him to see. He blinked several times, trying to focus. His vision cleared and he fired, drilling O'Kelly solidly with the last two bullets in his Remington.

The mad, murderous Irishman fell all asprawl, disjointed, like a split-open sack of oats. He landed in an odd position of tangled limbs and lay still except for the twitching of his dying muscles.

Blackness was wavering before Coffin's eyes as he dropped the Remington and pulled out the Colt Peacemaker and snapped off all five shots in the fleeing Holder's direction. None hit the outlaw, and as Coffin neared unconsciousness, his gun arm drooped and the shots fell lower and lower.

Then the blackness overwhelmed him.

Chapter 22

As Kate struggled to get out from under Coffin's weight, she panicked. He was dead, she was sure. He had to be. And the outlaws would be back soon to find her trapped and easy prey.

Despite the cold and snow, sweat beaded on her forehead as she fought to push up Joe's body, and her breathing was labored.

Then she heard a horse galloping, and she craned her neck. Between the trees she could see flashes of Reno Holder, riding low on the horse, slapping the animal with the reins, racing south toward the trail down into the deep canyon.

Kate relaxed a little. Bill Curly had taken off earlier, and Ian O'Kelly was dead. She would be safe from them now, she told herself over and over. But the terror did not entirely subside, as she strained to free herself. It was a panic born of facing more loss—she was certain Coffin was dead, and so she would be utterly alone. And it meant she would have lost everyone she had ever loved, and all within the span of but a few weeks.

She fought back tears, and finally stopped struggling so hard, allowing herself a few minutes to rest. As she did, she could see the strong pulse throbbing in Joe's temple. He's alive! she thought with a flash of hope.

She put more effort into freeing herself. He was alive! And he would need help! It took a while, but at last she managed to squirm out from under his dead weight. She lay back, breathing hard from all the exertion.

She stood, and looked down at her man. Fear bit into her

157

again as she saw all the blood on his back, and on his leg. She was near panic again, unsure of what to do, and so doing nothing.

"Damnit," Kate finallly snapped, furious at herself. She labored to roll him over, and finally managed. After a few moments' rest, to let her heart stop feeling as if it would thump right out of her chest, she lifted Coffin's shoulders. He groaned, though he did not regain consciousness. She tried dragging him, but made little progress.

She slipped in the snow and fell hard, hurting her buttocks. Frustration swelled up in her. She stood again. "Goddamnit, you are going to move your man into the safety of one of those tents, Kate McCoombs," she told herself sternly.

She took off his spurs, thinking it would make her job easier. Then she breathed deeply several times. Leaning over, she gripped Coffin under the arms. Straightening, she strained with every muscle in her back and legs. She sputtered, and her arms felt as if they'd be pulled from their sockets.

But Coffin moved, ever so slightly. Then more. And finally Kate was dragging the unconscious bounty hunter across the snow. Once she got him started, the going was fairly easy. When she made it into the tent, she let Coffin down as easily as she could. Then she slumped onto her knees, sucking for air, her arms and legs quivering.

Wearily she finally pushed herself up and headed out, back to where she had left the three horses and the mule. She mounted her horse, gathered up the others, and led them to the outlaws' camp. She unsaddled the horses, and unpacked the mule, taking all the supplies into the tent. All the while she steadfastly ignored the body of Ian O'Kelly.

Then Kate looked around the tent, seeing if there was anything usable left by the outlaws.

There wasn't much—some bacon, hardtack, beans, a few canned goods; several bottles of whiskey; tobacco; a few blankets, all but two of them well-used, foul-smelling, and filthy. Kate took the soiled blankets outside and dropped one into the fire. The others she dumped nearby, to be burned when she could get to it.

Steeling herself, Kate went back inside. It was eerie in the tent, with the sides flapping and snapping in the wind. But it was warmer. Kate pulled off her wool coat and tossed it aside. As she knelt beside Coffin, she thought how strange it was that she was so calm, acting so responsibly. Especially with all that had happened. But she was glad she was able to to do it.

With slightly shaking hands, Kate unbuttoned her man's blood-soaked coat. The exit wound, high up in the chest, in the triangle formed by the heart, breastbone, and collarbone, was still oozing blood. It didn't look good, particularly since Kate had nothing at hand with which to treat it. But it did not look as bad as she had feared it would either.

She unhooked Coffin's shoulder holsters and spread them out alongside the man, hoping it would make him more comfortable. Then she took his knife and slit open his pants leg, baring the wound there. It was ugly, with the little raised mound of flesh and the dark, leaking hole. Kate checked and found that the bullet had gone clean through, and no major arteries had been hit.

The enormity of her situation began to dawn on her. She was alone, God only knew how far from the nearest town, with no medicines and a man who looked as if he was near death. And on top of that, there was a gang of outlaws roaming around.

Kate shook her head. She could not—she would not!—think of that now. There was much yet to be done. Kate knew there was no way she could manage to hoist Coffin onto a horse and then travel with him till they reached a town. And she did not think she would be able to rig up a travois for him either. It was all up to her, then, to save him.

She put her coat on and grabbed their small, folding shovel. Outside, she stepped off into the chill wind, not hesitating to find a direction. If she did that, she knew, she would begin to think of what was happening and become helpless with the fear. Fortunately, she thought, it had stopped snowing.

It took a while, but she finally found what she was looking for—the thin, winter-browned, lacelike leaves of some Western yarrow, poking up through the snow. She dug up several plants, roots and all, and hurried back to the tents, a sense of urgency pushing her.

Inside, she rummaged around in the outlaws' supplies—not

allowing herself to think about what she was doing—until she found an old cast-iron pot that was almost clean. With anxiety growing in her, she hurried to the spring nearby and filled the pot with water. She boiled up some of the yarrow root on the fire.

As she waited for it, she struggled and fought to get Coffin's coat, shoulder holsters, and then shirt off him so he was bare from the waist up. She folded his blood-soaked shirt and put it under his back, so the wound was not touching dirt; and she folded the coat and made a pillow of it for him. He began to shiver, for it was cold even inside the tent, and she laid two blankets over him, tucking them tightly around his sides.

She went back outside, but the concoction was not ready yet. She fought back the despair that built up in her belly and splashed through her body. She shuddered, and tried to tell herself it was only from the cold wind. But she knew better.

Kate went and got the coffeepot and some beans. She filled the pot at the spring and set it on the fire next to the bubbling pot of yarrow root. Finally the medicine root was ready. With a folded-up shirt she had found inside, she picked up the pot and carried it in. She let it cool a while before lathering it heavily on Coffin's wounds—front and back.

It was hard work, trying to prop him up to get the stuff on the back wound. It got no easier when she had to wrap a torn-up shirt around his chest as a bandage. When she was done, she fell back into a sitting position, leaning back on her locked arms. Breathing was difficult, and she was sweating. But she had gotten it done.

It was, she knew as she pushed herself up, all up to Coffin now whether he would live or die. There was little more she could do other than to keep the poultices fresh. She went outside and poured herself a cup of the coffee. She went back inside to drink it since the wind was kicking up even more out there—and she also wanted to be close to Coffin. She was deathly afraid that he would die, and she was sure she would not be able to handle that.

When Kate finished her coffee, she realized she was hungry. Almost automatically she made herself some food, her mind unconsciously taking note of the fact that supplies were low and that if they were stuck here for a while—with winter full on them—they might be in serious trouble.

She ate without tasting her food. The more she sat, the more her mind played bad tricks on her. She tried desperately to keep the morbid thoughts away, until finally she scowled and tossed aside her empty plate. "Damn fool," she mumbled.

It was dark, and Kate finally lay down and covered herself with blankets. From outside, she heard the sound of wolves—or maybe coyotes, she was not sure—tearing at flesh, and she shuddered, figuring that she would not have to look at O'Kelly's body come morning.

At last she slept, exhaustion brought on by mental trauma, worry, overwork, and long hours at last overcoming her. But she awoke unrefreshed, having been kept awake by dreams in which hordes of leering, drunken, evil men wielding knives and guns ravished her repeatedly, without end, while all around her, friends, family, and her man died and died and died. . . .

With a sinking feeling Kate went outside. It had snowed again overnight, but not much. Fortunately, some coals were still hot, and it was not hard for her to build up the fire again and make some bacon, corn cakes, and coffee.

She found her brother's gun, which she had dropped the afternoon before, and Coffin's two pistols. She cleaned them and made sure they were loaded. It had occurred to her that since supplies were low, she must think of hunting to supplement her—no, she told herself sternly, *their*—larder.

Kate changed Coffin's poultices and then made sure he was well covered. She picked up her brother's Winchester. Bundled in her coat, Kate left on foot. She went to the far side of the spring, figuring any deer that might be in the vicinity would be coming for water sooner or later, and that the animals would know if humans were on the other side. Perhaps this way she could surprise them.

It was a long, cold wait, but soon after noon had passed, with her stomach growling with hunger, she heard the dainty footsteps of a deer coming. She flattened out on her belly on the cold snow, resting the barrel of her rifle on a small rock. Within moments a small buck wandered down a barely discernible trail and into her sight. Taking a deep breath, she held it, and carefully squeezed the trigger.

When the smoke cleared, she could see the buck, still standing, hooves splayed. It was hunched up, hit in the lungs, and it was not long before the animal collapsed.

Happy, Kate tried to drag the carcass to their small camp. But she could not. Finally she shook her head at her stupidity. She trudged back to the camp quickly, hoping all the while that some scavenger would not find the deer. In the camp, she got Coffin's knife and the mule. She returned to her kill, relieved to find the deer untouched. She butchered it where she had shot it, wrapped the meat in some of the bloody hide, and then packed it on the mule and returned to camp.

She checked on Coffin, but he had not moved. His breathing was still shallow, but he looked as comfortable as could be expected. Kate went back out and carved the deer meat up into manageable portions, stringing most of it high in a tree. She carried the ripped-up hide and other small, inedible parts far from the camp so they would not attract scavengers.

In the next several days, Coffin began to worry her. He lay unconscious for nearly a week before he awoke, weak, subdued, and confused. Two days after that Coffin went into delirium, with his fever rising rapidly. He thrashed around and mumbled inanities, moaned, and occasionally shouted things Kate could not understand.

Worried, Kate pulled the blankets off Coffin, exposing him to the cold of the tent. She opened the flap of the tent so the cold wind could blow in. That and putting old yarrow leaves all over him, since that was supposed to bring a coolness to the body, were all she could think to do to try to break the fever.

It took almost three days for the fever to snap; three days in which she got almost no sleep as she tended to her man, watched over him, changed his poultices, and paced with worry tearing at her heart.

But finally he awoke, calm, his temperature normal. He looked blankly around, and Kate feared the worst—that his fever had reached his mind and had destroyed it.

Then he smiled that crooked, handsome little smile of his, and said, "You look good, darlin'."

She chuckled, and cried at the same time in her joy. She knew he was lying. She must look a fright. She had not brushed out her hair since all this happened, and it was too cold for her to do more than swipe a little snow on her face periodically. She and her clothes were filthy, her hands scratched and split from the cold. Her face was pale and her eyes rimmed from lack of sleep. But her smile was so bright that Coffin did not notice the flaws.

"Can you sit up?" she asked.

"Yep." He struggled to sit, but was too weak. "Maybe not," he mumbled.

"Wait," Kate said, her heart fairly bursting with joy. She got his saddle and lugged it over to where he lay. With a new strength that surprised Coffin, Kate helped lift him and shoved the saddle behind him so he had something to lean against. She piled blankets around him.

"Want to eat?" she asked.

"Just cook up the mule whole," he said, grinning. "And drag him in here."

"That hungry?"

"Yep."

They stared into each other's eyes, saying much to each other without uttering any words. There was nothing they had to voice—it was all there for each to see in the other.

Kate went out, and was back in within moments carrying a tin bowl full of stew. "It ain't the best I ever made," she said in regret as she sat next to him, bowl in one hand, spoon in the other. "Now open up."

He did, and took a sip of broth. It was flavored with sage, he could tell, and something else he didn't know. The next spoonful contained a piece of meat. He took it and chewed, eyes growing wider with each chew. "Where'n hell'd you get deer meat?" he asked in surprise.

"Huntin'," she said proudly.

"But . . . what . . . how . . . ?"

Kate laughed, and Coffin realized it was the first time he had ever heard her do that—*really* laugh. To him it was a wonderful sound.

"I ain't been sittin' around just waitin' for you to get

better," she said, lying some. "I've been busy. Huntin', cookin' for myself. Buildin' a cabin..."

"What?" he exploded, eyebrows reaching for his hairline.

"Makin' a cabin," she said, fairly bursting with self-esteem.

"What for?" he asked, still amazed at this beautiful, delightful, efficient bundle of a woman.

"We need it," Kate said, shoving a spoonful of stew into Coffin's still-gaping mouth. He clamped his lips shut and chewed. "I don't reckon we'll be goin' anywhere any time soon. It's lookin' like a nasty winter brewed up already. I just didn't figure this tent was gonna be good enough for you to be recuperatin' in."

"We'll be on the trail next week."

Kate wanted that, but knew it was impossible. "Don't you try'n play hardcase with me, Joe Coffin. You ain't goin' anywhere in a week except into that cabin I'm buildin'. You can't even get up to take care of... well, personal business." She giggled.

"I'll show you," Coffin said angrily. He put his arms down and shoved, trying to push himself up. Agony ripped through his chest and back, and he slumped, gasping.

She laughed, and the sound now infuriated him. "Just set back." She held out another spoonful of stew, but Coffin clamped his lips shut. Now it was Kate's turn to be angry. "Now you listen to me, Joe Coffin, goddamnit," she snapped, surprising him again.

"I know who you are," she continued, "and I know just how tough you are. But you've taken two slugs and have been unconscious more than a week and a half. Your body needs time to heal, and I'll not sit here and let you try'n hurt yourself all over again just to show me how tough you are. I ain't impressed with it. Now eat some of this stew like a good fellow."

Rage colored his face, and then he relaxed. Coffin was not one to like having his manhood impugned, but he was not stupid either. He didn't need to impress her; he did need to get better. "Yes, ma'am," he said quietly, opening his mouth for the spoon.

Chapter 23

It was bitter cold, snowing and with a wind howling down through the canyon. But Joe Coffin wanted to get away from there. They had been there nearly a month and a half, and Coffin felt he was fully recovered. Besides, he just didn't think he could sit anymore in that makeshift cabin.

Kate McCoombs had done an excellent job, considering, in building the cabin, which was actually more of a log lean-to. She had, somehow—and she never told him how—managed to get logs she had cut braced at an angle up against the west wall of the canyon. These she had covered over with brush to keep the snow and rain out.

The north opening—from where the wind most often blew—she'd covered with pine and aspen saplings into which she had jammed brush. She'd covered the whole with the tent they were not using, folding the canvas and "nailing" it to the logs with pegs, and tying the bottom to whatever was handy. It made a nice, tight cover on the one side.

The other—south—side she'd left mostly open. There she'd built a fire pit of stones, perhaps two feet high, opening into the lean-to. It meant they would be warm, and she wouldn't have to go outside to cook or heat up poultices.

Coffin was proud of her, and told her so, when she helped him hobble into the new structure four days after he had awakened. It was small, but that helped keep it warm, and snug.

The tent they had been using, Kate began using as a storehouse. She put whatever they did not need there, straightening it out so that she knew where everything was. She threw out—or burned—much of what the outlaws had left behind, including almost all their clothes that were there.

And she and Coffin had settled in for the winter. But before long Coffin grew fidgety. It was barely a week after they had moved into the cabin that Coffin got up for the first time and really walked around. He only walked around the interior of the lean-to twice, but it was progress.

Each day he did a little more. By the time they had been there a month, Coffin was almost back to his old self. He worked hard splitting wood and hunting. She had been furious when he told her he would be taking over the hunting chores.

"Don't you think I can do it?" Kate asked, voice bathed in anger.

"Sure you can. You proved that."

"Then why? Want to show off your manhood again?" There was a bitter tone in the words, and it stung Coffin more than he cared to admit.

"No," he said softly, slowly.

"Then why, damnit?"

"Because," he said calmly, not allowing her to see the hurt he felt, "I need to get back my shootin' eye and my shootin' arm. I've got to see if these wounds are gonna take away any of my skill with a gun—either pistol or rifle."

"Oh," she mumbled, feeling like an idiot. She fumbled a while before managing, "I'm sorry."

"It's all right," he said, but the hurt remained. He left and went hunting, using the Winchester. His wounds did not seem to have made a difference in his abilities, though the long layoff did somewhat.

When he got back to the lean-to, he put the quickly freezing meat into the tent, washed off his hands with snow, and then stuffed them into his pockets to dry and warm them, wishing for the thousandth time that he had not lost his gloves in the short, deadly gunfight.

He stepped around the fire into the lean-to, giving his eyes a moment to adjust to the gloom in there. He did not see Kate at first but as his eyes adjusted, he saw her in the blankets, looking up at the "ceiling." It made him angry, since the hurt from her earlier accusations still lingered in him. So, he thought, she's mad at me for taking away some of her sport and now she's just going to lay there and do nothing at all.

Coffin shrugged. It would mean more work for him, but he could handle it. He knelt to pour some coffee, when he heard her say, "Well?"

"Well what?" he asked sharply, turning.

"I got somethin' a heap better for warmin' you up," Kate said huskily, almost ashamed at her brazenness.

"Yeah?" he said in annoyance, replacing the pot on the fire.

"Joe?" There was a pleading in the single word.

Leaving the mug of steaming coffee on the ground, he turned, ready to say something sharply to her. And stopped.

Kate had flung the blankets off and was lying in the same position as before, stark naked. Her hair was newly brushed and glowed in the red of the firelight. The pale skin of her breasts, belly, and legs stood out in stark contrast to the dark scarlet of her hair, which spilled out around her on the blanket.

"Good Christ," he breathed. He clanked over to her. He was not wearing his shoulder rig, so it was but a moment before his gun belt was off. He stripped off his shirt and then sat, pulling off the boots and the small-roweled spurs with the little jinglebobs on them.

"I'm sorry about before," Kate whispered, running several fingers down his strong back.

He nodded, afraid to speak, lest his voice sound less manly than he was feeling right at this moment. He stood and pulled off his Levi's pants, and carefully lowered himself into the waiting, willing embrace of her open arms and legs.

"Forgive me?" Kate asked when they were done and lying entwined in each other's arms.

"Yep." He grinned.

"I hurt ya, though, didn't I?" Kate asked with a twinge of sadness.

"Yeah," he said quietly. "But I would've gotten over it sooner or later."

"I hope I helped you get over it . . . ?" She held her breath, waiting.

"Oh, yes, ma'am," he said, reveling in the feel of her smooth skin.

"I was afraid that I had hurt you," she said. "And it worried me sick. I thought you might leave me or somethin', and with good reason."

"I'd not ever leave you," he muttered.

"I was worried . . . I . . ." Kate couldn't think any more as passion flooded through her loins, and she surrendered herself willingly to it.

As Coffin pulled her atop him, he wondered how he could have gotten so angry at Kate.

Kate lay atop the hard, muscular body of Joe Coffin, her toes toying with his, her head tucked under his chin. She kissed the still-ugly spot where the bullet had left her man's body, and she suppressed a shudder. But then she smiled. She was happier than she ever was. "You want a family, Joe?" she asked suddenly.

"Never thought much on it," he said, stroking her back. "You all right?"

"A little cold."

Between the two of them, they got the blanket pulled up around her shoulders.

"Well, I'd like a family. What do you say to that?"

"Not sure. I never had much of a family myself. So I don't know much about such things."

Her head came up and she stared at him, her eyes reflecting concern. "What do you mean not much of a family?"

He shrugged, and she snapped, "Damnit, tell me about yourself, Joe. I want to know everything about you."

"There's not much to tell, Kate. Really."

"Tell me anyway," she ordered, nipping the end of his nose.

He felt a stirring down below, and he tried to ignore it. "Well, I was born in some minin' camp in California to a hard-luck gold miner and a good woman who just couldn't take the life my father gave her. She died when I was still pretty young, and my father dragged me all around, prospectin'. But he never even made back his stake, though he was always full of big ideas and such.

"He died when I was about fourteen, up in the Sierra Nevada. I buried him, threw away most of his prospectin' stuff, and rode out, headin' east. I knew I had some kin back in Pennsylvania, so I went there. They weren't happy to see me, so I joined up with some infantry of the Pennsylvania volunteers and went off to fight in the Civil War."

"You were only fourteen?" Kate asked, shocked.

"Yep. But I turned fifteen before my first battle."

"That must've been horrible."

"The war? Of course."

"Not only the war, but bein' so young."

"I reckon," he said, rubbing a small circle on her back under the blanket. "The fightin' in the war was like I'd never seen before, though I was used to usin' my fists, and even a gun some. Man's small as me, has to learn to fight early. There's always some goddamn big fool who thinks that 'cause you're small that you ain't really a man or somethin'."

"Poor man," Kate soothed.

"I fought for a little more than two years. When the war ended, I headed west, not sure of what I was gonna do. There was a heap of men there with the same thought. Most of them finally took to farmin' or workin' in stores and such wherever a town started. But I wasn't out for that. Since I was born, I'd lived most of my life outside. I liked it. Still do. Though," he added with a grin, "I never turn down a bed under a roof when I can find one. Especially if it's occupied."

"Those days are over for you, boy, since I'm fixin' to be the only one occupyin' your bed—whether it's under a roof or under the stars—from here on."

"Yes, ma'am." His eyes glittered with joy. "I got no complaints with that. So," he added, "I took to bounty huntin'. I was good at fightin', at killin'"—there was a little distaste evident in his voice at that, but not much—"and I liked life outside. It was either that, stay in the army, or hunt buffalo. I hated the army, and huntin' buffalo didn't pay enough."

"Yeah," Kate sighed, "but buffalo don't shoot back."

"That's a fact, ma'am. I been bounty huntin' ever since. And here I am."

"And I'm powerful glad too," she whispered, her mouth covering his. And then, "Hurry, please, darling Joe."

The next morning, though there was a blizzard swirling

outside, and Coffin and Kate could not get out of their cabin, Coffin began making plans to leave.

"But why?" Kate asked. "It's dead winter, we got us a snug, safe place to stay—"

"I thought you was the one who wanted to kill them outlaws more'n anything."

"I do," she said, the thought spurring a river of anger through her veins. But she managed to control herself. "But I can't see gettin' killed tryin' to find them. Your gettin' shot," she said slowly, "made me think about all this. I couldn't bear it if you was to die."

"I wouldn't be real happy with it neither," he said, trying to sound lighthearted.

"Well, then let's just stay here for the winter. Those bastards'll probably lay low for winter too." She was deathly afraid of losing Coffin now that their love was growing, and since he had come so close to dying.

"We're low on supplies," he said. "We got us enough meat from huntin', but we're out of near everything else. We don't have gloves or much else for warm clothes. Since we have to make our way out of here through the cold and everything else, we might as well just keep on after those bastards while we're at it."

Kate did not seem convinced, but Coffin shrugged. He had made up his mind, and that's all there was to it. She could either come along when he left, if she chose to, or stay here.

"When?" Kate asked.

"Few days. There's no big hurry. I just gotta get out of here. I can't stand bein' cooped up no more."

"Think you're strong enough?" Kate asked, worry filling her chest.

"Thought I'd settled that question yesterday," he said with a grin, hoping to soften the sternness with which he had been talking.

"Reckon you did," she said dreamily, thinking back on it.

And so, three days later, in the midst of the cold, they mounted up and rode out, Coffin not looking back, Kate looking back with mixed feelings.

Chapter 24

Joe Coffin and Kate McCoombs wound down through Oak Creek Canyon and into a land of starkly bright red cliffs, dusted over with snow. Soon they came upon the frozen-over Verde River. They followed the river southeastward, and in five very cold days had reached Camp Verde.

It was a bustling place—both the Army post and the town that had sprung up near it. Coffin stopped at the first hotel he came to, and he and Kate went inside, where Coffin registered them as Mister and Missis Joe Coffin, much to Kate's delight.

"That sounds real nice," Kate said as they walked outside to take the horses to the livery stable.

"What?" he asked gruffly, knowing full well what she meant.

She only smiled. Then she said, "Why don't we do it for real?"

"When this job's done and over," he answered seriously. He had never given it any thought before, but there was no longer any other choice for him. He had made up his mind, and that was that.

The two got some strange looks as they walked down the wide, snow-coverd dirt street. "What're all these people starin' at?" Kate asked in some annoyance.

"Us," Coffin said, not thinking it odd. "You, mostly."

"But why?" she asked, startled.

"'Cause you're so goddamn beautiful that all these women are jealous. And all the men," he added crudely, "are gettin' itchy just watchin' you sashay by."

Kate flushed in embarrassment, both from the compliment and the rude way in which it was framed. Then she realized that it probably was not so, since she was dressed in man's too-big pants and a bulky, too-large coat. Only her face—beautiful enough, she knew without being arrogant about it—and her hair, which also would bring some stares, were visible.

"That's nice," she said, thinking to get back at Coffin a little. "Perhaps I'll go see just how itchy some of these other men are getting by my mere presence." The impishness oozed from her voice.

"You do that and it'll be the last thing you ever do," he growled, not seeing any humor in it at all.

"Then tell me the real reason they're all starin' at me."

"The way you're dressed," Coffin said quickly.

"I thought so," she said ruefully. She thought for a few minutes, then said, "Do we have enough money for me to buy a dress?"

"Reckon so." He still had more than seven hundred dollars on him. He could probably buy the town. "Why, though? You were the one who wanted to keep wearin' pants and such."

"I know," she said, her face pinking. "But that was before everyone started starin' at me. Besides, once we leave again, I'll want to wear pants again, but here in town . . ."

"You didn't feel that way in Aspen Wells."

"Yeah, but they didn't have a dance." She gulped, hoping he would not be angry at her.

"A what?"

"Dance." She pointed to a large poster nailed onto a post holding up the overhanging roof of a building nearby.

He stopped in front of it and looked. "I'll be damned," he muttered. He had not realized it was Christmas.

"Can we go?" Kate asked, her blue eyes bright with excitement.

Coffin rubbed his belly outside the coat, thinking a few moments. Then he said, "Don't see why not."

Kate gave a little chirp of joy and happily rubbed her hands together.

"Just remember, Kate," Coffin said with a grin, "that I ain't known far and wide for my dancin'." In fact, he had no interest whatsoever in dancing, but Kate wanted it, and it might be a good place to pick up information.

"I don't care."

They got to the livery and turned over the three horses and the mule. From there they went to the wire office, where Coffin sent a telegram to Marshal Tom Pike, telling the lawman that Ian O'Kelly was dead and that the federal government owed Coffin another thousand dollars.

From there Coffin and Kate went to the largest general store, where they arranged to buy enough supplies for the winter, including new coats, long underwear, gloves, new pants and shirts—including some that fit Kate.

Coffin bought a suit, though he hated the thought, and string tie, new boots, and fancy dress hat. And Kate spent so long picking out a dress and all that Coffin finally gave the store owner some money. "Let her get whatever she wants," Coffin said. "Any money left over you give her when she gets through. If it costs more, I'll be down to the saloon."

"You're not angry with me, are you?" Kate asked Coffin when he told her he was heading for the bar. The concern that flickered on her face could not cover the elation she felt.

"No," he said with a crooked grin. "I just can't stand here no more while you're fussin' and fiddlin' with such things. You pick out anything you want. Whatever you need. I'll see you back at the room after a little."

She nodded, her mind already back on the joyful task looming before her.

Coffin shook his head and left. He wandered down the street, enjoying the crisp coldness of the air. A light drizzle was falling. A few doors down was a saloon, and he pushed his way into the noisy, smoky place, and headed for the bar.

Everyone was in a jovial mood, with the holiday the next day. Even the bartender was passing out a free drink to newcomers, and Coffin saluted him with the brimming mug of cold beer that the barkeep had set before him.

Before long, Coffin joined a poker game, playing without much enthusiasm for the game, since no one else seemed to be doing so either. Instead, he kept his ears open, alert for any word of the outlaws he was tracking.

Three beers and four shots of whiskey later he left, feeling a warm, rosy glow inside. Kate was back at their room, a bundle of packages, most of them ripped open, spread across the bed. Her face beamed with happiness; indeed, he had never seen her looking so joyful.

"You look terrific, Kate," he said, slurring the words only a little.

She beamed all the more, though she knew he was lying, since she was still clad in the shabby, dirty men's clothes she had been wearing for months. "Thank you, sir," she said, doing a little curtsy.

She came up and wrapped her arms around his middle, and pressed her cheek into the coat on the front of his chest. He was still wearing the old coat, having had the new one delivered with the other things from the store. But Kate did not mind the dried blood, the smells of wood smoke, grease, and sweat on it.

He in turn placed his powerful arms around her shoulders and clumsily patted her back and hair, his hands made somewhat awkward by the alcohol in his system.

"Not now," she whispered, suddenly a little shy. Now that she had some fine, womanly clothes, and they were back in civilization, she wanted to look her frilliest, fanciest, laciest, satiniest best for him. She wanted to be clean and powdered. She wanted her teeth shining from a good scrubbing of tooth powder. She wanted to smell good for him, with the bathwater and perfume she had bought.

"Huh?" he asked, eyes droopy with sleep. It was one of the features that endeared him to her. Coffin was a man who could go for days on end without sleep, if the situation called for it. But as soon as he let down his guard and relaxed a little, he became tired, and could fall asleep in an instant.

Kate smiled at him. "I'm not all fixed up," she said, feeling funny about it.

"So?" he grumbled, the words slurred a little more, though now it was more from tiredness than drink.

"There'll be plenty of time later. Get some sleep. Take a nap, while I go about tryin' on clothes and things. I want you to be fresh and ready, not tired and a bit drunk later, when we . . ." She let the words hang there, inviting, with promise for the night.

"I ain't drunk," he mumbled, but he knew damn well she was right. And seeing how lovely she looked now, he thought of how she would look cleaned, her hair sparkling from a good washing and combing, with fancy lace and satin clothes. He felt a warming in his groin, and he gulped.

Shuffling to the bed, he shrugged off his coat and shoulder holsters. He sat and pulled off his boots before stretching out. By the time Kate bent over and lightly kissed him on the lips, he was asleep, snoring softly.

He awoke feeling great several hours later. Kate was sitting in the chair by the window, humming quietly and reading a newspaper. Coffin was mildly surprised to see that she was wearing a plain, brown high-necked dress. She smiled brightly when she saw him awake. "I'm hungry," she said. She waved a hand at her dress. "I bought this just for goin' out to eat. I didn't want nothin' too fancy, but I didn't want people talkin' about me and starin' at me while I ate."

"You look good in it. Ya know, it's the first time I ever saw ya in a dress." He smiled. Coffin put on new Levi's and shirt and his new coat.

Kate gathered up a wool wrap, and they went out. They feasted on steaks and potatoes, bread, beans, and coffee. After dinner they strolled back to their hotel through the light snow. Kate stopped at the desk, and talked to the people there for a few minutes.

"What was that all about?" Coffin asked, curious.

"Gettin' a tub set up for the room."

He grinned. "We gonna take us a bath together?" he asked, leering just a little.

"Nope. I'm gonna take a bath there. You, however, are gonna go over to the barbershop, where you can have a bath. Then you're gonna have this"—she flicked his long, dirty hair—"trimmed and get yourself a shave. By the time you get back, I ought to be done, and we'll be ready to go."

"Yes, ma'am." He went upstairs with her, and waited until the tub was pulled into the room. He assured himself that two women would be handling the chore of bringing in hot water before he left, carrying a package containing his new suit.

He felt a sight better as he walked back to the hotel, trimmed, washed, shaven, awash in lime aftershave, attired in crisp white shirt, wool vest, pants and jacket, new black boots, and derby hat.

At his hotel door, he stopped a minute. Taking a deep breath, he knocked, and said, "Kate, it's me, Joe."

"Come in."

With a little trepidation—unusual for him, but this woman seemed to bring out all the bad traits in him—he opened the door and stepped in.

Kate wore a sky blue satin and silk dress that accentuated her figure and highlighted her eyes. Her shoulders were bare, though her bosom was well covered with darker blue lace that seemed to be transparent. Her hair fell in a crimson cascade over her freckled shoulders.

Coffin grinned.

"Is it all right?" Kate asked, a touch of concern in her voice.

"Perfect. You're perfect."

He reached for her, but she skipped out of the way. "Later," she whispered, giggling.

They walked to the dance, which was just gearing up. The band consisted of a guitar, fiddle, harmonica, and squeeze box. The building was decorated with festive ribbons and pine wreaths.

Kate's eyes were bright, and people fixed their eyes on her as she walked into the large room.

"They're starin' at you again, ya know," Coffin said in mild amusement. He swung her into a dance, and several more, before he finally said, "Let's go get some punch."

As they sat, he said, "I'm sorry, Kate. I told you I wasn't much of one to dance. Did I hurt you any?" He was embarrassed.

"Not so's I'd notice," she said bravely, though both her feet ached from where he had stepped on them numerous times. But she didn't care. After they sat out several numbers, an older man walked up and, in diffident tones, asked Kate to dance with him.

Kate looked at Coffin. "Would you mind, Joe?" she asked. She liked to dance, but she would prefer to sit there all the night watching everybody else rather than getting Coffin mad at her.

Coffin looked a little angry at first, then relaxed when he realized this old, balding banker was no threat to him. "Naw, go on," he said gamely. While his woman was dancing, Coffin sneaked a few nips from the small bottle of whiskey he kept secreted in his inner suit pocket.

He spent much of the rest of the night sitting there, watching with rapt eyes as a variety of men spun Kate around the room. Or he wandered around, listening in on conversations, trying to see if he could learn any information about Reno Holder or any of his men.

Coffin kept his calm about all the dancing Kate did, knowing that he would be the one taking her home later, and the one making love to her. Most of the men she danced with would offer him no real competition, except for one. He danced with Kate several times, always holding her more tightly than he should have. And with each successive time, he was more reluctant to let her go back to her seat. Indeed, one time he even tried to tug her physically with him.

He might have succeeded too, if Coffin had not been keeping such a close eye on Kate as she danced. He stepped up to the man, who towered above him in height, but was turning rapidly to fat. The man had a nasty look about him, as if he was used to getting his way simply because he was bigger, meaner, and maybe tougher than anyone else—or because people were dumb enough to believe he was all those things.

This would be his first real test, Coffin thought, since he had been wounded. He thought he had all his strength back, but he was not certain. He grabbed the tall man's wrist and squeezed. His bull-like strength seemed to be completely back, and he could hear the small wrist bones grind. He felt much better about himself.

"Best let her go, pard," Coffin said calmly, though anger burned in his dark eyes.

The man stared down at him, trying to frighten him off with his fierce gaze. It didn't work, and he finally released Kate's arm. She stood rubbing her arm.

"You've had your last dance with my wife," Coffin said. "Don't come 'round askin' again."

"We'll just see about that," the tall man growled and stomped away.

Two dances later the tall man loomed in front of Kate and Coffin. There was a man at each side of him. "Time to dance again, little lady," he said, grabbing her arm.

Chapter 25

The people were reeling around the floor in joyful gaiety. Those who were not dancing sat watching in rapt attention or talking animatedly. Coffin, noticing it, stood, and slammed a short jab into the tall man's stomach, partially doubling him over.

The two men with the tall man reached for their pistols, but Coffin stared them down, his Colt halfway out of the holster. He shook his head, and they understood that they were dead if they drew. Each let his hand drop, and they stood with anger-filled eyes, watching.

Coffin turned back to the tall man, who was still partly bent over, his ear near Coffin. The bounty hunter leaned over and said in the man's ear, "Now, listen to me, boy, and hear me well. 'Less you want your guts splattered all over the dance floor, you're gonna let my woman's arm be, and you're gonna take yourself away from me'n her and stay away, understand?"

The tall man released Kate's arm. He turned malevolent eyes on Coffin. "I'll kill ya for this, ya short-legged son of a bitch," he said with a snarl.

"Anytime you're ready, pard."

"Now!" the man hissed, straightening.

The song was winding to a halt, as Coffin said, "Outside. Soon's the next dance starts."

The tall man nodded curtly, spun, and stalked away, his two companions in his wake.

"What'd you say to them?" Kate asked.

"Just told them to leave you alone. That you was spoke for, and there'd be trouble if they didn't leave off botherin' you."

Kate wasn't sure she believed him, but there was nothing she could say about it.

The next waltz started, and the elderly, balding banker asked Kate to dance again. She looked at Coffin, who nodded, and then said, "I'll be back in a little. Got to visit the privy."

She nodded, still wondering, and went off to dance.

Coffin walked outside into the cold. The bracing air sharpened his senses. He saw footsteps in the snow. He followed them around to the back of the building. The three men stood, waiting, several feet apart with the tall man in the center.

"I want the woman," the tall man said. "You don't like that, we'll settle it here and now."

As Coffin strolled up to within twenty feet of the three, he unhooked the hammer of the Colt—and the Remington too, just in case. "You really ain't that goddamn stupid, are you?" he asked.

"Damn." The tall man went for his pistol. Seeing the move, his two companions did so too.

Coffin's hand was a blur as he whipped the Colt out and fired all five shots he kept in the cylinder. Two bullets punched holes in the tall man's chest; one hit the man on Coffin's right in the forehead; and the last two hit the other man, one in the throat, one in the belly.

All three went down. Only one of them had been able to pull off a single shot, which ricocheted off a weather vane several buildings down as the man fell.

Coffin slid the Colt into the holster and pulled the Remington as he walked up. All three were either dead, or would be within seconds. He smiled a little. While he might not get any enjoyment from killing, there was a certain amount of satisfaction in a job well done. It did not bother Coffin at all that he had just gunned down these three.

Calmly, Coffin slipped the Remington away and hooked the small leather strap over the hammer. He strolled unconcerned to the outhouse on the other side of the building. Inside, he emptied his spent shells into his hand, and dropped them into the foul-smelling hole and reloaded the Colt. He relieved himself and wandered back to the dance.

The waltz was just ending, and he was waiting for Kate as she finished and thanked her flushed partner. "Havin' a good time?" he asked, smiling.

"Yes," she said, breathless. "You aren't, though, are you?"

He shrugged, wanting her. "There's things I'd rather be doin'." He grinned in comfortable lechery.

"We'll leave, if you want."

He could hear the disappointment in her voice, and said, "Naw, we'll stay around a while longer. Think you can stand to dance with me another time or two?"

"Yes, sir."

He swung her around the floor, trying harder this time not to stomp on her toes. He had limited success, so it was a little more enjoyable for Kate.

As they reeled into the second dance, a man, looking flushed and excited, entered the room and looked around. Spotting the sheriff, he went to him and gesticulated.

Coffin almost grinned. It was obvious to him that the man had found the three bodies outside. The sheriff, two deputies, and the man left. All but the sheriff returned shortly and spoke with the mayor. No announcement was made, but word of mouth passed the story around very quickly, and there was much excited buzzing from small groups of people that formed to discuss it.

"You know anything about this, Joe?" Kate asked, suspicious.

"Would it make a difference?"

"None," Kate said with a smile. "But I'd like to know."

"It was the tall fool, and the two idiots he brought with him. After that last time—when he grabbed you—he challenged me. I obliged." It was said almost cruelly, as if he was daring her to be offended or bothered by it.

But he should have known by now that Kate McCoombs was not a typical woman. "I thought it might be that way," she said. "Well, they got no better than they deserved," she said, dismissing the whole affair.

"Ready to leave yet?"

"Yes," she breathed, a touch of lust flickering in her eyes. "But do you think it would look right?" He stared at her blankly, so she said, "Well, they just found those three outside. You and me leave right now, it might look a little funny."

"Reckon you're right."

Coffin let others dance with Kate, while he kept a watchful eye out. Once or twice, he danced with another woman—most of whom were happy when he asked, since he was a handsome man, but regretted it as soon as his clumsiness became apparent.

After a decent interval, when the dance seemed to have forgotten the troubles of the three dead men, Coffin and Kate made their way to the hotel.

Kate stepped into the room and, as Coffin closed the door behind them, she spun several times. She stopped, facing him, her eyes snapping with lusty fire. Then, with a flicker of guilt and fear at her shamelessness, she slowly stripped off the long blue dress and the several petticoats underneath.

Coffin tried to say something, but his mouth was too dry. When she finally slid out of the simple chemise, she whooped and grabbed out to lock her arms around the back of his neck. With ease, Coffin carried her to the soft, quilt-covered bed. Then he pulled back and began unbuttoning his shirt. Moments later she said with a lecherous grin, "I can see you're getting a little itchy yourself." She motioned for him to lie down on the bed beside her, and then she was plunging down onto him, as a burst of passion exploded in them both.

"Well, Joe, where do we go from here?" Kate asked. It was still dark outside and they could hear the soft sighing of snow.

"Don't know. I didn't hear anything to help us either in the saloon yesterday or at the dance last night."

"Me neither. I even tried cautiously asking some of the men I danced with"—he looked at her in surprise, and she grinned—"but no one seemed to know anything."

She lay with the covers pulled up almost to her chin against the chill of the room, thinking.

"Let's try Phoenix," she said suddenly.

"Phoenix?"

"Yep. It's south of here, in the desert. Hotter'n three hells in the summer, but real nice in the winter. It ain't a real big place, like Prescott, but it's one of the bigger places down that way. Maybe they went down there to get away from the winter."

"Well, Phoenix will be as good a place to start lookin' for them again as any. They ain't there, we'll head farther south—unless we hear something. Hungry?"

"Starved."

Though it was not yet dawn, and Christmas Day, they found a restaurant open, where they ate well. Soon after, they managed to rouse the hungover owner of the general store and get their supplies. They packed the mule, and the extra horse. Bundled up against the cold and snow, they rode out of the sleeping town.

They followed the well-marked road westward, until it forked, and then they headed south. This road was still defined as a road, but it was not nearly in as good shape as the other. It had stopped snowing, but that night Coffin and Kate made a camp in a thundering rain. It was one of their more unpleasant camps, since they were soaked through from the long ride.

The next morning it was bitter cold, but the rain had stopped. The entire world around them glittered in ice. The slick, rocky ground made the going slow that day. But they made it as far as the little mining town of Bumble Bee, where they stayed the night.

With clean, warm clothes, slightly higher temperatures, full bellies, and a good night's sleep behind them, Joe and Kate rode out the next day in a better frame of mind, following the road that led almost due south. They passed through, around, and over small, humped-up mountains covered with rocks and cactus but little else. The farther south they rode, the more and more of the huge, multi-limbed saguaros they began seeing. In a few places, they laughed at the incongruous sight of snow on the giant cactuses.

The rocky road and many canyons and washes made the riding slow, since they did not wish to injure the horses. But eventually the land began to flatten and warm. There was more grass there for the animals, and even some water from streams or springs, though these often were dried up. Wood for the fires was scarce too, since all that grew there was brush and some stunted mesquite and green, spiky paloverde trees. With the flat ground, covered with short, golden grass, purple-brown sage, and other scrub brush, the going went much faster.

The days were warm, with a bright, seemingly always shining sun. The nights were still chilly, though, with a dazzling blanket of stars overhead. Coyotes howled close by, and there was plenty of game and birds—including noisy blackbirds, bright cardinals, majestic eagles, swooping red-tailed hawks—and jackrabbits galore.

Coffin and Kate finally rode into Phoenix, a small, but quickly growing city. It was warm, and the city dusty and dirty. A brown place, like so many places in the deep Southwest, with many homes made of adobe, and others of brick. Victorian architecture was beginning to show its spiraled, curlicued, and fancied face in many of the homes rising up not far from the Salt River.

There was much carriage traffic, but no one paid much attention to either Coffin or Kate. They turned their horses in at the livery stable and then found a room at a fancy hotel.

It was late afternoon, and so they went straight off to dinner at a nearby restaurant. Afterward, Coffin left Kate at the hotel, and headed for Phoenix's version of Whiskey Row.

He wandered into the first saloon he found and ordered a beer. Sipping it, he looked around the smoky, raucous room. He spotted no one he knew—and no one he was looking for. After a little while, he wandered around, pretending to watch a poker game here or a faro game there, but really just listening to people talk, hoping to hear something that might help him.

Nothing there, so he went to the next, and the next and the next, doing the same at each one, spending only a little time. Finally he overheard a bartender, talking to a customer, say, "Goddamned fat half-breed son of a bitch come in here with two dirty-lookin' whites lookin' fer a drink. Threw 'em the hell out."

"You gotta watch them half-breeds, Milt," the customer said. "They're worse'n full bloods, fer chrissakes."

Milt the bartender tapped the Colt Peacemaker he wore in a shoulder holster, then reached under the bar and came up with a scattergun. "I ain't scared of no goddamn Injuns, half-breed, quarter-breed, or full goddamn breed. Even if they are with a couple Injun-lovin' asses who talk tough."

"What'd they say?"

"Said they rode with Reno Holder's bunch up north. You believe that crap?" He laughed and walked away to serve another customer.

Coffin stood stock still, letting his emotions cool. It was some of Holder's men, he told himself. It had to be. He finished off his beer, and then strolled out, heading for the next bar. If they were around, they'd most likely be trying all the saloons to see if any would serve Bill Curly.

But Coffin had no luck, and knowing he was past his limit on alcohol for one sitting, he headed back to the hotel and the waiting arms of Kate McCoombs.

In the morning, the couple went to breakfast in the same restaurant as the night before. After a filling and satisfying meal, Coffin and Kate walked out into the warm, bright sunshine. As they started walking up the dusty street, Coffin saw Bill Curly.

The half-breed looked at him and at Kate, recognition blooming in his eyes.

Chapter 26

In that flash of an instant in which time seemed to freeze, Joe Coffin recognized Pete St. Johns and Will Greenaway. He also saw the light of remembrance that sprang into Bill Curly's eyes.

Then Curly pointed at Coffin and shouted to his two companions, "Kill him!"

Without question, the two white outlaws followed the lead of their half-breed companion and reached for their pistols. It made no difference to them why Curly wanted to kill this man here in the street; they only knew that a friend had made the call, and that there was a killing to be done.

But Coffin was not frozen. As Kate McCoombs screamed, "It's them!" Coffin grabbed her just above the right bicep with his left hand and shoved her as hard as he could.

The woman staggered sideways a few steps and fell, but Coffin was no longer paying any attention to her. Even as Kate was falling, Coffin had dipped into a crouch facing the three outlaws. The Colt bloomed in his right hand, and came up, steady and sure, at arm's length. His left hand came up and braced the right on the pistol butt.

Several shots rang out, sounding as one. Then the noise burst forth as four men fired randomly. Coffin was surprised he had not been hit.

He saw St. Johns, who was to Bill's right, turn a fraction as he fired his Remington. Coffin had a flicker of fear for Kate, who would appear to be St. Johns's target. Coffin swung the

Colt in his direction, and placed two shots through St. Johns's chest, knocking the dying outlaw flat onto his back.

As Coffin swung back, he saw Bill Curly running. The half-breed knocked down a man and then a young, well-dressed couple who were in his way. He reached the nearest horse—and Coffin was sure it was not the half-breed's—leaped on it, and spurred the animal viciously.

"Goddamnit!" Coffin roared as he brought his pistol around and put three shots into Greenaway, who was slammed back a step or two as each hammer blow of bullet hit him, first in the belly, then in the chest, then in the side of the head as he fell.

Coffin dropped the Colt back in the holster and snatched out the big, powerful Remington, with the seven-and-a-half-inch barrel. He braced it in both hands and fired off three rounds at the quickly fleeing Bill Curly. He thought he saw the half-breed flinch, but he was not sure at this distance.

He dropped his arm to his side, breathing heavily. It had lasted perhaps twenty seconds. He stepped off to make sure Greenaway and St. Johns were dead. As he did, he called out, "You all right, Kate?" There was no answer, and he spun, a fear that he had never experienced running icily from his stomach into his limbs. "Kate? *Kate?*"

He ran, the fear palpable, squeezing his heart, threatening to choke him. He skidded to a stop next to her, and knelt. She was on her side mostly, and partly on her front, facing away from him. Grabbing her roughly, he turned her to face him.

She was dead.

There was a bloody hole in her temple, the scarlet fluid seeping into her fiery mane of hair. There was another in her heart, the blood staining the plain brown dress she had wanted to wear in town to look more ladylike.

"Kate!" he screamed, tears awash on his face. "Kate!" He clutched her to him, heedless of the blood that soaked into his shirt. "Kate," he mumbled over and over into her hair.

People began to gather around. Some looked concerned, some shocked. Still others were offended that such things would happen here on the streets of Phoenix so early in the morning. After all, this was not Tombstone.

The full-mustachioed, powerfully built sheriff bulled his

way through the still-growing crowd of morbid onlookers, shouting, "What the hell's goin' on here?" He didn't really want any of the answers some people shouted at him.

Finally he loomed over Coffin, who was gaining some control over his emotions. "She's gone, boy," the sheriff said, putting a hand on Coffin's shoulder.

Coffin looked up, the fires of hate blazing his eyes dry. He stood. "Get your goddamn hand off me, Sheriff, before I rip it off."

There was a gasp from the crowd at such language as the sheriff, surprised, dropped his hand. Coffin shoved past the sheriff. Will Greenaway was dead, but there was a flicker of life left in the fat, drunken Pete St. Johns. Coffin knelt and looked at the flabby folds of flesh on the man's face. This was probably the man who had killed Kate, and he was certainly the bastard who had, with his knife, tortured Irene after his pal Will Greenaway had abused her, killing her so savagely.

"Where'd Bill Curly head out?" he asked, his voice dripping hatred and ice.

St. Johns tried to shrug, but the effort made him cough up blood.

"Answer me, you fat bag of buffalo shit, or I swear to Christ I'll cut off your balls here and now and jam them down your throat," Coffin snarled, hate clipping the edges of his words.

"I'm gonna die here anyway," St. Johns said with another bloody cough.

"You got a chance if the doc gets to you fast enough," Coffin lied. "But I ain't gonna let him near you, 'less you tell me."

There was a flicker of hope in St. Johns's eyes. "Wet Beaver Creek, up in Long Canyon," St. Johns gasped as blood filled his punctured lungs. "We got us a place up there. A cabin. Buck Schiebel's up there, and Reno's supposed to be there soon too."

Coffin stood. The rage that coursed through his veins was something he had never experienced before. It almost made him dizzy. He had flashes before his eyes—scenes from the past several months: bodies scattered along a long trail of blood; a girl, butchered like a hog after having been ravished by a pack of uncontrollable beasts; Kate McCoombs, roped to a wall and left to die after having been abused beyond belief; himself lying in the cold and snow with two bullet holes in him; Kate, naked and lusting, squealing and squirming atop him; Kate dead in the dust.

Coffin spit full on St. Johns's face. He shifted the Remington to his left hand and slowly drew his butcher knife. He knelt again, not caring how many people were watching him, at about St. Johns's belt level. The fat man tried to lift his head, and finally managed. His eyes were wide with fear, but he was too weak to move.

"Hey, what're you gonna do there?" the sheriff called as Coffin hefted the well-made knife. The lawman stepped into Coffin's range of vision.

"Well, Sheriff," he said slowly, "this fat pig used to be real fond of usin' knives. Ain't that right, Pete?"

"You know this man?" the sheriff demanded.

"Pete St. Johns. One of Reno Holder's bunch. Now, as I was sayin', this fat son of a bitch used to like usin' knives. 'Specially on young girls. Ain't that so, Pete? Used to take one of his knives and stick it right about here." Coffin placed the tip of the blade on the material of St. Johns's pants at the crotch, just under the fly. "Ain't that right, Pete?"

Coffin knew there was ice running in his veins now, instead of blood, for he was as calm and as lucid as if sitting in a front room yarning with old friends.

"Ain't that right?" he roared, demanding an answer.

"Yes," St. Johns gasped, fear filling up the huge bulge of his stomach. There was a jumble of noise from the crowd, which moved back a step.

"So, I reckon, it'd be a fittin' way for you to meet your end, you fat windbag. Ain't that right, Pete?"

"I can't let you do that, mister, whoever the hell you are," the sheriff said, starting to unlimber his pistol.

Coffin's left hand flicked up, the Remington cocked and steady. "I got two slugs left, Sheriff," Coffin said in a voice that raised the hairs on the lawman's neck. "One for each of your eyes, if you make one move."

The sheriff did not like being taken down in front of all these people, but he was not an idiot. He carefully took his hand off his pistol and folded his arms across his chest. He looked grim, but he understood Coffin's feelings.

With visions of a butchered young Irene floating before him, Coffin jammed the knife in. Two people in the crowd vomited as St. Johns's piercing scream rent the still air.

By the time Coffin was finished and pulled the knife free several minutes later, the street was almost clear. Only a few people still watched—and the sheriff.

Coffin wiped the blade of his knife clean on the leg of St. Johns's pants, and put it away. Then he stood. Throughout the whole thing, the Remington had never wavered from the spot on the sheriff's face. Now he put the weapon away.

"What am I gonna do with you, boy?" the sheriff asked.

"Not a goddamn thing," Coffin answered, his face blank. "I'm gonna see to my woman, gather up some supplies, send a wire, and then ride out."

The sheriff nodded. "I gonna have any more trouble with you?"

"Not if folks keep out of my way."

The lawman nodded again. Then he shot his chin out, saying, "Mister Philipps, the undertaker, is on his way."

Coffin dipped his head and started backing away.

"I ain't gonna back-shoot you, boy," the sheriff said. "Not over scum like these two." He jerked his head at the two bodies.

Coffin stared at the sheriff, and then decided he could believe the lawman. He spun on his heel and walked the short distance to where Kate's body lay. He arrived at the same time as Mr. Philipps, who looked nothing like what an undertaker was supposed to. He was short—shorter even than Coffin—with a full head of blond hair. He was rather young, with a wispy blond mustache. Most women probably thought he was handsome.

As the sheriff walked up, he said, "The other two go in paupers' cemetery, Mace." After Philipps nodded, the lawman said to Coffin, "Wire office is down there." He pointed. "You know where everything else in town is?"

"What I need to know."

The sheriff nodded, and cracked the barest of grins. "You need more help, boy, you come see me."

"Sure." Coffin turned back to Philipps, who asked, "You got enough money to bury her proper?"

Coffin seethed, but held his temper. "Yep."

"Want the works?" Philipps asked. The man's voice was professionally cold. It didn't matter to Philipps whether it was a beautiful young woman with her whole life ahead of her lying here, or one of the filthy outlaws.

"Yep. Stone too. When?"

"Three o'clock all right?" Philipps asked, looking up at Coffin for the first time. His face went white when he saw the look of Joe Coffin.

"Reckon it'll do." Coffin stood and walked away. There was a sick feeling growing in his stomach, an ache of loss he had never known. It was as if someone had punched a hole in his chest and yanked his heart out and left nothing in its place.

However, hate was rapidly filling the hole, and would soon spill out until he was almost consumed with it.

Back at their room—*theirs!* he thought bitterly—he took out everything of Kate's. There was precious little. Most could be thrown or given away. The blue dress she had worn to the dance back in Camp Verde he would bring to the undertaker's. Kate would go to her last rest in it, Coffin decided.

Also to be buried with her, Coffin decided, was his red bandanna: the one Kate had used so often in their early days together, when all she did was cry from the hurts she had suffered. It was their earliest link, and so must go with Kate to the grave. And her brother's pistol, and the man's pants and shirt she had worn.

Coffin gathered up those things and walked with heavy heart, depression weighing on him, to the undertaker's.

"I dislike asking at this time," Philipps said, "but I'm afraid I do not know your name—or hers." When Coffin looked at him blankly, he added, "For the headstone."

"Ah. Kate. Kate McCoombs."

"Thank you, Mister McCoombs. Now what are—"

"I ain't Mister McCoombs."

Now it was the undertaker's turn to stare questioningly.

Coffin smiled and said, "Sorry, we've been married only a few days. McCoombs was Kate's family name. It might be best to use that. . . ." He paused. "And maybe put my—our—name after. Kind of separate somehow."

"All right." Philipps's expression had not changed. "And what would that be?"

"Coffin."

Philipps's facade cracked, but he said nothing.

"Will the stone be done today?" Coffin asked.

"You in a rush?"

"I'll be leaving town tonight. Tomorrow at the latest."

"It will be done then."

Coffin gave the man the dates, and on the spur of the moment, a little saying to be chiseled into the stone. "You'll still be able to have it done on time?" he asked.

"If it ain't, I'll bury the stonemaker's ass myself at three-fifteen," Philipps said, suddenly human.

Coffin nodded. He went back to the hotel, gathered up the rest of Kate's things, took them to the trash heap outside, and tossed them on, keeping as a memento only the turquoise necklace she had frequently worn.

He worried about getting rid of all her things, but he knew he had to do it, and do it now, or he would never be able to do it. But he did not feel better about it.

Back in his room he cleaned, oiled, and reloaded his weapons. Then he went to the telegraph office, where he sent a wire telling Marshal Tom Pike that Will Greenaway and Pete St. Johns were dead, and that the others would be dead soon.

Coffin ate without tasting the food, and went back to his room for a short rest. At two-thirty, he walked to the livery, saddled up the chestnut horse, and rode to the cemetery on the west side of town. It was a simple ceremony, with only Coffin—and the sheriff—attending. The preacher said some words and the two Mexican grave-diggers began shoveling dirt in the hole onto the box.

Coffin kept himself in tight check as they did so, but he stayed until the two men were done. Then he waited until the stone was put into place. It was a simple one of gray, polished stone:

> Kate McCoombs (Coffin)
> September 5, 1862–January 3, 1889
> She walked in beauty
> and courage
> R.I.P.

He rode back into town and got smashing drunk alone up in his room, and he slept a drunken sleep full of gun-toting demons and beautiful, naked, red-haired, writhing women.

The next morning, Coffin sold Kate's horse and the extra horse, filled up on some supplies, and rode out fast. His head pounded and his stomach churned. But hate and the lust for revenge drove him.

Five days later he carefully entered Long Canyon, with its high walls of reddish stone. He smiled like death himself when he saw a trail of smoke.

Chapter 27

It was a little warmer in the canyon as Joe Coffin splashed across shallow Wet Beaver Creek, cracking through the rim of ice. About a mile farther on he worked his way up the red sandstone, horse and mule hooves clacking sharply on the rounded rock.

He stayed well back from the eastern cliff above the creek so as not to skyline himself as he moved from the bare stone and into the pine trees. Snow covered the flat sections that were dotted with brush, small pines, and cedars. It was a quiet, peaceful place, though colder than down in the canyon itself.

He spotted more smoke, and knew he was getting closer. Finally he hobbled the horse and the mule, letting them crop the little brown bunch grass left between the trees, as well as the shrubs. Grabbing a pair of binoculars from his saddlebags and his Winchester from the saddle scabbard, he slithered to the edge of the cliff.

He peered over, watching the ramshackle cabin. It sat on a bare shelf about seventy-five yards away, across the creek. A little to Coffin's left, the creek pooled. The pond was coated with ice. The cabin was backed up against the reddish cliff, which probably, Coffin thought, formed the rear wall of the shack. The cabin was made of badly cut pine logs with two crudely hacked-out windows covered with oiled paper. The door was of split logs, bark still on, hanging precariously on what Coffin figured to be two old shoe soles.

Except for the two horses off in the trees next to the cabin and the thin, wavering column of smoke from the poorly made chimney, it looked as if the cabin was deserted.

Coffin slid back a bit, then stood and walked to the mule. He took two blankets and some strips of beef jerky, and a few pieces of hardtack. He grabbed the canteen from the saddle horn of the chestnut horse and crept back to the cliff edge.

There had been no movement, so quickly, but still carefully, keeping as low as he could, Coffin spread out one of the blankets. Placing the Winchester, binoculars, food, and canteen within easy reach, he tossed his hat down and stretched out on his belly. He pulled the other blanket up over his back.

Coffin bit off a piece of jerky and held it in his mouth, letting his saliva wear at it. He was thankful that here in the winter, he did not have to worry about rattlesnakes.

And he waited.

Clouds drifted in, blotting the sun, but then fled before the wind as he watched, chewing slowly on jerky or hard biscuits. It was well past noon when the cabin door opened, and a rumpled man stepped out with a bucket in his hands.

Coffin whipped up his binoculars, and focused on Buck Schiebel, as the outlaw stopped just outside the door, breathing in the chill air. The outlaw shivered before heading toward the creek, a bucket in one hand, a hatchet in the other.

There was a tight-lipped, humorless smile on Coffin's face as he raised the Winchester. He easily levered a round into the chamber, cocking the rifle at the same tme. The well-oiled mechanism made little noise.

Coffin felt the comfortable fit of the stock against his cheek as he sighted down the short barrel of the .44/40. He squeezed off a shot.

Schiebel screamed as his right knee disintegrated, and he fell face down, dropping the pail and hand ax. He rolled over, clutching the shattered leg and howling, his cries piercing the otherwise still canyon.

Coffin had thought perhaps Bill Curly and maybe even Reno Holder were in the cabin, though there were only two horses to be seen, and right after his shot he swung the barrel of the Winchester toward the cabin door. Nothing seemed to move in there, and surely Schiebel's shrieking would have caused some activity in the shack.

Smiling fiercely, Coffin turned back toward Schiebel. The outlaw had rolled over on his back and was trying to push himself with the other good leg and his arms back toward the cabin, sliding on his behind.

Coffin fired again, and destroyed Schiebel's left shoulder. The outlaw screamed again and fell back, his head bouncing on the frozen ground. Coffin lay in his comfortable cocoon above and waited, watching.

Schiebel lay whimpering for a while, before making another effort at getting back to the cabin, his efforts severely limited by the wounds. He made little progress.

Satisfied that Schiebel was not going anywhere too fast, Coffin stood and put on his hat. He gathered up his things and repacked them before mounting his chestnut horse and following a rocky, narrow trail through a red stone passage down toward the creek. He came to the water a few hundred yards upstream from the cabin, where the creek was quite narrow. He clucked the horse into the ice-coated water. Both the horse and, a moment later, the mule, balked a little at the frigidness of the stream, but he coaxed them across.

Coffin approached the cabin cautiously, but there was no one around save the pain-wracked, moaning Buck Schiebel, who had made it perhaps five feet closer to the cabin. Coffin dismounted and tied off the horse and mule. Wary, he crept up to the cabin, Colt ready. He dove inside. But he found he was alone. Stepping outside, he strolled to where Buck Schiebel lay on his back, face screwed up against the agony.

"Howdy," Coffin said, looming over the outlaw. "Nice day, eh? A mite cool maybe, for my tastes, but nice, though."

The outlaw's eyes snapped open. "Who da hell are you?" he asked in a grumbling voice.

"Your executioner," Coffin said with false cheeriness. "How's it feel to have your own, personal executioner?" He didn't really expect an answer, and didn't get one. Squinting against the hard, bright winter sun, Coffin looked around, unconcerned.

When he looked back down, Schiebel was trying to pull out

his pistol with his left hand. Coffin sneered and stomped his heel down hard on the outlaw's mangled knee. Schiebel screamed and the blood drained from his face. His eyeballs rolled up into his head, and his body spasmed a few times, before he passed out.

Coffin walked into the cabin for a better look. The foul-smelling, dark, filthy den was, Coffin thought, an appropriate place for such men as Holder's bunch. Coffin found a bottle of whiskey. He pulled the cork out with his teeth and took a deep swallow. His eyes watered a little as the liquid burned a trail down his throat and into his belly.

He wandered back outside. Squatting, he placed the bottle down and rolled a cigarette and lit it. He sipped the harsh, cheap whiskey as he puffed. When he had stamped the cigarette out, he stood and grabbed the bucket and hatchet Schiebel had been carrying. He went to the creek, chopped a hole in the ice, and scooped up a bucket of water.

With a malicious smile, he poured the pail of icy water over Schiebel's head. The outlaw sputtered and snapped awake, choking out a mouthful of the water. Unthinking, he tried to get up, and shrieked again as pain seared through him.

Breathing heavily, he looked up to see Coffin towering threateningly over him.

"Where's Bill Curly?" Coffin asked. "And Reno Holder?"

"Don't know," Schiebel grumbled.

Coffin pulled out the Colt, and without hesitation, shot Schiebel in his other knee. Schiebel screeched and clutched the knee with his one good arm. "Jesus Christ!" he rumbled as agony tore at his insides. "Jesus Christ. Jesus Christ."

"Where's Bill Curly?" Coffin asked again. His voice and demeanor were calm, but the threat was evident. "And Reno Holder?"

"Goddamn half-breed's gone to Big Bug for supplies," Schiebel said harshly, his already growly voice made worse by pain.

"Where's that?"

"Southwest. Twenty, thirty miles maybe. Down past Camp Verde and Smithville."

"Why not go there for supplies?"

There was a rough, careful chuckle. "With all the troubles we caused in them two towns? Same with Piñon Springs, which is closer, though you got to cross over the mountain east a little to get there."

"You keep up this bullshit like you been doin', you won't have no place left to go."

Schiebel shrugged. There was always Phoenix and Tucson and Tombstone or west toward Cottonwood Spring and Truxton Spring or . . . Well, there was plenty of places.

"What about Holder?" Coffin asked sharply.

"I don't know."

Coffin raised the Colt, and Schiebel yelled, "Wait. Goddamnit. Don't! I don't know."

"Tell me what you do know."

"Reno was supposed to meet us here." Schiebel sucked in a breath as he moved his leg minutely and fresh pain ripped through him. It took him a few minutes to regain his composure.

Coffin took the time to get the bottle of whiskey. He knelt next to the outlaw and rolled another cigarette. He sipped and smoked, knowing the outlaw would desperately want both things. Coffin did not offer either.

"Reno was goin' down to Tucson for a little. He beds some Mexican bitch down there from time to time." He coughed, wincing as all three wounds throbbed. "Hey, mister, can I have me one of the cigarettes? Maybe a jolt of that red-eye?"

"No," Coffin said curtly.

Schiebel licked his lips, as if reluctant to speak anymore. "I really need some of that forty-rod," he said. "It's hard to talk, bein' so dry as I am."

Coffin lifted the bottle and tilted it so that it poured over the bloody shoulder wound. Schiebel's eyes widened so much that Coffin thought the outside edges would rip, and he gasped.

Again it took some time for him to settle down. When he did, Coffin said cruelly, "You've had your whiskey. Now talk to me. Is Holder still down in Tucson?"

"Don't reckon so. He can't stand that greasy bitch more'n a few days at a time." He tried to laugh crudely, but it set him to coughing. When he had calmed down, he said, "After that, he was supposed to go somewhere to meet the boss."

"The boss?" Coffin was truly surprised.

"Yep."

"Don't Holder run things?"

Schiebel grunted out a short laugh. "He's kind of like the ramrod—the field boss, you might say."

"Somebody else tells him what to do?" Coffin was taken aback by this new information.

"Hell, yes. The others don't know, though. Didn't know," he added remembering what Bill Curly had told him about a short, well-armed, deadly man who was decimating their little . . . "Oh, sweet Christ, you're the one, ain't you?" Schiebel asked, terror rising fully in his eyes.

"The one what?" Coffin asked with a blank face.

"The one who . . . You killed O'Kelly, didn't you? Pete and Will too. Curly told me when he got here. . . ."

"Tell me more," Coffin said evenly, knowing there was no longer any need to make threats.

"Like I was sayin'," Schiebel mumbled, fear grabbing his intestines, "the others didn't know."

"You did?"

"Yeah. Me'n Reno go back a ways."

"Who is this secret boss?"

"That I don't know." He was sweating despite the cold of the day. There was fear deep in those eyes, and he hurried on, before this vicious little man could do any more damage to him, "I really don't. I swear! All I know's it's some kind of lawman. Don't even know where."

"He never mentioned no names?" Coffin asked, eyes narrowed.

"No. Never. He was real close-mouthed about it all the time. Just every once in a while, he'd tell me he'd have to go meet this dude, and off he'd ride."

"You was never curious as to who it was?"

"Naw. Didn't make me no nevermind. Long's I got my cut from all the jobs we done." He was losing his fear. This short, stocky young man was friendly enough. If he could keep talking, maybe he could get this bounty hunter, if that's what he was, to help him out of the fix he had put him into.

"Yeah, and as long as there was some young women for you to ruin, eh?" The voice was measured, but fear sprang anew into Schiebel, puckering his groin.

Schiebel said nothing.

"Anything else you can tell me?" Coffin asked, suddenly tired.

"No," Schiebel muttered, barely audibly. He paused, then asked, "You think you could take me to Big Bug, mister? Maybe even Camp Verde? Let the doc try'n patch me up?"

"Reckon not." Coffin stood. He took another long drink of whiskey and then calmly shot Schiebel through the other shoulder. With dead eyes, Coffin turned to the cabin and went inside. He picked up the single kerosene lantern in it. He went outside, lit the lantern, and then threw it as hard as he could against the outside wall of the cabin.

Flames leapt up and spread rapidly along the splatter of burning kerosene. Black, oily smoke began curling into the air. Schiebel's two horses began squealing, trying to break free. Coffin went over and cut them loose, watching as they raced off.

Then he went to his horse and mounted. Grabbing the rope for the mule, he rode slowly down the canyon.

"Don't leave me here like this, mister!" Schiebel screamed. "Don't do this...."

Coffin ignored the voice as he rode away. He had no regrets. The outlaw would die soon enough of the loss of blood, or the cold. Or the coyotes would finish him off, or a mountain lion; perhaps even one of the many black bears in the area.

It bothered Coffin only a bit that he felt such little compassion. It was unlike him. Then again, he had never lost a woman he loved either, and such a reaction probably was expected. He did not worry about it. It simply was, and he would live with it.

He did not hurry. He didn't really want to find Bill Curly in a town. It would be much easier to find the half-breed riding along, unconcerned, on the trail. He also wanted time to mull over the information Schiebel had given him. A lawman giving the orders. Such a good idea, from the outlaws' standpoint.

It answered some questions Coffin had had. The outlaws

always seemed to be one step ahead of the posses, always seemed to know which towns to hit and when, what trains or stages were carrying gold. It could be any one of the many town marshals, or even the Yavapai County sheriff. Or perhaps a deputy. Yavapai County was so huge, there were a number of deputies. It could be easy for one of them to go bad.

The only other choices were a federal marshal or one of the federal deputies. But that was ridiculous, he thought. The only two in the area were Marshal Tom Pike and one named Sam Parson, who rode out of Snowflake over in Apache County. He didn't know Parson, but Coffin knew damned well Pike could not be mixed up in such doings. And Pike would have said something if he had any suspicions about Parson.

He wasn't sure of the deputies, though. They too covered a lot of territory, and knew many people, especially those who would have information about gold shipments, how much money was in some bank, which stages might be carrying cash, and other useful such things.

As he thought about it, he figured he would have to wire Marshal Pike when he got to Big Bug. Then he realized that might be stupid. If there was a deputy federal marshal involved in all this, the deputy might intercept the wire, or hear about it, and run for cover before they could put a stop to it.

No, Coffin decided, he would have to ride this trail by himself, and see where it led him. Once he knew that, he could bring in Tom Pike.

He made a cold camp that night, not wanting to give himself away by light or smoke, if Bill Curly was heading back toward the canyon hideout. But no one came along, and the next afternoon Coffin rode into the small town of Big Bug. He turned his horse and mule over to the man at the small livery at the edge of town and then, saddlebags over his shoulder and Winchester in hand, he headed for the only saloon in town.

He had a flash of *déjà vu* as he and Curly spotted each other at the same time. The bulky half-breed spun, ready to run.

Coffin fired a shot from the Winchester that kicked up dirt barely several inches to Bill Curly's right. The outlaw stopped and turned. "You're runnin' days are over, Curly," Coffin said harshly.

Chapter 28

Bill Curly raised his hands above his head. His obsidian eyes glittered with hate, and fear.

Coffin slowly levered another round into the Winchester, and raised the rifle to his shoulder. Curly began to sweat, and people on the frozen dirt street hurried for cover. Coffin applied only the barest pressure on the trigger. There was a dull look of hate in his dark eyes. He eased back on the trigger. "Drop your gun belt," he said roughly.

Curly dropped his hands to his belt, and then froze as Coffin said, "Slowly, boy. Nice'n easy."

The half-breed complied, inching his hands along, opening the buckle and letting the belt fall. All the while he was under the watchful eyes of Coffin, and the steady muzzle of the Winchester. Then he raised his hands again.

Coffin walked up to the outlaw, eased down the hammer of the rifle, and rested the barrel upside down on his shoulder. He looked up at the browned, hard face atop the tall, thickset body.

It had not been compassion that had stayed his hand. It was an undying, unrelenting hatred. Shooting down this outlaw from fifty feet with the Winchester would not be enough for Coffin. He must have more.

Coffin walked to the hitching post and hung the saddlebags over the rail, and set the butt of the Winchester on the ground, resting it against the hitching post. He turned and started walking toward Curly.

The half-breed almost grinned, and slowly started lowering his hands. This was better, he thought. He figured he would have no trouble taking on this short, but powerful-looking, young white man. One blow of his big fist, a grab and a squeeze, and the life would ebb out of the bounty hunter.

Curly's breath whooshed out and his eyes widened with shock as Coffin's balled fist slammed into his stomach, doubling him over. He stumbled back several feet, frantically trying to breathe. Each inhale made a wheezing, bubbling sound. Some numbness radiated from his navel, where Coffin had hit him.

As the half-breed staggered back, Coffin launched a pointed-toe boot, catching the outlaw under the chin, snapping Curly's head back. The half-breed flopped back, falling on his buttocks.

Coffin sneered, watching Curly sitting there in a heap. He unbuckled the gun belt with the Colt and the Remington and rolled it up and set it carefully on the ground next to the Winchester. A crowd was growing, people bundled in their coats and shawls and dusters. Coffin still wore his new hip-length, lined canvas duster, hiding the twin .36-caliber Colts. It was his hedge against treachery by the outlaw.

By this time, Curly had gotten back up. He looked a little shaky, but his wind was coming back fast. "You're goddamn dead now, son of a bitch bastard," Curly snarled, spitting.

Coffin said nothing, just flexed his fingers, thankful that he had his heavy leather gloves on. They would protect his hands. He moved forward slowly.

Curly curled up his hands and headed toward the bounty hunter. He feinted throwing a left hand, then came in hard with a sharp jab with the right. Coffin sidestepped the punch and hit Curly three times very fast, once in the nose, sending out a shower of blood; once in the mouth, cracking a tooth; and once in the forehead as Curly's head moved. The last nearly broke Coffin's hand, despite the thick gloves.

But the three blows had staggered the blocky half-breed, and Coffin moved in, aiming hard punches at the outlaw's head, stomach, chest, kidneys, anything he could reach.

Several punches staggered the big half-breed, and he went down on one knee. As Coffin moved in to finish him off, Curly locked both hands together and swung them as hard as he could at Coffin's left knee. The fists cracked into the side of the joint, and Coffin's leg buckled.

As Curly pushed up on thick legs, he smashed a hard, calloused fist into the side of Coffin's head.

There was a ringing in Coffin's ears as he fell to the side, and spots flickered before his eyes. "Christ," he muttered. He had been hit before, many times, but never that hard.

He rolled, and came to his feet, shaking his head, trying to clear away the clinging tendrils of fogginess. He had a reprieve, since his punches had taken their toll on Curly, and the half-breed's huge punch had sapped the little strength he had left.

The two men stood staring at each other, breathing hard from the exertion. There was no respect in either's eyes, only unremitting hatred. Then Coffin charged, shoulder lowered, and rammed into Curly's midsection. Both fell. Coffin landed atop Curly, but bounced a little and fell off to the side.

Curly rolled and managed to grab Coffin from behind in a bear hug. He grunted, trying to squeeze the life out of the bounty hunter. Coffin sucked in a last breath before his chest was so constricted he would not be able to. He could feel his ribs grinding. Whipping both legs forward as Curly stood, Coffin lashed out backward with his feet. The sharp round rowel of each spur caught Curly in the shins.

Curly yelped and relaxed his grip. Coffin burst free, landed on his feet, and spun, smashing the half-breed on the already broken, still-bleeding nose. He kicked Curly in the knee and, as the outlaw instinctively bent, Coffin slammed the side of each fist as hard as he could, one against each of the outlaw's ears.

The half-breed yelled as Coffin rushed in, swinging hard-fisted haymakers, pounding Curly's head, face, and body. The outlaw tried to cover up, but each time he did, he left another area exposed, and the bounty hunter would take advantage.

Curly began to fade some, and Coffin moved in more methodically. He jammed gloved thumbs into Curly's eyes, eliciting a scream, then boxed the half-breed's ears again. The outlaw slumped, landing with a thud. His breath rattled in through the mangled nose and down into the bruised chest.

"You best pray to whatever gods you got, boy," Coffin

rasped, "white or Navajo."

Curly mumbled something in Navajo that Coffin could not understand. Coffin snarled at him and walked up to finish the half-breed off. Suddenly Curly moved. His hand snaked down and pulled out a Bowie knife from his boot. He came up, blade reaching for Coffin's flesh, all in the same move.

Ice ran through Coffin's veins as he deftly, but barely, eluded the flashing knife. He slammed a fist into the side of the half-breed's head, knocking the outlaw off balance for a moment.

As Curly swung toward him with the knife again, Coffin turned and ran, leaping. He landed hard on his stomach, a few inches from his gun belt. He yanked off his right glove and snatched the Remington, which was on top, out of the holster.

As he spun up onto one knee in Curly's direction, Coffin saw that the half-breed had the same idea and had jumped for his own pistol. Since the outlaw's gun belt had been closer, he already had his pistol out and was standing, bringing the weapon around in Coffin's direction.

Coffin snapped the Remington Frontier up, and both men fired at almost the same instant. Coffin felt a bullet tear through his left sleeve, and when the smoke cleared, saw Curly standing, weaving. The half-breed still had his pistol in hand, but it was pointing mostly toward the ground, though he was trying to bring it back up for another shot. The front of his brown coat was covered with blood over the heart. Curly fired his pistol into the ground as his hand spasmed involuntarily.

Coffin stood. He thumbed back the hammer and coolly aimed. "Bye, Curly," he muttered as he put a bullet through the half-breed's forehead.

Coffin crouched, spun, and cocked the pistol in one smooth maneuver as he heard someone approach. The town marshal walked slowly toward him, pistol out but not cocked or aimed.

The middle-aged, medium-sized, nondescript marshal stopped in his tracks. He might not look like much, but he was not one to be afraid of some pistoleer, though he had enough sense to be cautious. Very carefully, not making any sudden moves, he placed his pistol in his holster. "Mind tellin' me what's gone on here?" he asked civilly.

Coffin straightened, uncocked the Remington. He stuck it in the holster and then began buckling on the gun belt. "Varmint huntin'," Coffin said calmly.

"I could use a little more detail," the marshal said.

Coffin liked the man immediately. There were no threats in his voice, and no fear. This was his town, and he had a right to know what was going on. Coffin almost smiled. He pointed at the body, "Yonder pile of shit is one of Reno Holder's gang."

"Damn," the marshal said, looking annoyed for the first time. "Now those bastards'll be comin' here lookin' for vengeance."

"You got no worries on that account, Marshal," Coffin said as he picked up the one glove and pulled it on.

"Eh?"

"'Cept for Holder himself, this bastard's the last of 'em."

The marshal's eyebrows rose in question. He looked hard at Coffin and knew the answer. He nodded. "Holder might get up another gang, ya know."

"I wouldn't worry about that neither, Marshal."

"Why not?" He thought he might know.

"Reno Holder's a dead man. I'll hound that prickly pear bastard from Mexico to Canada, from California to New York, if I have to. He ain't gonna have time for gettin' together no new gang."

The marshal nodded again. "Need the body for the bounty?" he asked without remorse.

"Nope. Just point me to your telegraph office. You mind if I stay the night in town?" He didn't have to ask, but in the few minutes since the marshal arrived, he had come to like the lawman, and thought it proper that he should give the man his due.

The marshal pointed down the street. Coffin looked and saw the sign for the telegraph office. He nodded.

"I don't mind if you stay. Just try'n stay out of trouble." He didn't really think there would be a problem. There was no one in town who would challenge this man after what they had just witnessed. "By the way, my name's Charlie Parks."

"Joe Coffin."

Parks touched the rim of his hat as he shouted, telling

everyone to leave, to let the undertaker do his job.

Coffin watched for a moment, his respect growing for Parks as he noticed the man's quiet dignity and efficiency. Then he turned and headed down the street, where he sent a wire to Marshal Tom Pike in Prescott, telling him Curly was dead, and that he would be looking for Reno Holder in the morning.

"You want to wait for an answer," the wire operator asked.

"Doubt there'll be one," Coffin said as he handed the man a few coins. "But if there is, I'll be either in the saloon or down to the hotel. You can fetch me there."

"Yes, sir."

Coffin left and got a room at the only hotel in town, a small place that was mostly empty at the moment. The town was quiet. It would, he figured, liven up considerable on the weekends, though, when the workers from the nearby mines came into town to blow off all the pent-up steam.

After bringing his things to the hotel, Coffin headed for a meal at one of the two restaurants. Then he headed for the saloon. There was a bad taste in his mouth from all the hate and rage that boiled through him, and he hoped to be able to wash it away.

He sat by himself, sipping whiskey and beer, puffing on cigarettes. A bargirl came over before long, but he was in no mood. She shuffled away in a huff. But an hour later, he called her over. She was all smiles again as he agreed on the price and went with her to her crib out back.

He felt some better about life when he returned a while later. His beer was flat, but the bartender, with not too much else to do, refreshed it quickly. Coffin sat drinking and smoking, thinking back over the past several months. He ignored the mutters and sidelong glances the few other patrons cast his way.

He was almost ready to leave when the wire operator rushed in. He stopped just inside the door and looked around. Spotting Coffin, he hurried over. "Reply to your wire," he said in self-importance. "Answer?"

"Wait a minute." Coffin read the message:

Holder in jail here. Thousand still yours. You scared him in. Pike.

"Goddamnit!" Coffin snarled. Looking up, he smiled grimly. "Sorry, mister." He handed the man another coin, saying, "No answer."

He was more enraged than before. He wanted Holder, and wanted him badly. There would be no pleasure in seeing the outlaw hang, or be put in prison. No, he wanted to kill the man himself. To see the shock of pain and knowledge that death was knocking on his door . . .

Well, maybe he would still have that chance, he thought. Tomorrow he would set out for Prescott. Perhaps it could be arranged for Holder to escape from the jail there. Or perhaps while Holder was being taken to court, there might be an accident. Or perhaps Coffin could even visit the outlaw in jail . . .

Yes, Coffin realized, there were ways, and he would have his revenge. He finished off his beer, feeling a little better. Almost content, he headed out of the saloon.

Chapter 29

Joe Coffin had fire in his eyes when he rode into Prescott. He headed straight for Marshal Tom Pike's office on the corner of Gurley and Cortez streets. He heard several shots, but since Pike's office was near Whiskey Row—and for good reason—he thought nothing of it.

But as he got closer to his destination, he found that people were running in the same dirction as he was riding. He spotted someone racing in the other direction, and he shouted, "Hey, mister, what's goin' on?"

"Reno Holder's broke out of jail," the man said, breathless. "Gunned down Marshal Pike and a deputy and rode off. The marshal's dead. I'm goin' to get the doc for the deputy."

"Hi-yah," Coffin shouted, jamming his spurs into the horse's sides. The chestnut leaped forward. The mule, caught up in it all, followed along, braying.

People cleared the way for the crazy rider as Coffin raced ahead. He slammed to a stop just off the wood sidewalk in front of the federal marshal's office. He bulled his way forward. One of the federal deputies—a blocky man, with big, chaffed hands and browned, weather-beaten face—stood in his way. "Goin' somewhere, mister?" he asked in a soft voice that rumbled like distant thunder.

"Get out of my way, goddamnit, before I splatter your ass all over the wall yonder."

"Ease off, mister," the deputy growled, unafraid.

"Let me in to see my friend, goddamnit."

"Friend?"

209

"Tom Pike, you goddamn fool."

"Who're you?"

"Joe Coffin. Now get the hell out of the way. I want to see my friend, pay my last respects before headin' out after the son of a bitch that done killed him."

"The hell you say," Pike's voice came from inside. "Cappy, let that short-legged son of a bitch in."

Coffin stood for a moment, stunned, even after Cappy moved his bulk out of the way. Finally he ventured in.

Pike was lying on his desk, a big, wood, flat-topped thing usually strewn with papers and clutter, now swept carelessly bare to form a makeshift bed. He was awake, but he did not look good. His face was pasty, and there was blood covering the chest of his drop-front shirt. His breathing was awkward—a large breath that wheezed out, then a struggle for other, smaller breaths, then finally the relief of a longer one again.

"You look about ready for the boneyard," Coffin said, trying to inject a little levity into the situation, and not altogether succeeding.

"Feel like it too." Pike coughed raggedly.

"Somebody runnin' for the doc said you was killed. He was gettin' the doc for the deputy."

"Well, I ain't dead yet, am I?" Pike coughed again, more harshly this time, and wound up spitting some blood. He lay back, wheezing.

"You're gonna be dead quicker'n hell you don't take it easy," Coffin snapped. "Can you tell me what happened?"

"Damnedest thing," Pike said carefully. "Things've been quiet lately with winter on us. Then there was a shootin' over to the Pine Tree Saloon. Some cowpoke full of bug juice gunned down one of the workin' girls when she started offerin' her 'favors' to another customer. As you can imagine, such doings were not looked on with a hell of a lot of favor by the other boys in the place, so the cowpoke lit out hell for leather.

"Since things'd been so quiet, me'n Cappy offered our services to the posse that went out after him.

"Anyway," Pike continued after a short pause to gather up his strength and breath, "we found that *loco* son of a bitch two days later off beyond Camp Verde. We made us a camp there, and the next mornin' just after we pulled out, we ran smack into Holder. Christ, I couldn't believe my eyes. Outlaw bastard was just saddlin' up his horse. He thought to run at first, but with near a dozen men facin' him, he just quit."

Coffin was so worried about his friend that he just listened. He would digest the information later, when he had time. He had already lost his woman; he didn't need to lose a friend too. Revenge—and Holder—could wait a bit, he reckoned.

"You're some weak, Tom," Cappy said in his gruff voice. "Set back and rest till the doc gets here."

"Hell, I might be dead by then." Pike waved a hand loosely in the direction of a deputy lying on the floor near the cells. His shirt too was covered with blood, but he did not seem nearly as bad off as Pike. "I had Parker over there check Holder over for weapons, then lock him up. Bastard bided his time for a day or two.

"Then, tonight, when just me'n Parker were here, he pulled a derringer on Parker when he brought in supper. Took Parker's keys, shot him, grabbed Parker's gun."

He coughed again, spitting up more blood. "Christ, Joe, it hurts. You ever been lung shot?"

"Came close. Just recent too. It's why you never heard from me for a spell there. When I caught Ian O'Kelly, he was with Holder and Bill Curly. I killed O'Kelly, but, while I was tryin' to protect . . . to save . . ."

His emotions began getting the better of him, something that had never happened before. He stopped, took several breaths to calm himself, knowing the others were looking at him strangely, before he went on. "Anyway, one of 'em—or maybe both, I ain't sure—plugged me. Took one bullet in the back, high up, almost in the heart. The other caught my leg. Hurt like all goddamn hellfire too."

Pike nodded. "Yeah." He sighed, then said, "Holder stormed out here and shot me good and right with Parker's pistol. He ran out the door, took a couple shots—don't know whether he was shootin' at somebody, or just whoopin' it up—stole a horse and lit out."

"I'll see to it, Tom."

"Hold here a while, Joe. Cappy's a good man, and a friend, but he'n me ain't *compañeros* like you'n me."

"Holder'll have more time to get away."

"You'll find him."

Coffin was torn. His friend needed him, but he could still hear Kate calling out from the grave for revenge. After battling himself mentally a while, he gave up and relaxed. He had found all the others; he would find Reno Holder again. Whether it was an hour from now, or a day, or a year, he would hunt down the outlaw leader and extract his own measure of payment from him.

"All right, Tom," he said quietly.

The doctor arrived.

"He gonna be all right, Doc?" Coffin asked. He was more anxious than he had expected to be, and it surprised him a little.

"He's gonna be dead if you don't get out of the way and let me do my job."

Coffin stepped around the other side, and watched for a while as the doctor examined Pike. But it made him uncomfortable, and he was eager to get on Holder's trail before it got cold. Finally he said, "I'm goin', Tom. You get better now, you hear."

"Yeah." Pike winced as the physician prodded the area near the ugly, seeping bullet hole.

Coffin walked outside, where a crowd still lingered. It was early afternoon, and cold, with gray, overcast skies. A cold wind whipped up particles of snow from the ground.

The deputy named Cappy walked out behind him. "I'll have a posse set in half an hour," he said in the low rumble of voice.

"Keep your goddamn posse."

"You ain't goin' alone."

"By the time you get a posse up, that bastard will be dead," Coffin said, squinting up at Cappy.

"You think you're pretty good, don't you?"

"The best. That's why Tom called me when you and your partners couldn't handle the job." It was not said nastily, though it might have been by some. It was stated simply as fact.

Cappy grunted in annoyance, the truth stinging, before saying, "Well, we'll be right on your heels, goddamnit."

"Just keep the hell away from me. I got first claim to that outlaw son of a bitch."

"Want the extra thousand dollars, eh?" Cappy almost sneered, but a touch of fear held it back partially.

"I got better reasons for finishing off that stinkin' pile of buffalo shit than a thousand dollars," Coffin said, the hate edging into his voice.

Cappy was taken aback by the vehemence in Coffin's voice, and the hard, icy look on the small man's face. "Somethin' personal?" he asked softly.

"None of your goddamn bus . . ." Coffin stopped and drew in a breath. He blew it out in a frosty cloud. "He and his men," the bounty hunter said very slowly, "killed my woman. They . . ." There was no point in continuing, so he stopped.

"I'm sorry," Cappy said softly, his words and demeanor contrasting with the deep, reverberating voice.

Coffin nodded, as Cappy said, "I still got to get together a posse. It's my job." He sounded apologetic.

"Go ahead. I'll be long gone by the time you boys leave. While you're roundin' up the men, see to my mule, would you?" He did not wait for an answer. He stepped off the wood step of the sidewalk straight into the stirrup. He swung onto the horse. "Which way?" he asked.

Cappy pointed northwest, and Coffin swung the chestnut in that direction. People moved out of his way as he spurred the horse into a gallop.

It was near dusk when Coffin ran Holder down in a clearing amongst the tall pines and firs in the Santa Maria Mountains. Holder's horse was near played out, and the outlaw, thinking that he had put enough distance between himself and any pursuing posse, was walking the animal, giving it some rest.

"That's far enough," Coffin called out as he edged into the clearing.

Holder stopped and turned. He was about halfway across the meadow, which was perhaps a quarter of a mile long, less than half that wide. There was nowhere he could run. Coffin rode up, and drew his Colt. "Toss down your gun," he said evenly.

"You're gonna kill me, ain't you?" Holder asked. There was some anxiety in his voice, but no fear. He was a handsome rogue, Coffin had to admit, better looking than in the picture on the Wanted poster. He could see why many women might fall for the outlaw.

"I'm gonna kill you whether you toss down your piece or not," Coffin snapped. "But I'd like to chat a while first. I got a few questions to ask you. I'd prefer to do that without havin' to worry about you drawin' that deputy's gun on me."

"I got nothin' to say to you, mister, whatever your name is."

"Joe Coffin," the bounty hunter said in clipped tones. "And it might be worth your while to talk to me. Now drop the pistol!"

Holder carefully pulled the pistol from his waistband and tossed it away. "Now the derringer," Coffin said.

"I dumped it a ways back. It was empty anyway."

Coffin didn't really believe him, but he was in no mood for debating it. "One of your *compañeros* told me you had a boss." He could tell by the sudden lifting of eyebrows, quickly caught, that he had scored a hit. "Said the man behind all this crap was a lawman."

"He was *loco*."

"Who is it?"

"I told you, whoever said that to you was loco."

Coffin sat a moment, trying to calm himself. "Look, Holder, there's a posse not too far behind. Tell me what I want to know, and I'll let you ride out."

"Bullshit!" Holder exploded. "You're gonna kill me soon's I say anything. I heard what you did to my boys down in Phoenix. I even heard of what you did to Buck Schiebel over in Long Canyon." He shuddered involuntarily. "You'll get nothin' from me. Just go on and kill me and get it over with."

"I did those things before I knew you had somebody behind you runnin' things. I don't want you—I want the bastard behind you. You don't mean shit to me."

There was a glimmer of hope in Holder's eyes. "How can I be sure you'll let me go?"

"You got my word."

"That ain't so good," Holder said, hope dimming. He was no fool.

"It's the best I can do." Coffin had no intention of letting Holder go, but he would tell the outlaw almost anything if it would help him learn who the lawman behind Holder was.

The outlaw pondered things for a while, before saying, "You wouldn't believe me even if I told you." He was stalling. He

214

knew full well this bandy, hard-eyed bounty hunter would kill him. He had escaped from custody once already—probably killed the federal marshal and one of his deputies to boot—so he figured he could do it again. At least his chances would be better. If he could stall long enough for the posse to get here, perhaps . . . or better yet, if he could distract Coffin for a moment . . .

They could hear the faint sounds of the posse approaching, and Coffin said urgently, "Tell me!"

The posse was almost to the clearing, they could hear. Coffin sat, waiting, but knowing that Holder was not going to tell him anything. He sighed, rage burning through him. He had no choice but to kill the outlaw. He could not risk turning Holder over to the posse. There was always a chance the outlaw would escape again, and the damage caused by the outlaw was already too great. Coffin thought back on the bloody trail left by Holder and his men: on a young girl, butchered with unbelievable cruelty; on a red-haired, vivacious Kate McCoombs; on . . .

Coffin's hand moved slowly toward the polished walnut butt of the Remington Frontier.

The posse burst into the clearing with a thundering roar. Cappy was at its head, and was shouting something, but Coffin was paying him no heed. Holder's right hand moved, and Coffin smiled grimly as he yanked the Remington out.

He fired twice. Both bullets plowed into Holder's chest, one in the heart, the other through the lungs. The outlaw went down with a wheezing gasp.

Cappy and the posse pounded to a stop. "What'n hell'd you do that for, goddamnit?" Cappy shouted. "We wanted to take that bastard back to face the hangman in front of the town."

Coffin put the Remington away, though several of the men in the posse had their pistols drawn. He stepped down from the chestnut, beckoning Cappy with his finger. When the deputy joined him, they walked toward the body. The other men in the posse rode on their heels.

At the body, Coffin bent and opened Holder's hand. In it was a cocked derringer.

Coffin sneered and mounted his horse. Without a word, he rode off.

Chapter 30

Joe Coffin rode into Prescott. His rage had not been eased much by the killing of Reno Holder. If there was a lawman—or anyone, for that matter—behind the late gang's rampage, Coffin would not be appeased until that man was dead too.

Coffin tied his horse outside the doctor's frame house on Leroux Street and went inside to see how his friend was.

"You can go in and see him," the doctor said, "but he's unconscious, and I don't want you disturbin' him."

"Sure." Coffin walked into the back room of the doctor's place and stared down at the still, waxy-looking figure covered up to his neck in crisp white sheet. Coffin shook his head in anger. Here was something else the mystery man behind the gang would have to pay for.

As he came back into the outer room, the doctor handed him a small wrapped package. "Marshal Pike said you'd be back," the doctor told him. "Seemed quite sure of it. Told me that when you did, I was to give you that package."

Coffin nodded, hefting it.

"Well, ain't you gonna open it?" the doctor asked, wanting to know what it was.

"Nope," Coffin said without even a glimmer of a smile. "I reckon I know what's in it." He walked out into the cold, windy street, and watched silently as Cappy and the posse rode in, carting Holder's body over a horse's back. Cappy touched his hat brim as he passed by Coffin, who nodded and returned the salute.

Coffin stuffed the package into a saddlebag and then rode

down to the livery stable. He took his Winchester and the saddlebags and walked up the cold, windy street to one of the several boarding houses and took a room for the night. Inside, Coffin opened the package. As he suspected, there was seven thousand dollars in it. Coffin grinned for the first time in quite a while. Now that all this was over, maybe his luck would take a turn for the better, he thought.

Then he thought again about the secret lawman behind Holder, wondering if it was true, or if Schiebel had been making it up. But the look Coffin had seen in Holder's eyes when he mentioned it assured him it was true.

He had a bath in a back room at the boardinghouse, and then roused the barber long enough to give him a haircut and a shave. With some new clothes, he looked almost respectable, and he headed for dinner.

After the meal, he went down to Whiskey Row, and entered the Cobweb. He was sitting alone, drinking a beer, smoking a cigarette, when Cappy pulled up a chair at the small wood table across from him and sat. "Mind?" he grumbled.

"No," Coffin said, glad for the company. It would keep his mind off things a little, he hoped.

"Well," Cappy sighed, the sound like a mudslide, "reckon it's finally over." He took a sip of beer and downed a shot of red-eye.

Coffin grunted and took another sip from his mug.

Cappy gazed at him as he pulled a cheroot from a shirt pocket. He scraped a match on the table and lit the small cigar. Squinting through the cloud of smoke, he said, "Something wrong? Seems like you think it ain't over yet."

Coffin hesitated. Cappy could very well be the one, as could any other lawman in the territory.

"I reckon you've rode a rough trail the last few months," Cappy said softly.

"Yep." Maybe having company wasn't such a good idea after all, he wondered.

They were silent for a while. Suddenly Coffin said, "One of Holder's men told me there was a lawman behind the gang." He was not sure why he had brought it out. Perhaps he was tired of keeping it bottled up; or maybe he just felt an instinctive trust of Cappy. Whatever, it was done now, and there could be no undoing it.

Cappy's eyes widened, and Coffin felt a little better. He did not think Cappy was acting. "Who?" the deputy asked, expelling the single harsh word with a lungful of smoke.

"Don't know," Coffin said in irritation.

"So it ain't over," Cappy breathed. He leaned back in his chair, thoughtful.

Finally he tossed down the cigar and stomped it out. "Maybe this'll help," he said, reaching into a breast pocket. He extracted a crumpled sheet of paper. "Just before I come over here," he said in the bass voice, "I was goin' through Holder's things. I found this. Thought it might be important, and figured I'd hold onto it till Tom got better, and then show it to him. But maybe you can use it."

Coffin took the paper and stared at Cappy for a few moments before uncrumpling the paper. He flattened it out on the table. It had been written by a wire operator. It said simply:

> You're the last. Meet you Canyon Diablo to find new recruits. L.B.

"Mean anything?" Cappy asked as Coffin looked up at him.

The bounty hunter shrugged, but a pinprick of hope and light pierced him. "Can't say, but I aim to find out."

"Figuring on a little trip over to Canyon Diablo?"

"Yep."

"I don't suppose you'd want a bit of company?"

"Nope."

"Didn't reckon so." He paused, then said, "I ain't known Tom Pike as long as you have, but I still figure he's a damn good friend. I don't reckon I got as much reason as you for huntin' down this bastard, whoever he is, but I do have *some* reason."

He held up his hand, as Coffin tried to speak. "Let me finish. Like I said, I got some reason. Not only did the gang pull all this nonsense in my territory, they also gunned down some friends, including Tom, and Parker. You need any help, you send a wire; I'll be there as quick as a horse can get me."

Coffin nodded. He didn't figure to need or want the help, but it was good to know it would be there should the need arise.

The two men—one a short, cocky, bounty hunter; the other a big, solid, gravel-voiced federal deputy—spent much of the night drinking and talking. Coffin still harbored some suspicions that Cappy might be involved in all the troubles, and might be trying to trick him with the note. But Coffin concluded as he went off toward his room that if it was true, Cappy had let nothing slip despite his alcohol consumption.

To be sure, though, Coffin spent the better part of the next morning asking—discreetly—around town about Cappy. But no one had a bad word to say about the rumble-voiced, giant deputy. Still just the littlest bit skeptical, Coffin rode out of town. But he only went as far as a nearby hillside, where he stood in the cold, hidden by a stand of pines, the wind cutting at his face, watching with his binoculars to see if Cappy left town.

The deputy did not, and Coffin finally made a cold camp. In the morning, he watched through his binoculars again. Only an hour later he saw Cappy wandering, unhurried, unconcerned apparently, through town.

Finally satisfied, Coffin saddled the chestnut and rode away. What supplies he had were carried in two pouches hanging from his saddle. He was in too much of a hurry to be slowed down by the cantankerous mule.

He fought through a blizzard and several snowstorms, faced hunger and biting, bitter cold winds. But two and a half weeks after he left Prescott, Joe Coffin rode into the town of Canyon Diablo. It was, as Cappy had told him it would be, a wild and open place. The first appointed town marshal had lasted a scant five hours; the second two weeks; the third barely a month. Cappy had not even known if there was a marshal in the town now.

It was a haven for outlaws, who practically ran the town. Murder, rape, robbery, fighting, and gunplay were commonplace. The few decent places in town were connected in some way to the railroad, which tried to watch out over its employees and its customers as best it could, though it was not easy. There could be no better place in all the territory to recruit a gang of outlaws.

Coffin stopped at a poorly tended livery. He unsaddled the horse. Carrying his saddlebags and Winchester, he strode up to the stable owner, and said bluntly, "Anything happens to that chestnut, and I'll cut your eyes out and feed 'em to the buzzards."

He spun and left. After getting a room at the only decent hotel in town—the one next to the train and stage depot—he headed for the first saloon he could find. It was dark, smoky, and foul smelling, full of noise and gambling; it was shabby and dirty.

The next one was much the same: a log saloon with a bar of planks laid on old whiskey and beer barrels. They didn't even bother to put up false fronts on these places. The next half a dozen were indistinguishable from the first two.

But in the ninth one he tried, he saw a familiar face. His eyes and jaw hardened. He knew he had found the man he sought.

"Hello, Joe," the man said as Coffin reached the table. He was not wearing his badge, but the scarred face had not changed.

"Why?" Coffin asked harshly, ignoring the other hard-eyed man also sitting at the table.

Lyle Bordus stared at the enraged Coffin, who stood across the table from the sheriff. "Why?" Coffin asked again.

"How'd you find out?" Bordus countered.

"Buck Schiebel told me Holder had a boss—a lawman. When I killed Reno, he wouldn't tell me who it was, but there was a wire in his pocket, signed L.B., saying to meet him here to form up a new gang. So I come for a look."

"What's this got to do with me?" Bordus said, trying to bluff it out.

"I'd wager all the money I got from killin' those other vermin that you're the only lawman in town here with the initials L.B."

"You're too smart for your own good, boy," Bordus growled. "You should've let it die with Holder and the others."

"So you could start up a new gang and let them take up where Holder left off? No goddamn chance."

"Still should've."

"I couldn't do that." Once again flashes of Kate McCoombs, and Irene, and ravished farms, and dead bankers flickered through his mind.

"Well, since you didn't, you'll not be leavin' Canyon Diablo alive to tell anyone about it." He waved a big hand at the man sitting to his left. "Meet my new partner," he said through his busted larynx. "Link Conroy."

Conroy was a hard-looking man with a broad chest and, as far as Coffin could see below the rim of the table, a thin waist. His face was rough and stony, with a broad, long nose, deep-set eyes, and generous, thin-lipped mouth. He wore a black derby with a red bandanna for a hatband. His shirt was brown cotton, dirty, and buttoned up all the way to the neck. One hand was under the table.

"I'd be obliged if you was to put that hand up on the table, Mister Conroy," Coffin said. There was steel in the words.

Conroy cracked a smile. From the movement made by Conroy, Coffin could tell the man was sliding a pistol back into a holster. Then Conroy placed both hands flat on the table top.

"You never answered my question, Lyle," Coffin said.

Bordus shrugged. "Times was hard after the war. What with all them goddamned carpetbaggers and such." There was anger in his voice. "It wasn't bad enough the South had lost the war, but then having to suffer the indignities of Reconstruction. Well, it was just too much. Especially for us boys who rode with Colonel Quantrill."

Bordus ignored Coffin's snort of disgust, and continued, "I knew Reno and a few of the others from servin' with the colonel in the fight for states' rights. After the war, four of us—me, Reno, Buck, and Pete St. Johns—headed into Texas. But with them damned blue-belly bastards runnin' things, life wasn't too comfortable for the likes of Reno and me. Without bein' left alone to run our farms we was in piss-poor shape.

"We took to rustlin' cattle and horses, sellin' 'em to the damn Union soldiers. They was the only ones with enough money to pay. After a few years, things started gettin' too hot for us. We split up and drifted our different ways. I took on as sheriff in a little minin' town in New Mexico. When the mines closed, the town died, and I moved on."

He paused and downed a shot. "There was a few more like that before I wound up as sheriff in Aspen Wells two years ago. I found out I could learn from other sheriffs when gold shipments and such were rollin'. Pretendin' I was on the lookout for Reno to arrest him, I sent a heap of wires out. Finally he caught wind of the wires, and figured I wanted to see him."

"After he rode into Aspen Wells, we got a hold of the other two boys from the old days. Buck had a couple other friends, Curly and O'Kelly, and he brought them along. And Pete brought along Will Greenaway." He shrugged, figuring that explained it all.

"Why all the killin'?"

Bordus shrugged again. He poured a shot of whiskey and downed it in one gulp. All this talking was making him thirsty. He didn't mind, though. Every man liked to crow about his accomplishments once in a while. This was Bordus's chance. And it would mean little, since Coffin would be dead soon anyway.

"It's plumb difficult," Bordus said with a smile, "to keep men like Pete and Buck and Curly from their sportin'." The grin widened, and Coffin wanted to smash him in the face. "Killin' gets in a man's blood. You should know that."

Coffin swallowed the bile. Bordus had no remorse in him, and the thought sickened Coffin. "Why'd you have 'em hit Aspen Wells? Twice?" he asked, fighting back the rage that threatened to envelope him.

Bordus grinned again. "Hell, that's simple," he gargled. "If every town in northern Arizona Territory was hit but Aspen Wells, things'd look mighty suspicious. Besides"—he laughed—"it was a good way of gettin' rid of people who were in my way."

"Like Harmon Tuck?" Coffin asked, seething. Not only was Bordus responsible for all those deaths, including Kate's, but Coffin also knew now that he had been used—completely and utterly taken in—by Sheriff Lyle Bordus. The knowledge sickened him, and his groin tightened with it.

Bordus laughed again. "Hell, yes. Saw it as a fine way of gettin' rid of that horse's ass. You played right into my hands, boy. Whole hog too." He guffawed.

Coffin bit back his rage—and the shame that boiled up under it. He never took his eyes from Bordus's face, but with his peripheral vision he kept a watch on Conroy. But the gunman had not moved.

"Why'd you let me go?" Coffin asked, the words clipped.

Bordus scratched his nose, thinking. "I was all set to kill you after you pulled that pistol on me. But then that mob formed up, and I reckoned it'd have to wait. You made it worse when you banged me on the head that night. Plumb spoiled my fun that time. She was a fine-lookin' woman that red-haired bitch was." He looked almost dreamy. "Was she as good as she looked?" he asked, goading Coffin.

Coffin used all his wiles to keep himself under control, but the look in his eyes made Bordus pause.

"But reason come on me," he said hastily. "I figured you'd come in useful if Tuck kept agitatin'. If he backed off, I'd let you ride out, and make sure you was killed on the trail somewhere. But, hell, you showed better'n I thought you would. After, I figured I owed you somethin', seein's how you saved my ass.

"Besides"—he chuckled—"after all the doin's in my town, if you showed up dead, I suspected your friend down there in Prescott just might get his dander up and come pokin' round town. I didn't need such pryin' eyes on my business."

Bordus downed another shot of whiskey and then leaned back in his chair, locking his hands behind his head. "I never expected," he said with a tinge of sadness in his voice "you to kill all them boys. I thought you might get one or two, and that'd help sharpen the others. But all six? Damn, you had me fooled too, boy, so don't feel so bad. I mean, you showed me against that mob you were somethin', but hell, to take on the whole Holder gang and wipe 'em out . . ." He whistled, and Coffin suspected there actually was some respect there.

"Well, Joe, y'all got any more questions?"

Coffin fought back the flood of fury raging inside him, as Bordus leaned forward, forearms on the table. All the mirth was gone, and his eyes glittered with hate.

Time seemed to be suspended, hanging dead in the fetid air of the saloon. The music and shouts and gambling went on as before. Coffin had his answers now; there was but one thing left to do.

Bordus and Conroy went for their pistols at the same time. But Coffin had never been faster. Still standing, and so unhampered by the table as were his two foes, he whipped out the Colt and fired four shots before either of the other two could get off a round.

The first two of Coffin's bullets punched neat holes in Conroy's face—one went through the left cheek, the other just over the right eye. Conroy had been, Coffin knew, a seasoned gunfighter, and therefore the more dangerous of the two, so he had fired at him first. The gunman's head snapped back and his chair fell sideways, dumping the twitching body on the dirt floor.

The second two shots slammed into Bordus's chest, knocking him—and the chair—straight back over. The noise in the foul saloon ground to a halt as Coffin walked around the table. With a boot, he rolled Conroy over onto his back. The gunfighter was dead.

Coffin stepped up to Bordus. The sheriff still lived. The lawman tried to say something, but no words came. Coffin glanced around the room, making sure no one was going to make a play against him. No one had so much as unlimbered a weapon. There was little hostility evident, though most of the flinty-eyed men—and the boozy, half-dressed women—watched with some interest.

There was no compassion in Coffin's eyes as he looked down at Bordus. The sheriff was having trouble breathing, and his eyes were cloudy with pain.

"Should've killed me when you had the chance, Lyle," Coffin said without mercy. He thumbed back the Colt's hammer casually. The room was quiet, except for an occasional cough or shuffling of feet—and Bordus's labored breathing.

"Go to hell, Coffin," Bordus choked out.

Coffin grinned, but it was mirthless. He aimed the Peacemaker and pulled the trigger.

Bordus's head jerked as the bullet drilled a small hole in the tiny canyon just above the nose. Coffin slid the weapon away and turned. As he walked out of the saloon, spurs clanking, the emptiness in his chest returned.

He would be glad, he thought, to get back to Denver.